STIRLING C

38048

D1138739

THE LAST DATE STAMPED P~

Jo~~~~ was ~~~

carriage, a prey to~ Domino was to be sacrificed on the altar of family duty and there was little he could do.

He was a disreputable man and could have no voice in her future. That kiss—those kisses, he corrected himself reminiscently—could only ever be an interlude. But what an interlude! It was ridiculous that his heart still sang.

How many kisses had he known in his lifetime? *Not like this*, a small voice within him argued, *not like this*. He had known instinctively that she was a girl of strong emotion, that beneath her modest exterior lay a sleeping passion waiting to be roused, and he had been right. He had wanted to kiss her until she begged him never to stop, and she had wanted him to. She desired him as much as he desired her.

Another conquest to add to the many, he thought acidly. All the more reason, then, to keep his distance. Otherwise he would hurt her—and hurt her badly. It was inevitable—for didn't he damage everything that became dear to him?

Isabelle Goddard was born into an army family and spent her childhood moving around the UK and abroad. Unsurprisingly it gave her itchy feet, and in her twenties she escaped from an unloved secretarial career to work as cabin crew and see the world.

The arrival of marriage, children and cats meant a more settled life in the south of England, where she's lived ever since. It also gave her the opportunity to go back to 'school' and eventually teach at university. Isabelle loves the nineteenth century, and grew up reading Georgette Heyer, so when she plucked up the courage to begin writing herself the novels had to be Regency romances.

Previous novels by this author:

REPROBATE LORD, RUNAWAY LADY
THE EARL PLAYS WITH FIRE

**Did you know that some of these novels
are also available as eBooks?
Visit www.millsandboon.co.uk**

SOCIETY'S MOST SCANDALOUS RAKE

Isabelle Goddard

All the characters in this book have no existence outside the imagination of the author, and have no relation whatsoever to anyone bearing the same name or names. They are not even distantly inspired by any individual known or unknown to the author, and all the incidents are pure invention.

All Rights Reserved including the right of reproduction in whole or in part in any form. This edition is published by arrangement with Harlequin Enterprises II BV/S.à.r.l. The text of this publication or any part thereof may not be reproduced or transmitted in any form or by any means, electronic or mechanical, including photocopying, recording, storage in an information retrieval system, or otherwise, without the written permission of the publisher.

This book is sold subject to the condition that it shall not, by way of trade or otherwise, be lent, resold, hired out or otherwise circulated without the prior consent of the publisher in any form of binding or cover other than that in which it is published and without a similar condition including this condition being imposed on the subsequent purchaser.

® and TM are trademarks owned and used by the trademark owner and/or its licensee. Trademarks marked with ® are registered with the United Kingdom Patent Office and/or the Office for Harmonisation in the Internal Market and in other countries.

First published in Great Britain 2012
by Mills & Boon, an imprint of Harlequin (UK) Limited.
Harlequin (UK) Limited, Eton House, 18-24 Paradise Road,
Richmond, Surrey TW9 1SR

© Isabelle Goddard 2012

ISBN: 978 0 263 89243 7

Harlequin (UK) policy is to use papers that are natural, renewable and recyclable products and made from wood grown in sustainable forests. The logging and manufacturing process conform to the legal environmental regulations of the country of origin.

Printed and bound in Spain
by Blackprint CPI, Barcelona

SOCIETY'S MOST SCANDALOUS RAKE

To Jackie
A generous friend and reader who loves Brighton

Chapter One

Domino de Silva raised her face to the warm sun and breathed a sigh of contentment. The gentlest of waves whispered along the pebbles at her feet and the wide blue dome of the sky spread itself with ease to meet a distant horizon. She closed her eyes in pleasure. For a short time at least she was free; all too soon she would have to return to the house on Marine Parade and her cousin's inevitable questioning. If only her father would send Carmela back to Spain, she might truly enjoy this last summer before the dreary future she was resigned to. But Papa would not do that. Her stern aunts back in Madrid had only agreed to her acting as his hostess if her cousin accompanied her.

'You seem to have dropped this.'

She was startled from her reverie by a warm

voice, disturbing in its intimacy. Shading her eyes against the sun's strong rays, she detected the outline of a slim but muscular form. The man appeared to be offering her a crumpled cambric handkerchief bearing all the marks of having been trampled in sand and sea.

She shook her head decisively. 'Thank you, but no. The handkerchief is not mine.'

'Are you quite sure?'

'I think I should know my own possessions,' she responded a little tartly.

'Naturally. But you had fallen into such an abstraction, I thought you might not realise if you had dropped something.'

She felt herself becoming ruffled. Whoever the man was, he was intruding on the few moments of solitude that were hers.

'As I said, sir, I fear you are mistaken.'

Her voice was edged with ice, but it seemed not to perturb him for he took the opportunity to move nearer. She became aware of a pair of shapely legs encased in skin-tight fawn pantaloons and a coat of blue superfine perfectly fitted to his powerful shoulders. Hessian boots of dazzling gloss completed an ensemble ill adapted to a provincial beach.

'It would seem I was mistaken,' he admitted, 'but I shan't repine. It's given me the opportunity to speak to a vastly pretty girl.'

She was astonished at his audacity. His voice and dress spoke the gentleman, but no gentleman of her acquaintance would have addressed a lady so.

'I would be glad, sir,' she said in the most frigid of voices, 'if you would leave me in peace to enjoy this wonderful view.'

He let out a low chuckle and for the first time her gaze moved upwards towards his face and she was unnerved by what she saw. She had not realised how young he was or how good looking. His fair hair fell carelessly over his forehead and a pair of golden-brown eyes lingered over her in a way that made her flush with annoyance. A small scar on his left cheek only enhanced his attractiveness.

The gold-flecked eyes considered her with lazy amusement. 'I'm not impervious to your request,' he drawled, 'but it places me in an awkward situation.'

'How is that?'

'My wish to gratify a lady is at odds with my strong sense of duty.'

Her determined silence did not deter him. 'My wish to oblige requires me to walk away this minute and leave you to your solitude.'

'Please do!'

'If only it were that simple,' he exclaimed mournfully, 'but chivalry requires I put my duty first. Since you appear to be entirely without an escort, it clearly behoves me to stay as chaperon.'

'How fortunate then that I can put your mind at rest! Trouble yourself no further. I am used to walking alone and am well able to take care of myself.'

At that moment she was far from feeling so. Her desire to venture out alone had never before exposed her to such persistent harassment. This man would not be shrugged off lightly.

'You're a mere slip of a girl,' he continued blithely, 'and it seems unlikely that you're quite as accomplished as you think in escaping unwanted attentions. Though a most comely slip of a girl, I grant you,' he finished after a slight pause. His eyes, glinting amber in the sunlight, danced with laughter.

There was nothing for it but to turn tail. He was impervious to disapproval and entreaty alike. She turned quickly to make her way back across the beach and her sudden movement impaled the flounce of her dress on a twisted piece of iron, which had detached itself from the groyne. She was well and truly caught.

'Allow me.'

And before she could protest he was down on his knees, carefully unhooking the frill of delicate cream lace from the iron stanchion.

She stood rigid with mortification, thankful for the cooling breeze on her heated cheeks. But there was worse to come. Before she could stop him, his hands began to rearrange the crumpled hem of her silk gown and for an instant alighted on her ankle.

'Thank you, sir,' she said in a stifled voice and fled towards the safety of Marine Parade.

'Must you go already?' he called after her. 'I feel we are only just getting acquainted.' He grinned at her departing figure. 'It's not every lady's ankles I get to see before luncheon, you know.'

She hurried away, more shocked than she cared to admit. That would teach her to walk unaccompanied. She must stop breaking the rules; within a year she would be married and there would be no more solitary strolls, no more escapes to the sea. And no chance meetings with impertinent strangers. Relieved, she reached the promenade and looked back to the spot she had just vacated. The man was still there, watching her every step, it seemed. He saw her pause and gave a cheerful wave. Impossible! She turned from the beach abruptly and hurried home.

Joshua Marchmain watched her for some time as she strode rapidly over the wet pebbles and began to climb the worn stone steps to the promenade. He had not meant her to flee quite so precipitately and just as things were getting interesting. He would have liked to spar a little more, for it was an unusual young lady who walked alone and disputed with strangers. And she had cut a most charming figure. The encounter had certainly provided a welcome break from the tedium of ministering to George's whims. How he had become so indispensable to the Regent he hardly knew. For years he had exiled himself from life among the *ton* and it seemed unlikely that on his return he would become a palace favourite. But he had, and quickly. At first it had been amusing to supplant long-serving courtiers in the Prince's favour, but now it was simply a dead bore.

A summer spent at Brighton had promised new interest, but the reality was proving very different. Or at least not different at all, that was the problem. The Prince's life revolved around banquets, gambling, horse racing, music and his love affairs, whether he were in London or Brighton. The sound of the sea was the only novelty. Joshua had spent that morning, as so many others, idling in the hothouse that was the Royal Pavilion but, faced with the six-course luncheon the Regent felt an appropriate midday snack, he had rebelled to play truant in the salt-tanged air.

Almost immediately he had seen her, a small, trim figure in cream silk and lace with a saucy villager bonnet on the back of her head, barely keeping her unruly dark curls under control despite an enormous bow of azure ribbon. Her face, when she'd raised it to look at him, had more than matched the promise of her figure. Her eyes, dark and tragic, set in a heart-shaped countenance, had sent an unaccustomed longing through him. She would never be a diamond of the first water, but her youth and vulnerability spoke to him in a way that perfect beauty no longer did.

The ripple of emotion was over in a trice. Just as well, he thought breezily. Suppressing inconvenient sentiment had made life a good deal simpler over the years. It might have been amusing to dally a while, but in the event the flirtation was over before it had really begun. Regretfully he retraced his steps; it was time to resume his duties before the Regent noticed his absence.

As soon as Marston opened the door to her, Domino knew she was in trouble. Her cousin was in the hall, an apron wrapped around one of the black dresses she habitually wore and a furious expression on her face. The butler made a strategic exit, winking conspiratorially at the young girl as he retired to the servants' quarters.

'And where exactly have you been?' Carmela's tone was as angry as her face.

Domino did not answer immediately. She had meant to provide herself with some excuse for her absence, a frippery purchased from the stalls in Bartholomews, perhaps, but in the flight from the beach she had completely forgotten. In any case her cousin hardly drew breath before the next onslaught.

'You do realise that your father is to host a reception here this very evening and you were supposed to help with the hundred and one things that have to be done.'

She did realise and felt a twinge of guilt. As the new ambassador for Spain, Alfredo de Silva was setting great store by tonight's entertainment. He had only recently presented his credentials at St James's; though the Court had abandoned a hot and dusty capital for the sea, it was vital that he continue his work among those who surrounded the Prince Regent. Only a few days ago he had confided a rumour to her that even George himself might attend this evening's event.

'I'm sorry, Carmela,' she said quietly, trying

in vain to mollify the angry woman, 'I felt a little unwell—you know how stuffy this house gets in the hot weather—and I thought it would help if I took a short walk in the fresh air.' Her cousin seemed unable to decide whether to look sceptical or shocked. In the end she managed a mixture of both.

'It's even stuffier outside,' she scolded, 'and how many times have I told you that you must not walk alone? You are imprudent, Domino. Why do you have a personal maid if it is not to accompany you wherever you wish to go? And why go anywhere today?'

'I'm here now, so tell me what I can do to help.'

'Nothing.'

'Nothing?'

'Everything is done. As always, I have worked myself to a standstill.'

It was difficult to see how Carmela had worked so very hard. She herself had planned the event days ago and had left the maids to arrange flowers and set tables. The catering firm and their own kitchen had prepared every morsel of food and drink necessary to entertain the cream of the *ton*. But she said none of this, unwilling to upset her cousin further.

She was sharply aware of the sacrifice Carmela had made. Her cousin was devoted to the family and could even be kind in her own stiff fashion. She had not wanted to come to England, least of all to a scandalous resort known throughout Europe as a den of extravagance, if not downright immorality. But come she had, putting her loyalty to the family before her own comfort and leaving behind the pleasing pieties of her Madrid home. Domino might wish she were alone with her father, but Carmela was part of the bargain, part of the price she had to pay for a few months' freedom.

Hurrying up the stairs to her bedroom, Domino locked the door with relief; she was out of reach here. Marriage, though unwelcome, would at least deliver her from the endless scolding of relatives. Her aunts had already presented her with the names of three suitors they considered eligible and all she had to do, they said, was choose one. Any of the three would make a highly suitable husband, able to oversee and conserve the vast estate she would inherit at twenty-one and certain to be assiduous in keeping the inevitable fortune hunters at bay. It didn't matter who she married. After Richard Veryan, it was utterly unimportant. She had loved and lost, and she knew even at this young age that she would never feel so deeply about any man again. It was enough for her to know that he was happy now with the wife he should always have had, and that she was in some small way responsible for bringing them together. But if only…

She was sunk in the customary forlorn dream when a knock at the door roused her. Fearing a resurgent Carmela, she opened it cautiously, but it was Alfredo de Silva who stood on the threshold, a beaming smile on his face and his arms outstretched in greeting.

'*Querida*, come with me,' he ordered, having hugged her until her ribs almost buckled under the strain. 'I have a little present for you.'

'I fear that I don't deserve a present, Papa. Ask Carmela.'

'Oh, Carmela—what does she know of deserving? I intend to spoil you to death now that you are with me again. I've missed you more than you will ever know.'

Her father was hustling her along the landing to his own room where the door stood open and a stunning gown of the deepest rose pink tumbled invitingly on the bed. She snatched it up eagerly and held it against her body. A glance at the cheval mirror in the corner of the room reflected back her creamy olive skin and burnished curls, their beauty heightened by the rich rose of the satin-and-gauze gown. Still holding the dress tightly, she waltzed around the bed laughing with pleasure.

'Thank you, thank you so much. It's quite lovely. But far too good for a mere reception, Papa. We should save it for a grand ball at the very least!'

'A ball? No, indeed. You can be sure that when the time comes, I will find something even better,' her father said mysteriously. 'Wear the rose pink tonight and your mother's amethysts. They will be perfect for the dress and perfect for you—you look so like Elena.'

His voice faltered a little and Domino took his hand and squeezed it comfortingly. 'I love being spoiled, but you are much too kind to me.'

'You should know, my dear, that I have an ulterior motive. In that dress you will entrance all my guests and then they will say how lucky Spain is to have such an excellent ambassador!'

She was glad now that she had returned to England to be with her father, despite Carmela and despite Lady Blythe's warning. Their English cousin had refused to continue as Alfredo's hostess once he left London; Brighton had been a step too far for Lady Loretta Blythe. *Raffish, my dear*, she had warned Domino in a letter to Spain, *please consider carefully whether you will be comfortable entertaining in such a place*. Domino had considered, but the prospect

of living with a much-loved parent again, free
of her aunts' strictures, had been too appealing.

Returning to her bedroom, she found Flora
in a fizz of excitement at the prospect of dressing her mistress for the evening's celebrations.
The abigail, the best of a mediocre selection
according to Lady Loretta, who had despatched
her from London, had never before acted as
a lady's maid and this evening would be a
test of the skills she had been practising so
assiduously. The rose-pink gown with its as-
sorted underpinnings was soon in place, the
very slightest brush of rouge applied to both
cheeks and a smear of rose salve for the lips.
Taming Domino's luxuriant curls into the popular Roman style, though, took a little longer,
and it was some considerable time before Flora
pronounced herself satisfied with the result.
Her mistress's raven locks now cascaded from
a carefully arranged topknot to rest lightly in
two glistening ringlets on the soft cream of her
neck. A careful fastening of the delicate neck-
lace of amethysts around Domino's neck and
the placing of matching earrings completed the
toilette. Both young ladies viewed the finished
result in the mirror and smiled with pleasure.
Whatever Domino might lack in willowy elegance, she made up for in sheer prettiness.

'I'm determined to enjoy this evening,

Flora,' she pronounced, her dark eyes sparkling with anticipation. She had begun to feel the old excitement returning even though she was once more about to enter the lion's den.

'Of course you are, miss, why ever wouldn't you?' her maid asked innocently.

'When I agreed to come to Brighton in Lady Blythe's place, the prospect of helping my father entertain seemed nicely distant. But now!'

'You'll be fine, Miss Domino, you always know exactly the right thing to say and do,' Flora soothed.

'My aunts have schooled me well, it's true, but this is the very first *ton* party I have ever hosted.'

And it had arrived rather too quickly, she thought. It seemed as though they had hardly settled themselves in the elegant town house on Marine Parade before Alfredo announced that he wished to give a reception. But it was more than that. Her last foray into the social life of England's top one-hundred families had ended in disaster. She saw the young girl she had been, so open to all the pleasures of that first London Season: balls, picnics, exhibitions, ridottos, Venetian breakfasts. How young and foolish! She had fallen in love with the wrong man and fallen foul of one who meant her nothing but dishonour.

'It's time you went downstairs, miss. I've just heard Miss Carmela's door close.'

The maid fussed around her, adjusting a tendril here, a fold of the dress there. Domino bestowed a warm smile on her. 'Thank you so much, Flora. You've had magic in your fingers this evening. I hope I shall live up to your handiwork.'

'You will, Miss Domino, for sure. You look fair 'ansome.' Flora grinned, betraying her rural heritage and forgetting for the moment the town bronze she was painfully acquiring.

The hall had been sumptuously decorated with tall vases of early summer lilac and as Domino walked slowly down the marble staircase, their perfume rose in a sensual spiral to meet her. The main doors were open and in the still evening air she could hear the rhythmic beating of waves against stone parapet. Her father and Carmela were already waiting by the front entrance to receive the first of their guests, her cousin having forsaken her usual black gown for a slightly less funereal mauve. They looked up at her approach and Alfredo glowed with pride; even Carmela gave her a tight smile of approval. So far, so good, but her nerves were taut. Would her planning stand up to the *ton*'s stringent demands? Could she perform the role of hostess with aplomb? She had not long to find out.

Lord Albermarle was the first to arrive and his bluff good nature put Domino immediately at ease. Most of their guests that evening would be men—an inevitable imbalance in a diplomatic reception—and she had not been certain whether to feel this as an advantage or not. But Lord Albermarle's gentle compliments and genial smile decided her. Far better to make her début without female whispers to disparage her efforts. Soon the ground floor of Marine Parade was throbbing with life. Most of the guests were involved in some way with the Court or with Parliament, but there were a few without any diplomatic or political interest who came simply to look over the new ambassador and his household. They appeared to like what they saw.

Sir Henry Bridlington spoke for many when he observed, 'Señor de Silva seems a very good sort and his daughter is bound to make a stir in Brighton this season.' He took a long pinch of snuff. 'The girl has looks, breeding and she's no fool. Refreshing to meet a woman with opinions!'

'It depends on the opinions, I imagine.' The

man who spoke was flaxen haired and his tawny eyes glittered with amusement.

'Nothing outlandish, I swear,' Bridlington responded. 'In fact, I thought she spoke most sensibly. And a very attractive face and figure, don't you know.'

'Ah, now you're talking sense. A woman's opinions are as changeable as the sea. But her looks! That's a different matter entirely. I must ensure I make the acquaintance of this nonpareil.'

So it was that Domino, busily circulating among her guests, came face to face with her tormentor of the morning.

He smiled lazily down at her while a flush gradually suffused her entire body as she re-alised who was barring her way. He had looked complete to a shade during this morning's en-counter. Now he looked simply splendid. He was dressed in the satin knee breeches and black long-tailed coat befitting a gentleman attending an evening party, but the way he wore them singled him out from every other man in the room. His clothes fitted him im-peccably—the work, she surmised, of a mas-ter tailor—and clearly suggested the perfect male body beneath. A dandyish silk waistcoat of maroon-and-grey stripes was countered by the restraint of a crisp white neckcloth, tied in an elegant *trône d'amour* and fastened by a single diamond stud. Her gaze travelled slowly over him, but always came back to those amber eyes, sensual and appraising.

'Miss de Silva, I imagine? Joshua Marchmain, at your service.' He bowed with a languid grace.

She bobbed a bare curtsy and inclined her head very slightly. His smile deepened at her evident reluctance to recognise him.

'Forgive my somewhat unorthodox approach. I lack a sponsor to introduce me at the very moment I need one.'

She remained tense and unsmiling, but he affected not to notice.

'I am forced therefore to introduce myself,' he continued. 'I would not wish to leave this delightful party before thanking my hostess— that would be grossly discourteous.'

'Discourtesy should not concern you, sir. You seem to have a fine stock of it.'

Her high colour was fading fast and she felt control returning. She was not to be overpowered by this arrogant man; she would make him acknowledge his earlier impertinence.

'How is that?' He was looking genuinely puzzled and she was reduced to saying weakly.

'I think you know very well.'

'But then I would not have been so discourteous as to mention our delightful...' he paused for a moment '...rendezvous.'

'It was not a rendezvous,' she remonstrated, 'it was harassment and you were abominably rude. How dared you accost a lady in that fashion?'

'But, Miss de Silva, consider for one moment, how was I to know that I was accosting a lady? No lady of my acquaintance would ever walk alone.'

'So you feel you have *carte blanche* with any woman you don't consider a lady?'

'Let us say that solitary females are not usually averse to my company.'

Domino seethed at his arrogance; he was truly an insufferable man. 'You deliberately trespassed on my seclusion,' she said wrathfully. 'Despite my pleas, you refused to leave me alone.'

The golden eyes darkened and not with amusement this time. 'But naturally,' he said in a voice of the softest velvet. 'How could I? You were far too tempting.'

She felt the tell-tale flush beginning again and longed to flee. But her training stood her in good stead and she drew herself up into as statuesque a figure as she could manage and said in an even tone, 'I believe, Mr Marchmain, that we have finished our conversation.'

He bent his head to hers and said softly, 'Surely not, Miss de Silva; I have a feeling that it's only just beginning.'

In an arctic voice she made a last attempt to put him out of countenance.

'I don't recall my father mentioning your name in connection with his work. Do tell me what your interest in this evening's event might be.'

He moved away from her slightly, but his manner remained as relaxed as ever.

'Which is a polite way of saying, what am I doing here without an invitation? You're quite right, I have no invitation. However, I believe the Prince Regent's presence was expected and I am here as his humble representative.'

'Then he's not coming this evening?' She felt a keen disappointment and, despite her dislike of Joshua Marchmain, found herself wanting to ask more.

'Did you expect him to?'

'My father was told that he might attend.'

'Then I'm sorry to disappoint you.' He smiled that lazy smile again. 'George is a somewhat indolent prince, I fear, and only rouses himself to action when he anticipates some pleasure from it.'

She was taken aback by his irreverence. 'You are a member of the Prince's household?'

'For my sins and at the moment, yes.'

'Then how can you speak so of a royal prince?'

'Believe me, it's quite easy. If one knows the prince.'

'It would seem that you hold the Regent in some aversion. If that's so, why do you stay?' she enquired with refreshing candour.

'That is a question I ask myself most days. So far I haven't found an answer. Perhaps you might provide me with one.'

She looked puzzled. 'I cannot see how.'

'One never can at the time,' he replied cryptically.

Domino was rapidly tiring of the continual fencing that Mr Marchmain appeared to find essential to conversation, but was too eager to learn of life in the Pavilion to walk away. 'Is the palace very grand inside?' she asked impulsively and then wished she hadn't. She had no wish to betray her gaucheness in front of this indolently assured man.

He smiled indulgently, seeming to find her innocence enchanting.

'Yes, I suppose you could call it grand; although I would rather say that it is eccentric. But surely you will see the Pavilion for yourself very soon and will be able to make up your own mind.'

'Perhaps. My father has not yet told me of his plans.'

'It is to be hoped they will include a visit to the palace. If so, allow me to offer my services as your guide.'

Domino had no intention of ever seeking his company, but she made the expected polite response. At least for the moment he was conducting himself unexceptionally. Then out of nowhere he disconcerted her once more with a passing remark.

'I understand that you have been living in Madrid.'

'How did you know that?' she demanded.

'I ask questions and get a few answers,' he murmured enigmatically. 'There's a wonderful art gallery in Madrid, the Prado. Do you know it?'

'My home in Madrid is close by.'

'Then you are most fortunate. To be able to look on the genius of Velázquez any day you choose.'

She stared at him in astonishment. 'You are interested in art?'

'A little. I collect when I can. I have recently acquired a small da Vinci—a very small one—so at the moment I am quite puffed with pride.

When you visit the Pavilion, I would like to show you the studio I have set up.'

'You are an artist yourself?'

'I am a dauber, no more, but painting is a solace.'

If she wondered why a man such as Joshua Marchmain should need solace, she had little time to ponder. Carmela had arrived at her elbow and was hissing urgently in her ear that they were running out of champagne and would she like to come up with a solution. The party had been more successful than they had hoped and people had stopped for longer to drink, eat and gossip.

Domino excused herself and Joshua swept them both a deep bow. Carmela glared at him fiercely before following in her cousin's wake. She must warn Domino to keep her distance from that man. She knew nothing of him, but every instinct told her he was not to be trusted and her young relative had spent far too long talking to him. At the best of times it would look particular, but with this man it was likely to begin gossip they could ill afford. Domino was to be married next year and it was Carmela's job to guard her well until such time as the wedding ring was on her finger.

Joshua watched them out of sight, smiling wryly to himself. He knew Carmela's type well. How many such duennas had he taken on and vanquished in the course of an inglorious career? But Domino appeared to have a mind of her own. That and her youthful charm made her a prize worth pursuing; the next few weeks might prove more interesting than he had expected. He weaved his way through the chattering guests to receive his hat from a stray footman before sauntering through the front door of Number Eight Marine Parade, his step a little livelier than when he had entered.

The next morning was overcast. The sun hid behind clouds and the sea looked a dull grey. The prospect of a walk was uninviting, but it was Sunday and attendance at the Chapel Royal was essential for the ambassador and his daughter. Carmela had refused point blank to accompany them; nothing would induce her to attend a Protestant church, she said. She would stay at home and follow her own private devotions. If Domino and her father felt a little jaded from the previous evening's exertions, a vigorous walk along the promenade soon blew away any megrims. Tired they might be, but they were also in good spirits. The reception had gone without a hitch and Alfredo was feeling increasingly optimistic for the success of his mission. Domino, too, was cheerful, seeing her father so buoyant. To be sure, entertaining the *ton* had been a little daunting, but she had come through her first test with flying colours. Apart from the impossible Mr Marchmain, nothing had occurred to spoil her pleasure. And even he had intrigued her. He was an enigma, a man of contradictions. She had thought him nothing more than a highly attractive predator, but then he had announced himself a lover of great art. He was sufficiently wealthy to laze the summer away in the Prince Regent's very expensive retinue, but seemed to lack the responsibilities that accompanied such wealth. And far from enjoying his exalted social position, it appeared to give him little pleasure.

A wind had sprung up by this time, blowing from the west, and Domino was forced to pay attention to her attire, hanging on with one hand to the Angoulême bonnet with its fetching decoration of golden acorns, while with the other she strove to keep under control the delicate confection of peach sarsenet and creamy tulle that billowed around her legs. They walked briskly, her father enumerating his plans for the week while she listened, but all the time her mind was busy elsewhere.

'Papa,' she said suddenly, when he fell silent for a moment, 'what do you know of Mr Marchmain?'

'Only a very little. He is one of the Regent's court, I understand, so no doubt expensive, idle, possibly dissolute.'

She felt dismay at her father's description. Marchmain was certainly persistent in his unwanted attentions, but dissolute!

'Do not concern yourself, my dear.' Her father patted her hand. 'Members of the Prince Regent's entourage are a law unto themselves. We will have dealings with them only when we must.'

She tried another tack. 'How is it that Joshua Marchmain is only a plain mister? Surely if he belongs to the Regent's company, he should have a title.'

'I believe the young man is related in one way or another to any number of the nobility and has inherited a wealthy estate, which he will certainly need if he keeps company with the Regent for long. But why this interest, *querida*?'

'No real interest, Papa,' she said stoutly. 'He just seemed an odd person to be attending the reception, a fish out of water.'

'I think we can say that Mr Marchmain's appearance at our small entertainment was the Regent's overture to Spain. We must accept the overture politely, but still maintain a distance.'

He took her arm firmly in his. 'Come, we

should step out smartly if we are not to be shamed by our lateness at church.'

They walked quickly on, the summer wind skirling around their feet and sending up dust and abandoned news sheets into a choking cloud. Brighton was a fashionable resort— almost too fashionable, she reflected—and Marine Parade was a less-than-ideal residence. It was too near the centre of town and attracted promenading society far too readily. She had quickly realised that lodgings close to the Pavilion were in general reserved for young bucks, looking forward to a lively few months by the sea, and for the sprinkling of dandies with their pencilled eyebrows and curled mustachios who were always ready to ogle any stray female who crossed their path. She had come to wish that her father had chosen a house on the outskirts of town but, this morn- ing, proximity meant they had only a short way to travel before they arrived at the church a few minutes before the last bell ceased tolling.

The Chapel Royal was a square building in the classical style with rounded sash windows and a row of Doric columns flanking the main door. It was the custom for visitors without their own pew to be charged an entrance fee and Domino and her father obediently joined a straggling line of people, all waiting to pay their shilling. The queue was moving slowly and they waited for some while to disburse their fee, but as they neared the imposing front door of the church, there was a sudden commotion behind them, a servant pushing his way forwards to clear a pathway for his employer. She turned to discover who this grand personage might be and received a terrible shock; she found herself staring into the eyes of the man she had come to loathe when last she was in England.

Leo Moncaster smiled grimly at her. 'Miss de Silva? Imagine that. And there was I thinking never to see you again.'

Her father had turned around and was looking with surprise at the sneering stranger. 'Is this gentleman annoying you, Domino?' he asked her quietly. She was quick to reassure him and he turned back to pay their shillings.

'I see you have brought reinforcements with you this time.' The sneer became even more pronounced. 'And is your aunt here also, ready to come to your defence at any moment?'

'Lady Blythe remains in London, sir, although I see no reason why that should interest you.'

'On the contrary, Miss de Silva, everything to do with you interests me. I have a long memory, even if you do not.'

And with that he pushed past beneath the pediment displaying the Prince Regent's coat of arms and into the church. She was left trembling from the encounter, but anxious that her father should not suspect anything amiss. She linked arms with him and smiled as bravely as she could.

'Shall we go in?'

Seeing Leo Moncaster had been a crippling blow. When she had agreed to play hostess for her father, she had never for a moment imagined that she would meet the man who had done her so much harm. If she had been thinking sensibly, she might have known he could well be here and living at the Pavilion. Moncaster was an inveterate gambler and it was said that fortunes were won and lost on a nightly basis at the Regent's tables. Where better for such a man to spend his summer? It was clear that his malevolence was unabated despite Lady Blythe having paid her niece's gambling debt in full. Of course, he had not wanted the money. It was herself, or rather her body, that he had wanted. That was the prize of which he'd been cheated. But how could she ever have thought him attractive? A shudder ran through her as though she were tiptoeing over a grave, fearful of disturbing dark layers of memory. Her only comfort was her father's assertion that they need have little to do with the Prince Regent or any of his cronies.

Certainly the Prince would not be in evidence this morning. Although he had laid the church's foundation stone some twenty-five years ago, he had stopped worshipping at the Chapel Royal when a sermon on immorality had offended him. But there was some compensation to be had. An enormous man with creaking corsets was heaving himself into the pews reserved for the Royal Family a few rows in front of her: the Regent's brother, the Duke of York. He kept up a constant muttering, hardly audible, but nevertheless highly embarrassing to his companions. Their attempts to stifle him made her smile; for the moment she forgot the dreadful meeting she had just endured and was emboldened to look about her. The galleried church was filled with decoration, its supporting columns and pulpit highly embellished, while a large organ in burnished copper thundered from above the altar. It was a rich man's building.

She looked sideways across the aisle, scanning a busy canvas of faces, hoping to keep out of Moncaster's sight. Immediately beneath one of the galleries a countenance she was beginning to know well swam into view. Joshua's gaze was on her, sporting an appreciative smile as he took in her situation just behind the noisy Duke. She noticed that he was dressed more soberly this morning, but the familiar lock of fair hair trailed over his brow and his sprawling figure exuded his customary confidence. Her glance moved on to the woman who sat next to him; there was something proprietorial in her posture. She was richly dressed in an ensemble of emerald-green Venetian silk and her hair was covered with a headpiece of ostrich feathers. The feathers swayed slightly in the current of air and their height ensured that those who sat immediately behind could see little of the service at the altar.

Domino did not profit from the parson's homily that morning. She was too conscious of both the men she wished to avoid and was relieved when the final hymn reverberated through the rafters and she was able to walk from the church into a burst of sunshine. The rector was at the door to greet his parishioners and once again they were forced to wait patiently in line before they could pass through the narrow entrance.

'Pious as well as pretty,' a voice said softly in her ear. 'It gets better all the time.'

She turned to face him, grateful that her father was engaged in talking to a fellow communicant.

'Still accosting unwilling women, Mr Marchmain?' she snapped back.

'Never unwilling, Miss de Silva.'

Her face flushed scarlet as she took in the implication of his remark. She was just about to retort angrily when another voice cut across their interchange.

'Joshua, why don't you introduce me to your delightful new friend?'

It was the richly dressed woman she had seen sitting next to him in the pew.

A look of irritation flitted across his face, but was gone in a moment.

'But of course. Miss de Silva, may I present the Duchess of Severn. Charlotte, Miss de Silva—the daughter of our new ambassador from Spain.'

'How delightful to have you in Brighton, my dear.'

Domino wasn't sure she liked the woman. She seemed to purr when she spoke and the glances she cast towards the waiting Joshua verged on the covetous. But she curtsied decorously and made her father known to the duchess.

'You must both come to one of my small soirées as soon as possible,' Charlotte Severn said smoothly. 'I will send an invitation this very week. I am sure Joshua will know your direction.'

Domino sensed a hidden meaning, but managed to smile politely and hope that her father would conjure some excuse for their not attending.

'She is a very fine lady, is she not, Papa?' she remarked as they made their way back along the promenade.

'Who?'

'The Duchess of Severn.'

'Finely dressed at least.'

'You don't sound as though you like her.'

'I don't know her, Domino, but I do not like the set she moves in. I would prefer you to have as little to do with her as possible.'

'Mr Marchmain seems to know her well,' she ventured.

'Indeed he does,' her father said grimly, then abruptly changed the subject.

She was left to puzzle over just what had vexed him so badly.

Chapter Two

Joshua turned abruptly on his heels and headed back towards the Pavilion, his temper frayed. He needed to be alone and Charlotte Severn could easily be left to the escort of Moncaster, whom he had noticed in the distance. He was angry with her for intervening in his conversation with Domino and even more annoyed that she had promised an invitation to one of her celebrated soirées. He didn't know why, but he wanted to keep Domino to himself, or at the very least not expose her to the intimacies of the Severn household.

He had no intention of seducing the young girl, that was not his style, but neither did he want her knowing a woman such as Charlotte. That lady might be the wife of one of the premier dukes of the land, but she had the soul of a courtesan. The role suited her well and she should stick to it, he thought, rather than attempting to befriend the young and inexperienced. The Royal Pavilion was a suitable milieu for her. Every kind of dubious pleasure was available there and she had a husband happy to look away while she played. His Grace was content in his declining years to puff off his wife's beauty and retire to the lure of the gaming table. He was one of the Regent's most assiduous companions, not least because he was so wealthy that it mattered little to him how much money he lost.

Charlotte had access to wealth untold—but that was not enough, Joshua reflected wryly. It hardly compensated for a dull and ageing husband. He remembered when he had first seen her two years ago—Wiesbaden, it was, at the town's most opulent casino, and seated at the hazard table. She had looked across at him, her eyes staring straight into his, their porcelain blue still and expressionless, but nevertheless saying all they needed to say. That very night they had become lovers and from time to time continued to meet. But for long stretches of the year the duchess could not shrug off the duties incumbent on her position and that suited him well. There were always others happy to keep him company and lengthy periods of absence had until recently staved off the inevitable ennui which acquaintance with any woman produced. Or any woman since that first disastrous love affair.

But things were changing. He didn't know if it was the sea air stirring his blood and making him restless, but something had altered in him. Charlotte Severn no longer beguiled him and his frustration at being part of the Regent's sycophantic court was beginning to acquire a sharper edge. And the girl—she had something to do with it, too. It wasn't just that he wanted to bed her; that was as certain as it was unlikely. It was, he thought, that he had enjoyed their encounters, enjoyed her vitality, her verve, the zest with which she resisted his raillery. He had met her on three occasions and each time behind his gentle mockery he had wanted to explore, to discover more, to begin to know her. Today she had looked enchanting in peaches and cream and yet another rakish bonnet, those dark tragic eyes looking out at him so scornfully from beneath its brim. They could be made to wear another expression, he was sure. If ever he felt mad enough to risk exile again, he would savour the challenge. Charlotte's companionship had never seemed more irksome; she had stepped between them, muddying the waters, placing her footprint where only his had previously been.

The duchess was waiting for him in the outer vestibule of the Pavilion. If his temper had improved with the circuitous route he had taken, hers certainly had not. He barely had a foot through the door when she addressed him in a voice crisp with indignation.

'There you are, Mr Marchmain. I had begun to think I had lost you.'

'Why is that, Your Grace?' He would be as formal as she.

'Not unnaturally, I awaited your escort from the Chapel Royal. But when I turned to call on your services, you had gone.'

'Forgive me. I felt in need of a slightly longer walk and I am aware that it is not a pastime you favour.'

'A walk with you is always a pleasure, Joshua,' she replied in a more conciliatory tone.

'Then forgive me once more. Had I known, I would certainly have requested your company,' he lied.

She fixed him with a cold, enquiring eye. 'How is it that you know the ambassador's daughter?'

'I was representing the Regent last night, if

you remember,' he said indifferently. 'We met at her father's diplomatic reception.'

'You seem already to be on good terms with her.'

'Why should I not be? I understand the need for England to maintain a good relationship with Spain.'

'Ah, so that's what it is.'

Leo Moncaster strode into the Octagon Hall as they talked and viewed the two tense figures with satirical amusement.

'Quite a breeze blowing out there,' he offered with an assumed bonhomie. 'That's the problem with being beside the sea, never without a wind. Still hopefully Prinny will soon get bored with coastal delights and leave for Carlton House within the month.'

His audience remained resolutely silent and his eyebrows rose enquiringly.

'Have I been guilty of interrupting a private conversation? If so, my profuse apologies.'

'Apologies are unnecessary. Your manners are never anything but perfect, Moncaster,' Joshua remarked acidly, unable to conceal his dislike. 'Her Grace and I were just about to part.' And with that he strode off to his rooms, leaving Leo Moncaster looking quizzically at the duchess.

'I realise I am hardly a favourite of Marchmain's, but, beyond my unwelcome presence, what ails him?'

'I imagine no more than a tedious sermon and a cold walk from the Chapel Royal.'

'He seemcd ruffled uncharacteristically so.'

'I may have annoyed him,' the duchess admitted, her voice carefully neutral.

'How so?'

'I invited a young woman who appears to have become his protégée to one of my soirées. That apparently is not something to be done.'

'And why not exactly?'

'Possibly he thinks I may corrupt her innocence,' Charlotte said with a knowing little smile. 'Would you be so good, Leo, as to escort me back to Steine House? A trifling distance, I know, but I prefer to have a reliable man by my side.'

Lord Moncaster offered his arm and they sailed past the waiting footman. He was not to be put off the scent, however, and as they walked through the Pavilion Gardens enquired, 'And what innocence would that be, if she knows Joshua Marchmain well?'

'Don't be so crude, Leo. Joshua is a gentleman.'

'You think so? Never trust a man not to sully innocence.'

'I suppose you should know,' she answered in a bored voice, 'your reputation precedes you.'

'At least I make no pretence to be other than I am,' he responded harshly. 'Marchmain is as much a rake; his pretence is to be something else.'

'Joshua is a man of the world, but he is not a rake. He has discrimination.'

'In seeking you out, dear lady?'

'In seeking out a woman who is mature and experienced and with whom he can enjoy life to the full.'

'As opposed to a girl who is young and naïve, yet sends his heartstrings singing.'

She bit her lip viciously, Moncaster observed with a sly glance. 'Don't say, my dear, that you've fallen in love with him. Not a good policy, not at all.'

'Joshua and I understand each other very well.'

'I wonder.'

'What do you mean by that?'

'I wonder how well. After all, you knew nothing of this girl.'

'That is because he made her acquaintance only yesterday.'

'And who is this paragon of unsullied innocence?'

'Her name is Domino de Silva. Domino, what a ridiculous name! Why, what's the matter?' The man beside her had stiffened imperceptibly.

'De Silva, you say?'

'Yes, do you know her?'

'Shall we say I have had dealings with her.' It was Lord Moncaster's turn to look grim.

'It sounds as though they were not entirely to your liking.'

'They were not. I have a score to settle.'

'I see.' Charlotte Severn glanced covertly at the polished man accompanying her. He took his time before he spoke again.

'Are you interested, perhaps? We might work well together.'

'We might,' she replied consideringly, 'but for the moment I prefer to see what I can accomplish alone.'

'Then let me give you a hint. Gaming.'

'Gaming? In what way?'

'A small chink in the armour. It is so fatally easy, is it not, when one is young and inexperienced, to find oneself adrift in a world one does not understand? Fatally easy to lose money, for instance, that one does not have. Then think of the shame, the scandal that would necessitate instant withdrawal from society.'

'You are a wicked man, Leo.'

'A practical man, my dear. And practical is what you should be. Marchmain may be the gentleman you profess, but he is a man, and a very attractive one, too. Think of that.'

The duchess did think of it. She hurried away to her chambers, a frown on her otherwise unblemished forehead, and immediately called for paper and pen.

Domino thought little more of Charlotte Severn. If her invitation ever materialised, she was sure she could depend on her father to rescue her. Alfredo was busier than ever and it seemed to Domino that whole days passed when she barely saw him. Looking for occupation, she decided to seek out one of the many art galleries that had sprung up in and around Brighton under the Regent's patronage. Prince George loved art and so, by default, did his courtiers—or, at least, they maintained the pretence that they did. But rather than attend the Picture Gallery on Grand Parade, which boasted an unrivalled collection of Italian and French art, she chose a newer and much quieter gallery situated to the north of the town. It was an unfashionable area and little visited by the nobility, but Domino had recently seen a flyer advertising the Grove Gallery's latest exhibition and had been intrigued by the more experimental art it was offering for sale. Mindful of Carmela's repeated injunctions, she took Flora with her.

It was a beautiful early July morning when they struck inland towards New England farm and the scattering of modern houses that had been built nearby. A delighted Flora chattered incessantly as they walked, for accompanying her mistress was a rare treat and she was determined to provide amusement on the arduous walk uphill. Listening to the unending flow with only one ear, Domino hoped fervently that her maid would run out of words well before they reached their destination.

Thirty minutes walking had brought them to the top of the Dyke Road, the main thoroughfare north out of Brighton, and Flora was still talking. They found the gallery easily enough, the only building apart from a scattering of new villas, set amongst fields where cows were placidly grazing amid the shadows. Not even Carmela could find dangers lurking in such a tranquil setting, Domino thought, and felt justified in asking the garrulous Flora to await for her outside. Gratefully she trod over the threshold and felt the silence fall like a gentle cloak on her shoulders. The interior was bright and airy, a large rectangular space, its walls hung with green baize and its floor covered by a rough drugget. The paintings were displayed seemingly at random, but the brilliant light emanating high up from latticed casements that encircled the entire top of the rectangle illuminated them perfectly. She looked about her with pleasure and began to relax.

The paintings were certainly unusual. She wasn't at all sure she liked them, though they were for the most part ingeniously executed. But there was one landscape that caught her eye and slowed her steps: the Downs on a tempestuous day, the grass, the bushes, the trees, all bending seawards in the westerly wind, seeming to tumble unstoppably towards the troubled and racing waters in the distance. A glorious sense of freedom, brought to life so strongly in the painting, swept through her. She wanted to awake every morning to that wild landscape, feel its energy and be invigorated. But the price tag was far beyond her means. Perhaps, she thought wistfully, she could return next year when she had inherited the very large fortune that awaited her—but then someone else would hold the purse strings. Perhaps that someone else would have a love of art too, would see how very special this picture was. But no, that was too fanciful. If he took any pleasure in painting, it would not be an English landscape that would hang in his bedroom.

Our bedroom, she thought, and quaked at the thought of the intimacies that must be shared with a virtual stranger.

'Are you going to buy it?'

Joshua Marchmain! The man seemed forever destined to disturb her peace. He had expressed a strong interest in art, but why had he chosen to visit this morning, and this gallery? The latter was soon explained.

'You would be doing a friend of mine a favour if you did—buy it, I mean.'

His voice was light and amused. She looked at him smiling lazily down at her, a shaft of sunlight pouring through the glass atrium above and reflecting pinpoints of light in the gold of his hair. As always he was immaculately dressed: a perfectly cut coat of dark blue superfine, an embroidered waistcoat of paler blue and close-fitting cream pantaloons. Despite the fashionable dress, he was no dandy. Domino was acutely aware of his body so close, so taut and hard, a body a woman could easily melt against. A wave of desire suddenly knotted her stomach and began its destructive trail through every fibre. She was genuinely shocked at her response and there was an uncomfortable pause before she was able to gather her wits together and wish him a prim good morning.

'I take it that your friend is the painter and this is his exhibition.'

'It is, and he is doing the painterly thing and starving in a garret.'

'Then, surely, you should be helping him.'

'I am very willing, but he won't hear of it. He maintains that he must live by his brush and his brush alone, and there are only so many paintings one individual can buy. So you see how important it is that you purchase his most treasured work. It's a splendid scene, is it not?'

He wondered if she would listen to the alarm bells clanging in her head, murmur something innocuous and move on, but her reply was one of genuine warmth.

'I think it wonderful—so wild and natural, so full of energy and joy.'

'Now I wonder why those qualities should appeal to you.'

The familiar flush flamed her cheeks and, seeing it, he made a vow to tread more carefully. He was intrigued by this delightful girl and, if he wanted to know her better, he would have to be sure to confine his remarks to the unexceptional. He offered her his arm.

'Since we are both here, Miss de Silva, do allow me to escort you around the rest of the exhibition.'

She hesitated for a fraction and he was relieved when good manners triumphed over churlishness. A lace-mittened hand was placed lightly on his arm and they began a stately progress around the gallery. He was hopeful that she would share his enthusiasm for the art and delighted when she willingly joined him in appraising the pictures they viewed, her dark eyes glowing with pleasure.

She was simply dressed in sprig muslin, but its soft folds and pleats revealed an exquisite young figure. From time to time her warm limbs touched his as they walked slowly side by side around the vast space and he felt his body stiffen in response. He wondered what those delightful curves would feel like beneath his hands and how soft that full mouth would be in meeting his.

'How have you become so knowledgeable, Mr Marchmain?'

Her words cut through this delightful fantasy and he was forced to administer a sharp mental shake before he could reply calmly, 'I think you might find the experts would quarrel with your use of the word *knowledgeable*. But I have travelled widely in Europe and have always made a point of seeking out the very best art each city could offer.'

'And have you kept travelling?' she asked wonderingly.

His voice when he answered was unusually sombre. 'There were a few years when I stayed put, years when I rented rooms in a Venetian palazzo. I found that an ideal location for painting.'

'It must have been. I've only ever seen pictures of Venice and I long to visit myself.'

'Then you must and as soon as possible. I would say that you were made for that city.'

And his gaze swept lingeringly over her: creamy olive skin, upturned nose and sorrowful dark eyes did not make a classical beauty, but something infinitely more charming. She blushed again and he silently chided himself. She was bewitching, that was the problem. She was so serious and yet so full of youthful energy that he wanted to open up the world for her and watch her smile. He was surprised by the force of his feelings.

'Do you still stay in Venice?'

'No longer, I fear. I inherited a property in England and it became necessary to return and become a responsible proprietor.'

'And where is your home now?'

'I would hardly call it home, but the house is known as Castle March. It's in Norfolk. Do you know it?' She shook her head. 'It is a large estate and needs managing. I ought to spend more time there, but ruralising in the depths of the English countryside is not exactly my forte.'

'I am sure that country living must have its own attractions.'

'Possibly—but only, I imagine, if you have someone to share them with.' Instantly he wished he had remained silent. That was the kind of remark that sent her into retreat. 'It can be pretty bleak in the fens for much of the year, so company is always welcome,' he offered, trying to retrieve the situation.

But she had taken alarm and detached herself from his arm. She adjusted the ribbons of her bonnet and thanked him prettily but firmly for his escort. In a moment she had disappeared out of the door and he was left to fume at his clumsiness. For a man of his address, he was managing extremely poorly, he thought. What was it about her that made him as maladroit as some untried adolescent? It could only be the enchantment of youth. For years he had strictly confined his most intimate attentions to experienced women; he had forgotten how utterly disarming innocent beauty could be.

The minute Domino stepped through the front door she saw the letter lying menacingly on the hall table and knew immediately from whom it came. The envelope was of thick cream vellum and bore a ducal crest. Charlotte Severn's invitation had arrived. The duchess's words uttered in the heat of the moment had been made good, but Domino had no wish to open the letter. She had taken the woman in dislike; why exactly she was unsure, but her father's condemnation had served only to underline the distaste she felt.

It was clear that the duchess was a close friend of Joshua Marchmain and he was certain to attend her social events. For that reason alone she would be reluctant to go. She had spent an engaging hour with him this afternoon, but he was a man she needed to avoid. He was dangerous to her peace of mind; the laughing eyes flecked with gold, the languorous gaze, had made her whole body burn in shameful response and promised the kind of pleasure she dared not think of. He was most definitely not a gentleman. He might dress as one and mix with ease in *ton* society, but he was rash and reckless and constantly put her out of countenance. How very unlike Richard, who was just as handsome but mindful of the proprieties and careful never to overstep the line. Joshua would not even recognise the existence of a line. He was undoubtedly a rake—a charming one, but someone with whom she should have no further commerce.

* * *

Her assumption that her father would prevent her attending the entertainment at Steine House proved false. When he walked into the dining room that evening, he was waving the duchess's card in his hand.

'The Duchess of Severn.' Then, seeing his daughter's long face, he said firmly, 'I think we must attend, Domino.'

'Could you not go alone, Papa?'

'I would prefer to, certainly. I am not at all keen that you further your acquaintance with the lady. But I fear we would give grave offence if you were to refuse.'

'But I am of no importance,' she persuaded eagerly. 'It is your position as ambassador that has prompted her to write.'

'I think not. The invitation was issued directly to you at the Chapel Royal. And my position, as you put it, means that I dare not offend anyone as influential as the Severns. The duke belongs to the Regent's inner circle.'

Domino made no reply, but sat erect, hands in her lap, and looked blankly ahead.

'Will it be such a trial, *querida*? We will stay no more than a couple of hours, I promise. And you will have me by your side the whole time.'

'I'm sorry, Papa, I'm being a goose.' Domino

leaned across the table and gave him a loving hug. 'I had hoped the duchess had forgotten me.'

'Unfortunately not. I only hope her remembrance does not signify that she wishes "to take you up", as they say here. Your standing would not be enhanced by her favour.' Alfredo sighed deeply. 'Negotiating our way successfully through the English Court was never going to be easy, but I may have underestimated the difficulties.'

A thought struck him and he brightened. 'Carmela can attend with us, then your being singled out for an invitation will not look so particular.'

Carmela, who had retired from the table and was sitting on the cushioned window seat reading an improving work, put her book down with a sharp slap. Her face glowered.

'I mean no disrespect to you, cousin, but nothing on earth would induce me to attend that woman's party.'

'Carmela, how is this? She may not be precisely to our taste, but she is a great noblewoman,' Alfredo chided her.

'Is that what you call it? We have a different word for it in Spain.'

He looked warningly at her and then back to Domino.

'What is that, Carmela?' Domino asked innocently.

Her cousin compressed her lips. 'Suffice to say that she is a married woman, but does not behave as one. She would not be welcome at any house belonging to our family.'

Domino looked shocked. 'You mean she has lovers?'

Carmela appeared to struggle with herself for a moment, but then decided where her duty lay.

'I do not generally indulge in idle gossip, as I hope you know,' she said repressively, 'but I think it right that you should be on your guard. In the few weeks we have been in Brighton I have heard disquieting things about the Duchess of Severn. I believe that her current lover has followed her here and is even now residing at the Pavilion.'

Domino glanced at her father, urgently seeking his reassurance, but no denial was forthcoming. His face was set and he refused to meet her eyes. Suddenly she understood. Joshua Marchmain was that lover. That was why he had been so irritated at the Chapel Royal. He had not wanted her to make the duchess's acquaintance, had not wanted her to know the truth of their supposed friendship. She felt herself flushing hotly, embarrassed at having been so naïve. Flushing, too, with a kind of pain. But why on earth did she feel that? Had she been stupid enough to think there was any kind of connection between them?

It was true that he had singled her out at her father's reception and engaged her in lengthy conversation. He had even talked sensibly and interestingly about art. But that was misleading. She should remember her first encounter with him as she walked by the sea; his conduct had been predatory, light-hearted and amusing, it was true, but nevertheless predatory. Even outside the church on Sunday he had not been able to resist throwing out lures to her. He was a womaniser for whom every female was fair game, even as his mistress was living a mere stone's throw away. The thought of visiting Steine House was loathsome.

A few days later, an unwelcome message arrived at Marine Parade. Señor de Silva was required to return to London immediately. News had arrived from Spain too confidential to be entrusted to a messenger and it was necessary for the ambassador to post up to Manchester House. He would spend only one night away, but it looked unlikely that he would return to Brighton in time for Charlotte Severn's soirée.

Alfredo was faced with a quandary. He had

no wish to expose his daughter to the malign influence of Steine House without his protection but, at the same time, he knew that it was essential he was represented at what would be a prestigious affair. He would let Domino herself decide.

'I hardly like to ask this of you, my dear,' he began tentatively, 'but would you be willing to go to the duchess's concert by yourself for a short while? I could no doubt arrange for an older lady to take you under her wing until I return. Once I am back in Brighton, I will make haste to join you at Steine House. Or perhaps Carmela could swallow her misgivings? If she would agree to attend, it would make things a great deal more comfortable.'

The women's despondent expressions hardly promised comfort. Attending the event without the support of Señor de Silva was the last thing either of them wished to contemplate. But they both found themselves agreeing to his suggestion, Domino because she loved her father dearly and knew that he would not ask this of her unless it was necessary and Carmela because the family's honour was at stake and that was sufficient to call forth her loyalty.

So it was that at six o'clock on a balmy Friday evening the two of them set off in a hired carriage for Steine House. It had an infamous reputation, for it was the home the Regent had purchased for his long-standing mistress and unofficial wife, Maria Fitzherbert. She still resided there and was hardly ever seen beyond its walls, though the Prince was said even now to visit her frequently, despite a legal marriage and many subsequent lovers. Rumour insisted that a tunnel ran via the adjoining Marlborough House to the basement of the royal palace. The Duke of Severn was an old friend of Mrs Fitzherbert and he and his wife were always made welcome in her home when they visited the town. The duke in particular could not bear to live permanently in the overheated Pavilion and always availed himself of this hospitality.

The whispers that swirled around Steine House could only sharpen the aversion both Domino and her cousin felt at having to enter its portals. But when their carriage stopped outside, they saw only a graceful white stucco building with an Italian-style façade and a trellised verandah and balcony. A balustrade of carved ironwork led up a single flight of steps to a heavily ornamented glass door. Domino pinned on what she hoped was a polite smile and made ready to greet her hosts. She received a courteous welcome, the duke seeming to her young eyes horribly withered and old.

No wonder the duchess looked elsewhere, she found herself musing, then promptly castigated herself for such an appalling thought. Steine House was already having a noxious effect. Once inside the main door, they were directed up a bamboo and iron staircase to a salon from which the strains of music could already be heard.

'This is the staircase Lord Barrymore once rode his horse up for a bet,' Carmela hissed in her ear.

Domino paused on the staircase, startled for a moment by her staid cousin's incongruous knowledge of *ton* gossip. Where on earth did she hear such stories? As she stood balanced on one foot, she caught sight of her reflection in the long pier glass at the top of the stairs. She was pleased with what she saw. The apricot silk she had chosen, trimmed with gold edging and worn with an overdress of cream-coloured gauze, set off the creamy olive of her complexion perfectly. Her glossy ebony curls hung naturally to her neck in ringlets this evening and her eyes were sparkling, if only in apprehension. Carmela leaned forwards and tapped her wrist sharply with her fan, a painful reminder that in her cousin's book any sign of vanity was sinful.

In a few moments they were in the large

salon, a huge scarlet cavern of a room hung with red satin curtains and upholstered in red plush velvet. A uniformed footman ushered them to one of the rows of little gold chairs that had been arranged in the shape of a wide semi-circle. Domino sat down gingerly on one of the tiny chairs.

'Be careful, Carmela,' she warned, 'these chair legs are so thin that one false fidget and the sound of matchwood will drown out the string quartet.'

Carmela permitted herself a slight smile and looked searchingly around the room. 'I see nobody who came to our reception,' she remarked disappointedly. 'How strange when a most famous soprano is to sing.'

'Evidently they have decided to miss the delights on offer.' Including Joshua Marchmain, she noted wryly.

She told herself she was glad that at least this evening she would not have to face him. Yet, unaccountably, she felt a pang of disappointment. She had enjoyed her tour of the Grove Gallery. True, she had been put out of countenance once or twice by his infelicitous remarks, but she had spent nigh on an hour in his company discussing nothing more incendiary than art and European travel. He was interesting and intelligent, and though he had visited places she could only dream of, he had not made her feel the gauche girl she knew herself to be.

But rumour had named him the lover of any number of married women, including Charlotte Severn. Could rumour have possibly lied? In her heart she knew it could not. Mr Marchmain was a thorough-going rake and, if the sensations of her own unruly body were anything to judge by, he did not have to work too hard for his success. The shaft of intense desire that had pierced her so suddenly and so unexpectedly signalled clearly that she was in danger of being drawn into a whirlpool of feeling, with him at its centre. It was well for her that he was not here this evening.

'My lords, ladies and gentlemen, I give you the illustrious soprano, Bianca Bonelli.'

The duke led the famous singer, who had journeyed from Milan at his request, to a raised platform, kissing her hand enthusiastically while the string quartet began to play the opening piece of music. Domino set herself to listen with what she hoped was a thoughtful expression.

A late-arriving Joshua, hovering in the doorway, spotted her immediately and almost laughed aloud at her face, screwed up in concentration—or was that pain? If it was, it was a pain he shared. He made a swift escape to the library, where he would not be disturbed, but from where he could still hear the concert's end.

And end it did, with a great deal of relief on Domino's part. Carmela wore her usual severe expression but her spontaneous applause made clear her enjoyment. Hardly surprising, Domino thought, for the music had evinced a moral seriousness sufficient even for her cousin. The latter seemed eager to meet the musicians personally and, when the duchess suddenly appeared at their side, Carmela was whisked away for introductions and Domino found herself led by Charlotte into an adjoining salon where liveried footmen were circulating with drinks and canapés.

Her Grace deftly lifted two large flutes of champagne from a passing tray and said with an enticing smile, 'I am so pleased you were able to come, Miss de Silva, as I collect your father has been forced to post back to London on urgent business.'

'Indeed, Your Grace. He sends his most sincere apologies and will make every effort to join us this evening.'

'I understand,' she cooed, 'and really it matters not. You are my prize, after all. I was entranced when we met at the Chapel Royal on Sunday and have spent all week wishing to know more of you.'

Domino doubted that very much. The woman's insincerity was blatant, but she managed a gentle smile in response.

'Tell me, do,' the duchess continued, 'how long are we to have the pleasure of your company in Brighton?'

'For the Season, ma'am. I have undertaken to stay with my father while the Court is absent from London.'

For a moment the expression on her hostess's face suggested she was not best pleased by this news, but she rallied immediately.

'How delightful, for we are also destined to be here until the Prince returns to Carlton House. Let us toast our new acquaintanceship, Miss de Silva. I am sure we will be the best of friends.'

Domino could not think so, but politely raised her glass. Champagne bubbles shot up her nose and she had difficulty in preventing herself sneezing.

'You see,' Charlotte continued, 'one meets so few new people in Brighton, the same dreary crowd year after year. So when a bright new star appears, one is drawn immediately towards them.'

Domino concluded that she must be the

bright star, but was at a loss how to answer. She need not have worried, for the duchess was now in full flow.

'You are so beautiful, my dear, and have such charming manners, that I prophesy prodigious success for you—you will be the toast of the town.'

This was so patently absurd that Domino was hard put not to laugh aloud. She knew herself to be well enough but, against the duchess's blonde perfection, she was nothing. And she certainly had no ambition to take Brighton by storm. Quite the opposite—she anticipated several agreeable months by the sea, close to her father, before she returned to Spain to make the decision of her life.

The duchess continued to talk while she sipped her champagne. The drink was gradually becoming more acceptable, and when her companion substituted her empty glass for another fizzing to the brim, she hardly noticed. When the older woman took her by the hand, she allowed herself to be expertly steered through the crowd towards a smaller chamber at the far end of the salon.

'In proof of my friendship, Miss de Silva— but may I call you Domino? Such a sweet and unusual name—I would very much like you to meet some particular friends of mine. Just a few congenial spirits whom I know you will esteem.'

Her head had begun to spin a little, but she retained enough caution to remind her hostess that Carmela should be with them.

'But naturally, my dear. I shall introduce you to a few dear companions and then collect your cousin and bring her instantly to you.'

They were through the door before Domino could protest further. The room they entered, though smaller than the salon, was still a substantial size, thickly carpeted and curtained, deadening all sound and cutting the space adrift from the outside world. A number of people were gathered around three large tables set at different angles in the room; even in her befuddled state, she knew instantly that this was a gaming room. She pulled back sharply.

'I am honoured, Your Grace, that you should wish to introduce me to your friends,' she stumbled, 'but I do not play cards or any other game of chance.'

'Allow me to advise you, my dear, since you are still so very young.' The duchess's voice was honey. 'You have undertaken to play the role of hostess for your father. In England, you know, polite society expects always to have the opportunity to indulge in games of chance and a hostess must be as well versed in them as her guests.'

'I thank you again, Your Grace, but I do not gamble.'

'Who said anything about gambling? Just a few friendly games, my dear.'

Domino felt deeply uncomfortable. She was finding it very difficult to continue refusing her hostess, but games of chance, whether money passed hands or not, were something she had sworn never again to engage in. She had learned her lesson all too well the last time she was in England. Gambling had a fatal attraction for her and she could not risk getting involved. But she could hardly say this to someone she barely knew, to a woman who occupied such an exalted position. Her head was definitely swimming now and her legs feeling decidedly unsafe. She felt the duchess's hand on her shoulder and began to sink downwards to the waiting chair. The faces around the table looked up at her expectantly. In the distance other faces at other tables blurred into a misty vision. She longed to get away but she could not, in politeness, leave. Surely just one hand of cards would not matter. She would satisfy the demands of hospitality and then depart straight away. She took hold of the arms of the chair, making ready to sit down, and the support made her feel slightly less shaky. She smiled hazily at the assembled company and then, out of the blur, a face swam into her vision. A dark, wolfish, horribly familiar face. Leo Moncaster!

Chapter Three

She gave a sudden choke, shaken by an irrational panic, and would have collapsed but for a supportive hand at her elbow.

'Miss de Silva? How nice to see you here,' Joshua Marchmain was saying smoothly. 'I hope you found the music to your taste.'

'Yes, indeed, thank you,' she stuttered.

He was holding his arm out to her and she took it. Nervously she glanced at the woman who stood at her left side. Charlotte Severn's eyes were narrowed, but there was no mistaking the daggers she was sending forth.

'The concert was delightful, was it not? And such a privilege to hear Signora Bonelli. I believe she is judged one of the finest sopranos of our day.' His voice was unruffled, but even while he spoke he was skilfully extricating the apricot silk from the entanglements of chair and table.

By now the duchess had regained her composure and, in a gesture of seeming warmth, clasped hold of Domino's other arm.

'But must you go already?' she addressed the girl directly, excluding Joshua from the conversation. 'I am delighted that you enjoyed our small concert, but do stay for the rest of the evening's entertainments.'

Her head still whirling, Domino was caught between the two and had no idea how to cope with the dreadful situation. It was one scenario that the etiquette books failed to mention.

Joshua locked glances with the duchess. His voice was imperturbable as ever, but there was an edging of steel that Domino had never heard before.

'It does not seem, Your Grace, that card playing holds much attraction for Miss de Silva, so I will engage to reunite her with her cousin.'

Leaving their hostess stranded with outstretched hand, he propelled Domino firmly towards the door and whisked her through it. Once on the other side he cut a swathe through the milling crowd to arrive unerringly at Carmela's side. Her cousin wore a worried expression, which rapidly turned to exasperation once she saw Domino safe and well. She nodded curtly to Joshua and grabbed Domino by the arm. Social politeness was brushed aside and, without waiting to bid their hosts goodbye, Carmela made for the bamboo staircase. The carriage had been ordered and was already waiting outside.

Catching her breath at the head of the stairs, Domino had only time to glance briefly over her shoulder. Joshua Marchmain had not spoken a word as they'd threaded their way through the crowded room, but now she saw him in conversation with the duchess, their heads close and talking animatedly together. Her heart lurched as she took in the intimacy of the little tableau. But why did the image cause her such distress? All the while Carmela was bundling her down the stairs and into the coach, she struggled to find an answer. Why on earth should Joshua's relationship with the duchess matter? She knew them to be lovers— naturally they would have much to say to each other. He would be keen to explain his absence from the concert and to excuse his intervention with Domino, even keener no doubt to make an assignation with his mistress for later that evening. It all made perfect sense, but it only served to intensify her misery.

* * *

Unknown to Domino, her departure left the two locked in a furious exchange.

'What exactly were you thinking of?' Cold anger permeated Joshua's voice.

'I don't pretend to understand you.'

'I think you understand me perfectly. Miss de Silva is still a minor and yet you were encouraging her to break the law by gambling.'

'Don't be ridiculous.' The duchess fairly spat the words. 'I merely suggested to her that she might like to join a select gathering and play a few rounds of loo.'

'A select gathering—is that what you call it?' He snorted derisively.

'I take it that you finally decided to put in an appearance this evening for reasons other than to be unpleasant.'

'It's as well I did. It was clear that the girl did not want to stay and just as clear that you were intent on forcing her.'

'What rubbish. How could I ever force her to do anything she did not wish? If you had not interrupted us in that nonsensical manner, she would be happily playing cards this very moment.'

'Playing cards, I am sure, but happily I don't believe.'

'I say again, how could I make her play cards

if she did not wish it?' The duchess's expression was scornful.

'I imagine a few judicious glasses of champagne might help to do the trick, together with pressure from her hostess which she would find difficult to resist.'

'You talk as though she were an innocent. It won't have been the first time that she has supped champagne, I'm sure, and from what I hear she has been more than happy in the past to engage in games of chance—even, dare I say, to accrue considerable debts.'

'How can that be?'

For an instant Joshua appeared less composed and the duchess watched him with a gloating expression. 'Why don't you ask her? The two of you seem remarkably thick with each other. And why are you so late? The concert is long finished.'

'I am devastated to have missed it,' he said with barely concealed irony, 'and naturally I apologise. I was visiting—an artist friend—and was unexpectedly detained.'

'That must have been important,' came the brittle rejoinder, and she walked away to mingle with her guests in the inner sanctum. Leo Moncaster was waiting for her.

'I can see why you wanted to handle the matter yourself.' His smile was sardonic.

'I was wrong. She was far more stubborn than I gave her credit for. But I think I would have succeeded in the end if Marchmain had not turned up at that moment and spoiled the game.'

'And you still feel that she is of no interest to him?'

She did not answer him directly, but said slowly and deliberately, 'I need to get rid of her.'

There was a slight pause before Moncaster said in a heartening voice, 'Don't be too discouraged, Charlotte. It would have been difficult to coax her to stay once she saw my face. There must be more subtle ways to catch our little bird.'

'You have some ideas?'

'I have some ideas. Shall we now work together?'

Charlotte Severn's nod was almost imperceptible but Lord Moncaster retired that night a contented man.

Domino slept fitfully and woke unrefreshed to a new day. The events at Steine House still crowded her mind, filling it with jangled impressions only half-understood, but all of them contributing to her despondency. How was she to make sense of such a dreadful evening? The concert had evoked stifled yawns, but at least it had been innocuous. It was the Duchess of Severn herself who had seemed far from innocent. She had appeared to be so friendly, so keen to make Domino's acquaintance that she should have felt flattered. Despite her dubious reputation, Charlotte Severn was enormously influential and her notice of a mere ambassador's daughter would for most be a cause of pleasure and gratitude. But Domino had felt neither pleased nor grateful. Instead she had felt manipulated, even coerced. She had not wanted to abandon Carmela, but the Duchess had been insistent. She had not wanted to enter the inner room, yet had found herself propelled through its doors unable to protest. And once there her fears had multiplied. Seeing Leo Moncaster had been the final straw. His malevolent face still lowered in her dreams. Three years ago he had been her undoing and here he was once more, ready to do her harm if he possibly could.

Rescue had come, but at what cost? Just when she'd decided that on no account must she have further dealings with Joshua Marchmain, he had made her beholden. How shameful to be dependent on a rake for rescue! He had said not a word as he'd walked her towards her cousin and sanctuary, but he must have thought her a silly and naïve girl, out of her depth and drowning. It was evident that he had been angry with the duchess—at one point Domino had felt literally pulled between the two of them—and she might have found comfort in that, but for the last glimpse she'd had of the pair.

They had stood as though closeted, their heads so close that his cheek was almost grazing the woman's hair. Any animosity had vanished. They had been talking easily together and she had a sinking feeling that she had been the main subject of their conversation. Her face burned; they would decide that she was a foolish young girl who had become hysterical when invited to partake in a game of chance. Then a worse thought struck, making her face burn even brighter. What if she really had been that foolish, foolish enough to imagine the whole thing and misinterpret the duchess's conduct? This high-born lady had gone out of her way to be friendly and her seeming coercion might simply be a desire to encourage a reluctant young guest to enjoy herself. The duchess would not know her unfortunate history with Lord Moncaster; she would be ignorant of the dread he evoked. And how had Domino responded to Charlotte's overtures? Blind, inexplicable panic and a dreadful lapse of good manners. She and Carmela had left the party without a word of thanks or indeed a word of farewell. It was appalling.

She told herself that she must not dwell on such harrowing thoughts, but dwell on them she did. The evening's events continued to revolve in her mind until they began to assume hideous proportions. She wished that her mother was by her side to guide her. She knew that she could have told Mama everything—well, nearly everything, she amended inwardly. Her feelings towards Joshua would have remained under wraps. She did not even understand them herself. How could she feel this strong attraction to him when Richard had been the only man she had ever loved?

Remember him, remember him, she told herself fiercely. Richard, the new Lord Veryan, and she a whirling figure in pale blue, dancing with him at Almack's for the very first time. How wonderful that had been. She hugged the memory, warmed by its still-powerful glow, chasing Joshua and her confusion away. But then another image emerged: Richard dancing that very same night with Christabel, the woman he contended he despised, the woman who had so cruelly jilted him, but the woman he still loved. Domino had known even then, deep in her innermost self, that his feelings for the flame-haired beauty had not died and that he was deceiving himself in thinking he was free of her power. But how resolute she herself had been in refusing to see the truth of the situation, wishing, hoping that he would turn his head and see the girl who was so often by his side through those long summer months, the girl who idolised him. But all he saw was a scrubby schoolgirl, without guile or wisdom, too spontaneous for her own good. Was that what Joshua saw? Was this another situation in which she was blind to the truth?

For much of the day she stayed cloistered in her room, venturing downstairs only at meal-times, though in truth she had little appetite. At the table Carmela made no mention of yesterday's tribulations and Domino could only assume that her cousin had vowed herself to silence. Señor de Silva seemed to have taken the same vow. He had arrived from London in the early hours of the morning and Domino had expected to find him eager to hear details of their visit to Steine House. But not one question did he ask. Perhaps Carmela had alerted him to the wretchedness of the evening. Domino had committed a serious impropriety in disappearing for some considerable time without a chaperon, but neither her father nor her cousin appeared to blame her.

Indeed, they both treated her with unaccustomed gentleness and, during the days that followed, were careful never to comment on her fondness for her room and her refusal to venture out for even a short walk.

It was Alfredo who finally broke the impasse on a morning that sparkled with light.

'The weather is so fine, *querida*,' he said heartily, embracing her in one of his bear hugs. 'Why don't we walk on the Downs, perhaps even take a picnic?'

Carmela nodded silent approval and he continued persuasively, 'The breeze will keep us cool and we should easily find sufficient shade to enjoy our meal.'

She said nothing, but her expression was downcast. Her father, though, was not to be defeated. 'Just you and I,' he coaxed.

She did not wish to disappoint him, but shrank at the idea of walking on the Downs, or indeed anywhere in the vicinity. What she wanted most was to hide away—from the duchess, from Moncaster and particularly from Joshua Marchmain. Every time she stepped outside the door, she risked meeting with one or other of them. Brighton was not a large town.

'If that is too far for you, we could take a short walk through the Lanes.' Alfredo would not be dissuaded, and she saw how concerned he was. 'It's not good, Domino, to be confined in these four walls for too long.'

She knew he was right. Eventually she would have to emerge from her refuge and face whatever or whoever came her way. She was compounding her folly at Steine House with even greater folly. And showing a drastic lack of spirit too, she castigated herself. She needed to regain her usual vitality and show the world that she was ashamed of nothing. She could do that, must do that. If she met Charlotte Severn, she would smile and curtsy and leave it to the other woman to set the tone. If she met Lord Moncaster, her father would be there to defend her. And if she met Joshua— but she would not, she was sure. She had been shut away in Marine Parade for nearly a week and had heard nothing of him. He had his own tight little circle and would not have noticed her absence from the social scene.

'I need to change my books at the library, Papa,' she offered, 'and if you are agreeable we could walk there.'

The library she patronised, one of the many that were dotted across Brighton, was in the west of the town and would furnish a satisfying stroll. On the way, there was the distraction of any number of tempting shop windows filled with exquisite silks and laces, almost certainly smuggled from France. She chose her dress with care, searching for as plain a gown as possible, and ended by donning a simple but stylish jaconet muslin. Once out of the house, she kept her eyes lowered beneath the deep brim of her straw bonnet, but she need not have worried, for the *ton* were out of town that day it seemed, enjoying themselves elsewhere. They walked through near-deserted streets while her father told her of his trip to London and the worrying news from Spain.

'A change of government usually means a change of everything else,' he confided to her. 'I am no longer certain of my position. It could be that I am recalled to Madrid very soon and perhaps reassigned elsewhere. I am sorry, if that happens, *querida*. Your holiday by the sea will come to an abrupt end.'

She squeezed his arm reassuringly, but felt a tremor of foreboding. Leaving Brighton would mean separation from her father when they had so recently been reunited. It would mean an inevitable return to Spain and the future that awaited her. The life she had agreed upon just a few weeks ago seemed increasingly dreary. Nothing had changed and yet everything seemed different. She was still pondering this paradox when they arrived at the fashionable new subscription library, which fronted the western end of the promenade.

Usually its coffee rooms and lounges were filled with residents and fashionable visitors but, as with the rest of the town today, it was nearly empty. A few ladies were browsing the bookshelves and a small card game was in play at one end of the smallest saloon. Another gentleman was busy sifting through music sheets, evidently keen to find something new for the musical evening he was planning.

'All at the Race Ground,' he explained succinctly when Alfredo mentioned the scarcity of people. 'The Regent's Cup today, y' know. Big prize money.'

'I wish we had known…' her father turned to Domino '…you would have enjoyed the meeting. That's what comes of staying too close to home.'

She could only feel gratitude that her father had not heard the news. At the race course she would have been sure to see everyone that she most wished to avoid.

Thirty minutes of browsing the floor-to-ceiling bookshelves secured a neat pile of small volumes and they made ready to leave. They were almost out of the door when her father spied a tattered poster taped insecurely to the wall.

'Look, Domino, Henry Angelo has set up a new fencing academy here in Brighton. I was tempted in London to try a lesson or two with him.'

She could not help but smile. Her father's physique in middle age was hardly conducive to fencing.

'Why do you smile, little one? You think I couldn't do it?'

'No, Papa, I am sure you could, but wouldn't you prefer to watch rather than participate?'

'Perhaps you are right, though in my youth I was a match for anyone.'

'Yes?'

'I actually beat the legendary Don Roderiguez.'

She looked questioningly.

'You wouldn't know of him. It was well before you were born, but he was worshipped in Madrid for his skill. I took him on as a wager and nobody expected me to win, but I did.'

'And Don Roderiguez?'

'I have to admit that he was probably not quite himself. I managed to fight him after a particularly boisterous party.'

They both laughed and she said wistfully, 'Gentlemen are so lucky; they have many channels for their energy. All we have is embroidery or the pianoforte.'

'I don't notice either of those featuring heavily in your life, my dear.'

'Exactly, Papa, that is just what I mean. Fencing would be far more enjoyable.'

And it would get rid of some of my restlessness, she thought, even perhaps beat the blue-devils that have been plaguing me. Yes, men were lucky. A woman had simply to sit, to watch and to wait.

Unbeknown to her, Alfredo had taken note of his daughter's interest and promptly committed to memory the address of the new fencing school. He would arrange a small treat for her. Lately she had seemed unusually dejected. He knew the evening at Steine House had not gone to plan, but he was in the dark about his daughter's true state of mind. Anything that would distract her could only be good.

So it was that Henry Angelo had an early morning visitor the next day. The request was unusual and certainly unconventional, but he had a business to establish and an ambassador was too important a personage to offend in these early days. His school had already attracted the attention of those members of the *ton* spending the summer in Brighton, but

Señor de Silva could prove useful in bringing new clients from the diplomatic circles in which he moved.

Summoned to an early breakfast, Domino found her father already at the table, seething with barely suppressed excitement.

'What have you been doing, Papa?' she asked guardedly. 'You look like a naughty schoolboy.'

'This morning I have important papers to clear, but this afternoon, Domino, we are to play truant together!'

'And Carmela?' Her cousin had not yet put in an appearance.

'Carmela and playing truant are not compatible, I think.' Señor de Silva smiled happily. 'This is just for you and me.'

'Not a picnic on the Downs?' she asked in some alarm. Despite her resolve to be brave, she still feared places where she risked meeting the world and his wife.

'No, no picnic. The wind today is far too strong even for the English to eat outdoors.'

Through the windows she saw the grey surf breaking harshly on the sea wall and spilling through the iron railings that defended the promenade. A few hardy souls, determined to complete their daily constitutional, were making their slow progress along the seafront. They were bent nearly double as they headed into the fierce wind, clutching wildly at flying garments.

'Then indoors somewhere?'

'Indeed. But you must probe no further. It is to be a great surprise!'

She had hoped to spend the day curled on the sofa reading some of the library's offerings, but it was evident that Alfredo had made special plans and she was sufficiently intrigued to hurry upstairs after a modest nuncheon and change her dress. Choosing suitable raiment proved difficult, for she had no idea where she was going. Eventually she settled on a primrose sarsenet flounced with French trimmings: modest enough for an informal outing, yet not too plain. She quickly threaded a matching primrose ribbon through a tangle of black curls and joined her father in the hall.

'We will go by carriage,' he announced as Marston battled to hold the front door ajar. 'The weather is far too rough to walk.'

Soon they were bowling past fishermen painting boats that had been pulled high on to the beach, past their women tending the nets and then past Mahomed's much-patronised Vapour Baths, until they reached the end of

East Cliff. The imposing mansions that lined the road gradually became far less in number as they travelled eastwards, but just before they reached open countryside the carriage pulled up at a small establishment tucked between two much larger white-washed dwellings. An arched wooden door painted in luminescent green beckoned a greeting and, even before they had taken a step out of the vehicle, a sprightly, dark-haired man bounded out to greet them.

'Welcome, welcome,' he enthused, executing a deep bow. 'I am most honoured by your visit.' Domino supposed him to be the proprietor of whatever establishment they had come to.

'Follow me, please, come this way.' The man ushered them into the house, fairly dancing down a narrow passageway to a small but comfortable sitting room. All the time he kept up a stream of lively chatter.

Looking around her she saw a pair of highly polished rapiers crossed above the fireplace and all four plastered walls closely hung with prints of sword fighting. Her father had brought her to none other than the fencing academy they had seen advertised! It was hardly the outing she would have chosen, but she owed it to him to look pleased. For days he had good humouredly tolerated the Friday face she had been wearing and must have gone to some trouble to arrange what he clearly thought an interesting diversion.

Henry Angelo proved an attentive host. She had to suppress a smile; this most Italian of men was intent on solemnly observing the rituals of an English tea. He did it with aplomb, pouring the steaming liquid himself and handing around the Crown Derby teacups with a splendid flourish. Small delicate scones with a selection of jams were offered, followed by pastries and fruit cake. The whole time Signor Angelo bubbled along with his tea.

'My father moved from Paris, you know, forty years ago to set up a fencing school in London. It was a gamble, but he has been very successful!'

'So I understand,' Alfredo acknowledged, 'and you are continuing the family tradition, I see.'

'I hope so. These new premises in Brighton are a venture, but I am gradually becoming known. And it helps that my father has many powerful friends. He knows the great boxer, Gentleman Jackson.'

'Really?' Alfredo appeared genuinely interested.

'Yes, indeed. He numbers Mr Jackson among his closest friends. Years ago he helped him establish a boxing club next door to our Fencing Academy in Bond Street.'

Reminiscences of the Gentleman's many successful prize fights, and a listing of all the great and the good that had frequented both establishments, followed at breakneck speed.

'The Regent himself honoured us with a visit to Bond Street,' the younger Henry announced breathlessly. 'We hosted an exhibition of fencing just for him, you know, and he asked for a set of foils used by the master fencer of the day. Masks and gloves, too!' he concluded triumphantly.

The heat of the small sitting room, combined with the unbroken flow of small talk, was making Domino's head swim. She was heartily glad when their host danced once more to his feet and made ready to show them around the Academy of which he was inordinately proud.

Once in the school proper, there was far more space and air and she breathed more freely. Signor Angelo led them from one practice room to another. The building was far larger than it appeared from outside, stretching back seawards a considerable distance. Each room was flooded with natural light, the ceiling consisting almost entirely of glass panels open to the sky. Collections of foils, their guards decorated with a variety of acanthus leaves, anchors, cherubs and serpents, filled the corners of each room. Still voluble, their host was explaining at length the distinctive style of French epées, Italian rapiers and English swords. From a large oak cupboard in one room face masks and padded bibs spilled out on to the floor.

'*Señor*, please, try one of these,' he invited Alfredo, holding up a stiff white corset. 'It is the very latest in design.'

The body padding was a cause of some humour since Señor de Silva's rotund figure defeated all attempts to accommodate it. Alfredo smiled ruefully.

'My dream of fencing is again dashed!'

They had passed through a series of such rooms when their host suggested that they might like to see a demonstration.

'I have just now one of my best instructors engaged in a training bout with a most proficient amateur. They are upstairs in an arena I keep for more serious competition.'

Alfredo looked a little uncertain, but Domino smiled easily and they mounted the steps to a large room that filled the whole of the first floor of the building. Signor Angelo waved them to the chairs situated at the very edge of the room. The two combatants were at some distance, but immediately she became aware of the sheer volume of energy crackling in the air. Their white-clothed figures circled each other, lunging, parrying, occasionally retreating to recover position. It was impossible to tell who was the instructor and who the pupil, since the opponents were so well matched and first one man, then the other, gained the advantage.

She found herself being pulled into the drama of the fight. It was a practice session only and the buttons were firmly secured to the top of the men's foils, yet there was a sense of restrained danger. Both men were at the prime of their fitness: one small and angular, buzzing forwards and backwards like an angry bee, the other slim but muscular, agile and menacing in his weavings. She watched his body tauten and slacken in response to the other's constant teasing, his muscles hardened and contouring his body. He had such natural grace and such power in his limbs that she was mesmerised into following his every movement, imbibing his male strength almost like a drug. She would have liked to reach out and touch him, stroke the line of his rippling arm, his slim waist, his powerful thigh. For a moment she found herself breathless, liquid with desire.

Then she shook herself awake. She had not felt such a powerful emotion since Richard had smiled at her and turned her body to water. With a shock, she realised she had not thought of Richard once during the past few days. Somehow he had begun to drift into the distance, remote from the pressing concerns of her life. And thinking of him now no longer evoked the same eager yearning that it had always done. What could that mean? That she was ready to give herself to another, ready perhaps for the husband who was even now awaiting her return to Spain? Would he evoke the same intense desire that had just shaken her? It seemed unlikely.

The bout was over and the opponents shaking hands. Signor Angelo rushed forwards and congratulated his pupil.

'That was *magnifico*, *signor*. You get better all the time.'

The man addressed laid down his foil and raised his mask. Of course, it could only be him, she thought.

Joshua Marchmain smiled across the length of the room and walked slowly towards her. She drank in his shapely form. Really, fencing clothes left little to the imagination. He wiped the beads of sweat from his forehead and smiled that leonine smile.

'If I'd known I had such an audience, I would have finished off Guido in double-quick time!'

He bowed courteously and raised her hand to his lips, just grazing the surface.

She found herself unable to speak. His touch had reignited the earlier fire and she was helpless to dampen its ravages. It was left to her father to fill the silence that spread between them.

'Thank you for a splendid display, sir. I have not seen such skill for many years.'

'You fence yourself?'

'I used to.' Alfredo smiled wryly. 'But tell me, was that the Italian style?'

'Always the Italian style,' Henry Angelo put in. 'Mr Marchmain fences like a professional.'

'I had to wait until I reached Italy before I learned the true art of fencing,' Joshua said in explanation.

'But now you don't have to do it for real, eh?' Henry interrupted. 'English husbands are more complacent.' And he waved his hand at the scar that Joshua bore on his cheek.

The barely disguised reminder that this man was an out-and-out rake brought Domino back to her senses. In seconds she had recovered her poise.

'How often do you fence, Mr Marchmain?' she asked in a neutral voice.

Still flushed with annoyance at Angelo's intervention, Joshua turned to her, suddenly smiling so sweetly that hammer blows again began to afflict her heart.

'As often as I can, Miss de Silva. Are you interested in the sport?'

'I have never seen it until today, but I can understand why men find it so exciting.'

'But not women,' he mocked.

'I am sure if we were allowed the necessary freedom, sir, we too might find it exciting.'

'Any time you wish to strike for freedom and would like a lesson, Miss de Silva, I am at your service.'

The golden eyes darkened and she felt his voice caressing her with a warmth akin to velvet. She was quite certain that it wasn't only fencing he had in mind.

Her father was frowning, looking from one to the other, and when he spoke his tone was brisk. 'I am sure it is an excellent way of keeping fit, but my daughter enjoys riding. In Argentina she was constantly in the saddle.'

'And do you still ride in England?'

'A little. The fresh air is beneficial, but trotting tamely on Rotten Row is hardly exacting.'

'Then perhaps you should try something else.'

'What would you suggest?' she challenged, hardly daring to imagine what form of exercise he had in mind.

'For something a little more demanding, why don't you try sea bathing?' His voice was bland, but she felt sure he was laughing just below the surface.

'I hardly think that would be suitable,' her father interrupted.

'I assure you it is all the fashion. The ladies have their own part of the beach, you know, and are well looked after by the "dippers"—the bathing attendants.'

'But still, it would not do. Your aunts...' Alfredo left the sentence unfinished.

'They would certainly not contemplate sea bathing.' Domino's face lit with amusement at what those very proper ladies would make of such a suggestion.

'But should you not enjoy all that Brighton has to offer before you return to London?'

'My daughter will not be returning to London,' Alfredo said decisively.

Joshua did not look at him, but instead fixed Domino with an intense gaze. 'You will not be staying in town this autumn?'

'I will be returning to Spain,' she said quietly.

'That is sad news.' His voice held genuine regret. 'But before you go, you can surely spare us a few weeks in the capital?'

Her father once more intervened. 'I regret

not. My daughter has a very important date to keep and must leave for Spain immediately when the Brighton season ends.'

Joshua looked at her enquiringly.

'I am to be married, Mr Marchmain, and must return to Spain to meet my bridegroom.' She touched her father's arm and, with a brief bow in Joshua's direction, they were gone.

For a moment he stood motionless, hardly able to believe her words. Then he wheeled around abruptly and made for the changing room, his mind buzzing noisily. Married? But to whom? She had said that she was going to Spain to meet her bridegroom, which meant, dear God, that she did not yet know the man. She did not know the man with whom she was destined to spend the rest of her life. An arranged marriage! Fury welled up in him and he slashed blindly at the walls as he strode along the passageway. Whatever Charlotte had intimated, the girl was an innocent. How could her father dream of sacrificing her in such a way; how could she think of agreeing to give herself to a stranger? The idea that any young woman might offer herself to a man she did not know sat uneasily with him, but this was Domino. Domino! A girl so enchanting, so full of youthful joy, that he could have wept iron tears. He dressed quickly and every layer of clothing was donned in rage. He did not understand the fury that was shaking him, but he could not remember ever feeling so angry.

He had to get himself under control. He hardly knew the girl—it was madness to react so strongly to an arranged marriage. In his world they were frequent; indeed, his personal world was built on them, he thought cynically. Loveless partnerships were the hunting ground for any self-respecting rake. And that was what he was—an ugly label, but one that suited him. A rake never pondered the past, for he had no past. He suffered no confusion, for he knew exactly who he was and so did the women who chose to tangle with him. And what he also knew was that innocent buds such as Domino were best avoided. That particular lesson had been seared early on this rake's soul. He should need no reminding.

Seated beside her father as they rattled their way home, Domino was gratified that she had startled Joshua from his customary calm. He had looked genuinely shocked when she had announced she was to be married. Could it be that he cared for her, or was it simply that he found appalling the idea of an arranged marriage? Hardly. Over the years he must have benefited from any number, the comforter of wives who had no love for their husbands. Yet his face had shadowed with the news, as though he would wish to save her from that fate. Or preserve her for his own dishonourable intentions—that was more likely. He could not have developed a *tendre* for her, she reasoned. Rakes didn't do that; it was more than their career was worth to care for the women they made their lovers.

Her father's words had brought home to her how swiftly the weeks were passing. Marriage was ceasing to be an abstract notion and rapidly becoming reality. Once Richard had disappeared from her life, she had not cared who she wed. She would endure the intimacies of married life, impassive and acquiescent. But the events of this morning suggested otherwise. Joshua Marchmain's face and body were his stock in trade but, even knowing that, her response had been intense. Hungry, even. She had loved Richard passionately, but she had never experienced the sheer elemental need that just a short while ago had swept through her. And it was not the first time that she had been in danger of succumbing to this magnetic attraction. Every time Joshua arrived on the scene she had to exercise the tightest control over her emotions. Today she had lost that control. Surely she could not be seriously attracted to such an arrogant user of women. Yet those golden eyes had only to settle on her, that lazy smile flicker her way, that hard muscular body move close to her, and she became someone she hardly recognised.

Her restlessness reached a new peak in the days that followed. She needed to be constantly on the move and forgot her earlier reluctance to be seen abroad. Every morning she set off with her maid in tow to explore an unknown part of the Sussex landscape, winding through the town and up the hills to a viewpoint far above the sea, or along the shoreline itself, or following the pathways that circled the foot of the Downs. Poor Flora was hard put to keep up with her mistress. On one of their walks along the seafront, they came to the ladies' beach that Joshua had spoken of.

'Look, Flora.' She drew her maid's attention to the horse-drawn bathing machines carrying the swimmers into shallow waters. From there the professional dippers helped their female customers into the sea.

Her maid shuddered. 'It's not proper, miss.'

'The women change in the carriages and then just slip into the sea. It seems quite modest,' Domino said thoughtfully.

Flora sniffed, unconvinced. 'Mebbe, but I

don't reckon Señor de Silva would be too keen, nor Miss Carmela neither.'

'But if so many women take part, it must be acceptable,' Domino pursued, her interest now thoroughly aroused.

'You're never thinking of joining them, Miss Domino.' Flora's tone was scandalised. 'And think how dangerous it must be.'

A number of apprehensive women, clad in flannel gowns and caps, emerged from the carriages and cautiously dipped their bare toes in the water. Courage gained, they were soon venturing further out and in no time at all a flurry of bonneted heads were bobbing up and down in the waves.

'I don't think so,' Domino reasoned. 'The water is shallow close to the shore and the dippers are there to provide security. Once the women are used to the sea, they're all right. Just look at them.'

She had a sudden longing to be there with them, to ride the waves thundering into the distance, to cleave her way through the surf out to the far horizon, to swim to an escape.

But seeing Flora's concerned expression, she only laughed and said reassuringly, 'Don't fret, it's merely a silly fancy.'

The next day she excused herself from accompanying Carmela to a lunchtime recital at St Nicholas's Church. Her father, too, was engaged, dealing with the daily round of official business, and she was able to slip out of the house unseen. Flora had been given the afternoon off and was already deep in the excitements of the stalls at Bartholomews. A ten-minute walk brought Domino to the ladies' bathing beach and another five saw her slipping into the flannel bathing costume provided by the attendant. She gave a little gasp as she glimpsed her bare arms and legs but, peering out of the carriage doorway, she saw other women happily disporting themselves, seemingly without anxiety for their unclad state. It was female territory after all, she comforted herself, and the water looked delightful.

It was. Soon she was luxuriating in the feel of the flowing tide, her body tingling to its touch. At first she bobbed up and down amid the waves, allowing the foam to swirl and curl around her toes. But then, more daringly, she began to cut a path through the undulating waves, feeling the sun warm on her bare face and arms. She was lighter than air, her body and mind at one in a weightless existence, all her troubles and confusions suspended. She swam effortlessly, on and on as though she would reach the horizon. But there was a strict time limit imposed on the bathers and all too soon she was forced to begin the return.

The horse-drawn carriages once more loomed into close view, lined up on the shore like so many sentries watching over precious treasure. Reaching the shallows, she found her feet and picked her way carefully over the pebbled seabed. The wet costume clung tenaciously to her body and a thrill of womanly pleasure passed through her at the sensuous form it revealed. Tearing the cap from her head, she waded the last few yards ashore, black curls streaming wildly down her back. For an instant before she reached the shelter of the bathing machine she looked towards the promenade and turned scarlet with vexation. Joshua Marchmain again! How dare he! This was an area reserved only for ladies and all men were banned. Of course, he would not care for that. He cared for no convention. He would embarrass anyone he wished for his own pleasure. He had suggested to her that she should try sea bathing; it was clear now why. Not from any wish to afford her enjoyment, but so that he could view her better and nearly naked. Her anger turned to chagrin. How could she have imagined that he might harbour any genuine feeling? He was a rake through and through.

Chapter Four

She had looked like a water sprite from the deep and Joshua, watching her voluptuous progress ashore, had to restrain himself from wading out into the shallows and catching her in his arms. He had barely seen her since that evening at Steine House, just those few moments at Angelo's when he had reacted so angrily to news of her future marriage. He had known then that he should put all thought of her out of his mind and had tried very hard to do so. Nevertheless he'd found himself looking for her at every gathering and her unexplained absence had only increased his interest. His desire for her was becoming insistent. All too familiar, but this time complicated by something else, something deeper and unfathomable. Desire he knew, but not this nagging need to take her in his arms, to protect her from harm, to kiss her tenderly awake to the passion he was sure lay dormant within. Caught by her magic, transfixed by her fluid movement up the beach, he had remained in full view long enough for her to see him.

He was still there, an appreciative smile on his face, when she emerged fully dressed from the land side of the bathing machine. She did not speak and made to walk past him with a bare nod of acknowledgement, but he was too quick for her and barred the way.

'Did sea bathing live up to its promise, Miss de Silva?' he enquired laughingly.

She turned abruptly and her voice sliced the air. 'Did ogling female bathers live up to yours, Mr Marchmain?'

He looked taken aback by her words and the fury in her voice, but in a moment had recovered his poise. 'One bather did!'

'You are insufferable!'

'Because I appreciate female beauty? That is hardly fair.'

'Because you seem intent on pressing your attentions on unwilling women.'

'As I've mentioned before, they are not always unwilling,' he said drily.

'Let us be clear, sir. Whatever your customary experience, I find your attentions wholly distasteful.'

'And what attentions would they be? All I have done is stand on this small spot of promenade and enjoy the pleasurable sight of women, for once free of the shackles imposed on them.'

Since she was so much in tune with this sentiment, she found it difficult for the moment to continue the quarrel. But not for long.

'The only reason you told me of the sea bathing was to enable you to spy on me.'

'An over-dramatic interpretation, I think. I am no spy.' His voice was no longer amused.

'Call it what you will. I have no intention of being ogled by men, and particularly not by a man with your reputation.'

'And what reputation would that be?' he said dangerously.

'I have no wish to continue this conversation. Please allow me to pass.'

He made no move, but instead looked her fully in the face grimly.

'You are a delightful girl, Domino, but young and naïve. You know nothing of me or my life, so take care in passing judgement.'

'I am not so naïve that I cannot recognise a rake when I see one.'

There, she had said the shocking word, and to his face. She waited for the explosion, but none came. Instead he was smiling down at her with a condescending expression on his face.

'A rake, am I?' he drawled. 'And all because I dared to see one second of your beautiful body in a bathing costume—and not a particularly revealing one.'

She flushed scarlet. 'You have done nothing but distress me since our paths first crossed.'

'A somewhat overwrought statement, wouldn't you say? I have simply been going about my usual business. It is you who appears so eager to suffer distress.'

'Are you suggesting that I have no cause for complaint?' she fumed.

'I am suggesting that you may be a little too prone to exaggerate my interest in you. Forgive me, but encouraging such fancies cannot be healthy.'

She longed to hit him very hard, but by a supreme force of will managed to stay her hand. Instead she took a cold, calm breath and launched the most wounding insult she could think of.

'You claim to be a gentleman. If you are indeed such, then you will leave me alone, now and in the future.'

She saw him stiffen. It was one thing to fling at him the insult of rake but the insinuation that he was not a gentleman would cause the deepest rancour.

'I regret, Miss de Silva,' he said in a newly aloof manner, 'that you have found meeting me so distasteful.'

'I have.'

'Then I will no longer discommode you with my presence. As far as I am able, I will stay out of your sight.'

'Please do.'

'Dare I enquire,' he asked, his tone now heavy with irony, 'if you intend to be at the Lewes race meeting tomorrow?'

'I believe my father has reserved places for us.'

'In that case you can be certain that I will spend the day a hundred miles from Lewes.'

'I am delighted to hear it,' she flung at him and stormed past, her cheeks still flaming and her head held high.

A blind rage had sustained her on the short walk back to Marine Parade, and it was only when she was in sight of the house that she began to question why Joshua Marchmain's conduct had so infuriated her. His blatant voyeurism was, after all, only what she would have predicted. Why, then, was she so out of temper? Or was it that she had expected better of him? Somehow she must have held a secret hope that the stories about him were exaggerated, that gossip had distorted his true nature. In short, she had wanted to believe he was the kind of man she could trust. How very stupid! He was right, she was naïve. He was and always would be an inveterate rake, for, even though she might acquit him of deliberately luring her to the bathing station, he had still gazed his fill. An honourable man would have turned away; an honourable man would not even have been there! She wondered wearily how many disappointments she must endure before she finally accepted that she was a very poor judge of men. Once back in Spain, she would trust her aunts to choose a husband. They could do no worse than she.

Deep in these unpleasant thoughts, she walked through the door of Number Eight to hear her father's voice raised in protest.

'It is simply a day out, Carmela, a social occasion, nothing more.'

'Naturally I realise that in this society a day at the races is just one more entertainment…' Carmela shuddered '…but you cannot deny that a racecourse is a place of sin.'

'Come, I know that you have—definite views.' Her father phrased his words carefully.

'But in this instance, are you not being just a little severe?'

'I think not. Gambling wherever it occurs is sinful.'

'Domino will not be gambling and neither will I. We will enjoy a day in the fresh air and the excitement of seeing horses compete.'

'But you will be surrounded by every kind of vice!' Fired by moral zeal, her cousin was not giving up easily. 'We should be doing all we can to protect Domino from the work of the Devil, not exposing an innocent girl to temptation.'

'Enough!' Alfredo held up his hand. 'I am taking my daughter on an outing of pleasure whether you approve or not. And I will personally guarantee that she returns as innocent as she went.'

He strode along the hallway to his office, his shoulders stiff with annoyance, and closed the door rather too noisily. Carmela sniffed just as noisily and hastened back to the purity of her own room. Even after they had both disappeared, the atmosphere crackled with irritation and Domino was left thinking that for all kinds of reasons it might be a good idea to return to Spain sooner than she had hoped.

However, the next morning she had changed her mind. A perfect English summer day greeted her, cotton-wool clouds drifting lazily across an azure sky, and the green perfection of ancient downland rolling out its smooth carpet to welcome them as they drove the few miles inland to Lewes. The racecourse, some five hundred feet above sea level, was idyllic on a tranquil day such as this. Shaped like an elongated horseshoe, it ran along the crest of a valley and then downwards towards the sea, its natural undulations making it a test of stamina and tactics for both horses and riders.

A decidedly mixed crowd had already gathered by the side of the track and Alfredo silently wondered if he had dismissed Carmela's qualms too readily. Every type of person, it seemed, had come to the Lewes races that day: prosperous farmers and their wives; rural workers in smocks and gaiters; smartly dressed professional men and their clients; sellers of every kind of food and drink vociferously shouting their wares and any number of ragged urchins. As their hired vehicle drove on to the course, he saw with relief that the cream of society had decided on keeping a comfortable distance from this ragbag of humanity. A large white-painted grandstand was alive with the colourful swathe of silk gowns and feathered hats. It seemed that the Regent and his party were already ensconced in commodious chairs with an unparalleled view of the entire course.

As the races began, Alfredo felt even greater relief. The gambling that Carmela had so feared was modest and conducted with decorum, so much so that, towards the end of the programme, he was encouraged to place a wager on a likely looking horse. The result of the race was in doubt right up to the finishing point and Domino, immersed in the spectacle, cheered on her horse with such verve that her father was delighted they had come. For some weeks, he fancied, she had not been herself. In his presence she tried to be bright and talkative, but whenever she thought herself unobserved, she fell back into a preoccupation that he could not fathom. Now the glorious weather and glorious landscape, the sheer excitement of the chase, had prompted her to throw herself into the moment as only she could. Her arms waved wildly in the air as their horse breasted the finishing post first. With difficulty she restrained herself from jumping up and down.

'I see you have been a clever girl and backed the winner. I fear that my luck is completely out today.'

Domino looked round at the woman who had spoken and her heart sank. She had been relieved to find that Joshua had kept his word and stayed away. Now her father had chosen the worst moment to collect his winnings, leaving her to face the duchess alone. This was the first time she had met Charlotte Severn since that dreadful evening at Steine House. But the older woman, resplendent in sapphire satin, was smiling invitingly at her and patting her hand in what Domino supposed to be a motherly fashion.

'Such energy needs sustenance.' The duchess's voice had taken on the cloying tone that was so discomfiting.

'Do accompany me to the marquee,' she persuaded, 'we must take tea together.'

The girl began to demur, but Charlotte immediately linked arms with her and urged her forwards. 'Don't worry about your papa. When he returns he will be sure to know where you have gone and will come to collect you.'

Very quickly Domino found herself seated at one of the small ironwork tables that dotted the interior of the marquee, a waiter pouring the pale straw of China tea into delicate white porcelain.

The duchess fixed her with eyes that smiled through a pool of ice.

'I am so pleased to see you again, Domino,' she was saying sweetly. 'I do hope I may call you by your first name.'

Domino was hypnotised into assent.

'I was most upset by the way that we parted at Steine House. Such a dreadful misunderstanding on my part. I had no idea that you were so averse to cards—though obviously not to gambling in general.' Her voice momentarily lost its honey as she nodded pointedly towards the races still taking place.

Her victim squirmed, remembering her gauche behaviour that evening. And to be discovered now in the very pastime she had rejected so publicly!

But Her Grace was continuing smoothly, preparing her ground with the girl she was seeking to undo. 'I am so very sorry,' she trilled, 'if anything I did or said at the time upset you.'

Domino could hardly reject the older woman's plea after this show of contrition. The duchess's deep blue eyes held hers in a seemingly sincere appeal and she found herself softening towards their owner.

Her natural good nature won over whatever reservations she still harboured and in a small voice she confessed, 'I am sorry, too—my conduct must have seemed a little strange.'

'No, my dear, absolutely not.' Charlotte Severn was determined on complete abasement. 'The fault was entirely mine. But I hope we can mend our fences. I so much wish us to be friends.'

Domino would have liked to believe her, but could not. An older female friend—someone she could confide in, someone with the maturity and experience to guide her through the pitfalls of English society—was a luxury she must do without. She had lost the person who might have filled the role admirably; Christabel was long married and living many miles away.

'It is as I told you, my dear,' the duchess was saying pleasantly, 'there are very few new people in Brighton. An old hand like myself can become seriously blasé, not to say boring, if we are not kept on our toes. I adore young people and you are so bright and lovely.'

Charlotte was having an effect. Today she appeared more genuine and more approachable. 'You know, if Mr Marchmain had not interrupted us that evening, I am sure we would have quickly resolved our differences. But Joshua is always so hot-headed.' She gave a soft sigh of pain. 'Have you not found that also?'

'I hardly know Mr Marchmain.' Domino stammered.

'Really? I understood that you were a good friend of his.'

'Indeed, no, ma'am,' she replied indignantly.

'I hope you are not too cross with him. I know he can be a little unconventional.'

'As I said, I hardly know him.'

The girl's flushed face warned Charlotte not to pursue her line of questioning and she changed tack.

'Tell me what you have been doing since we last met,' she invited.

Relieved at the turn of conversation, Domino gladly searched her mind for something to report. 'Nothing very noteworthy, I'm afraid—reading, walking—and I did try sea bathing,' she ventured.

'You are so brave, my dear. I would be utterly scared of immersing myself in water.'

'I learned to swim as a child—we lived by the sea in Buenos Aires.'

The duchess looked questioningly at her, hoping to probe a little more deeply.

'In Argentina,' Domino said helpfully.

'Yes,' the duchess responded a trifle waspishly. 'I am aware of that city's location.' Then, quickly recovering, she cooed, 'I have the greatest admiration for ladies who can boast such sporting prowess. As for myself, all I can claim is to ride well and I do pride myself on that.'

'I adore riding, too. Papa put me on my first

horse when I was three. But riding in Argentina is very different,' Domino confided wistfully.

The duchess scented an opportunity. 'How is that?'

'Once out of the city you can gallop forever—the pampas stretches for miles. And on a proper saddle, too, just like the gentlemen use here.'

Charlotte repressed a shudder and murmured encouragingly, 'How wonderful.'

'Here—' Domino warmed to her theme '—one feels so constrained. Always having to ride sidesaddle and so tamely. Ladies are not permitted to gallop and certainly not to race.'

'If it were possible, would you do so?' the duchess asked cannily.

'It would certainly be fun!' and Domino threw back her head and laughed aloud.

Seeing the girl's dark eyes alight with merriment and her shining curls dancing in pleasure, the older woman felt a surge of envy.

'Of course one would not race openly, but maybe a race in a more secluded place?' she suggested, apparently absorbed in stirring her tea.

'Wherever would that be, ma'am?' Domino's voice conveyed interest and the duchess moved in for the final scene of the little drama she had been busy staging.

'Have you heard of Prince George's famous wager?'

The girl shook her head.

'He bet that he could drive a coach and four down Keere Street, just a short way from here. It is the steepest and narrowest of roads in Lewes. And do you know, he won that wager!'

'He must be very expert.'

'Yes,' her companion said judiciously, 'but I have it in mind that we women could undertake something even more masterly.'

'How could we do that?'

'Why, by racing our horses down Keere Street,' the duchess produced triumphantly.

Her companion at first looked nonplussed, then her face fell into a frown. 'But surely that would be dangerous.'

'Skilful, shall we say?' Charlotte said in her smoothest voice. 'We would not be hurtling down the road pell mell. It would take considerable expertise to negotiate the steep gradient and find a clear way over stones and cobbles. A very considerable feat!'

'It would certainly be a test of horsemanship.'

'So what do you think?'

'You mean that we should race?'

'Why not?' The duchess smiled as warmly as she could. 'I am longing to do something a little more daring than attending routs and receptions; it seems that you feel similarly. You said a moment ago that you have been in the saddle since you were three years old, so now is the chance to prove it.'

'I would love to, Your Grace, but I doubt that my father would allow me to undertake such a race.'

'Charlotte, my dear, call me Charlotte. It's really quite simple. Say nothing to your father and I will tell no one either. It will be our little secret.'

'But how could we prevent people knowing?'

The duchess's patience was wearing thin, but she made one last effort. 'We ride over the Downs to Lewes very early in the morning before anyone stirs. It is a shame that we will never be able to boast of our exploit, but we will have the satisfaction of knowing just how clever we have been.'

Domino was seized with a sudden panic. 'Are you quite sure that it's possible to ride down that road?'

'I would not have suggested it if I had thought otherwise, but if you are fearful then, of course, you must not attempt it, my dear.'

Annoyance rippled through Domino as her courage was subtly brought into question.

'And we will not tell anyone?' she asked, seeking more reassurance.

'Not a soul. No one will ever know—just we two.'

'When shall we hold the race?'

A silent joy engulfed the duchess. She had caught her fish at last. 'What about the day after tomorrow? That will give us the opportunity to choose suitable horses.'

'And when shall we meet?'

'Just after dawn I think, around five o' clock. The Downs will be wonderful at that time.'

'And we will both come alone?'

'Completely alone,' Charlotte reassured her. 'We will meet at the crossroads that lead into the town and then ride the few paces to Keere Street together.'

She paused for a moment and then said musingly, 'I think I shall make a laurel crown for the victor—though whoever wins will have to keep it hidden!'

Domino laughed brightly, but her determination to win the laurel crown was strong. She had agreed to the duchess's wild suggestion because she had not wanted to appear cowardly, but she was filled also with a fierce desire to beat the woman. A sharp *frisson* of pleasure had shot through her at the idea that in this one respect she might vanquish the duchess, even though she could not rival her in love. It was not a thought she intended to examine too closely.

Her father was walking towards them and bowing courteously. 'Your Grace. The races are nearly over, *querida*. Shall we go?'

'You are not cross, Papa?' she enquired, as he led her back to their place in the grandstand.

'No, my dear, I am not cross, but don't make a habit of spending time with that lady.'

Domino said nothing but consoled herself with the thought that she would be spending only an hour or two with the duchess and that, in any case, no one would ever know.

As the last folds of Domino's jonquil gauze cleared the tent flaps, Leo Moncaster appeared from the shadows and took her vacated chair.

'Well?'

'It's fixed, I have caught her. The day after tomorrow.'

'So I can spread the good news?'

'As quickly as you can, Leo. Make sure one of your cronies opens a book and encourage all your acquaintance to wager on the result. When the scandal breaks, I want it to be as big as possible. But don't let the news get to her father.'

'Isn't she likely to mention it?'

The duchess smiled wryly. 'How little you know! Girls never divulge their misdemeanours to their papas. In any case it's to be "our little secret".' She screwed up her face in distaste. 'The sooner I rid the town of the *señorita*, the better!'

'To have men betting heavily on the race will destroy her reputation completely,' Moncaster muttered grimly. 'She will be the only topic of gossip for months ahead.'

The duchess's smile creased her face until her companion continued, 'But what about you? You will be subject to the same gossip.'

She looked at him stonily. 'I think, Leo, that my credit will stand me in better stead than our young friend's.' Then, shrugging her shoulders, 'There is no way I will ride that road. It's a death trap.'

'So you won't turn up?'

'I shall meet her as planned, but only to lead her straight to the audience waiting at Keere Street. You must invite the most inveterate gossips you can find as witnesses. I will be the good friend who is trying to protect her from scandal. I shall be outraged that she should have considered such an exploit!'

Leo looked doubtful. 'That's all very well, but she is bound to expose your part in setting up the race.'

'She may try, but nobody will believe her. I shall say that she was intent on persuading me to race. I tried to deter her but without success. I have come now only to make one last effort to save her.'

'I like it,' Leo mused, rubbing his chin thoughtfully. 'You will be seen as a saintly Samaritan and she a reckless girl who cares nothing for her reputation and is happy to outrage the *ton* for some shocking spree.'

'Exactly. When she sees that everyone is against her, she will flee English society. I warrant she will be on the next boat to Europe.'

'Very neat, Charlotte. It will destroy her utterly, but leave you glowing with virtue.'

'Admit it, I am as good a conspirator as you!' the duchess blazed with pride.

'Don't forget that I was the one who revealed her weakness to you.'

'And how has that helped today?'

'Simple. With her predilection for gambling, it was always probable that she would be seduced by a likely wager.'

The duchess was in benevolent mood. 'Let us call it a draw. If all goes the way I have planned, we will both end content.'

Domino started to entertain doubts even before she regained Marine Parade. This mad adventure offered her a last exhilarating grasp at freedom, but it began to strike her as being a little too mad. Still, it had been Charlotte Severn who suggested this daring exploit and, though her father did not approve of the duchess, she was a great lady and moved in the very best circles. Nothing she did could ever be truly wrong, or rather, Domino corrected herself, ever be truly challenged. And the race would wrongfoot Joshua. While she was revelling in the company of his mistress, he would still be abed and unknowing. For once she would be free of his interference.

Nevertheless, the more she considered the matter, the less sure she felt. She could not tell her father what was afoot, certainly not Carmela, and it would be wrong to involve Flora. It was a secret she must keep alone. She hugged the knowledge to herself, gradually building the pleasures of the race in her mind. She was an accomplished horsewoman and there was a good chance she would beat the duchess. Charlotte Severn would make a satisfying adversary; to defeat her would be worth every one of Domino's present anxieties. She could not warm to the woman and the spectre of her liaison with Joshua was never far from mind. Even if she were to lose, forbidden pleasures were in store: to ride at full stretch for the first time since she had left Argentina, to feel the wind in her hair and herself lone mistress of the Downs.

And so it proved. She had taken the precaution of ordering a horse from stables some way from Marine Parade. They were situated at the very beginning of Juggs Way, the winding path used by Brighton fishwives on their way to sell their menfolk's catches to the good citizens of Lewes and surrounding villages. It was a lengthy walk from the seafront and meant Domino had to rise very early. The sun was only just emerging from a dawn mist when she swung herself up into the saddle and coaxed the neat bay she had hired over the courtyard cobbles on to the Downs. She had been assured that the pretty mare was the swiftest in the stables.

It was a glorious morning, the air still and translucent, with the sun's emerging rays only just beginning to warm her face as she headed eastwards. Small hedges fenced the lower slopes of the Downs and were filled with the scent of honeysuckle and the sound of birdsong. Once clear of them, she allowed the horse to stride into a canter over the close-cropped grass and rolling folds of the hills. She wanted the mare to be fresh for the race, but not too fresh.

The miles had melted as though by magic and within half an hour she could see the roofs of Lewes beginning to appear. She wondered if the duchess was already at the crossroads.

A figure appeared just breasting the misty line of the horizon; it must be Charlotte come to meet her. That was unexpected, but it would be companionable to ride into the town together. As the form drew nearer, though, she could see the figure was not that of a woman and began to feel uneasy. She was still a long way from any dwelling and there was no other soul in sight. The man was cloaked against the morning chill, but bareheaded; in the shaft of sunlight that flooded suddenly over the hills, she could see the colour of gold. It could not be. It was.

'Good morning, Miss de Silva,' the figure hailed her.

She found herself clenching her fists until her fingernails drew blood. Was she never to be free of his intrusions? As he drew closer, she saw his face. It was unsmiling and his bow was brusque.

'Forgive my trespass, ma'am. I have been at pains to absent myself, but find that today I must break my own rules.'

She recovered from the shock of seeing him sufficiently to execute a minimal bow. By now they had both come to a halt, their horses beginning to sidle against each other.

'And why have you found it necessary to encroach yet once more, Mr Marchmain?' she enquired in a freezing voice.

'I understand that you have engaged yourself in a contest. I've come to warn you that you should not take part.'

Her eyebrows lifted. 'I was not aware that I had appointed you the arbiter of my conduct.'

'It will not be I who judges your conduct,' he said grimly. 'Although it will be judged—and harshly.'

'And why is that, pray?' Her anger was tangible and filled the space between them.

He allowed himself a slight smile. 'Ladies do not engage in races, nor do they risk breaking their necks as you assuredly will.'

'What makes you so certain?' His smile was infuriating her. 'Your arrogance is breathtaking. You should know that I am accounted an excellent horsewoman.'

He did not respond directly, but instead said bluntly, 'Have you seen Keere Street?'

'No.'

'Then you should before you accuse me of arrogance. To race a horse there would place you in certain peril—and not just you, but that delightful mare you are riding.'

'I understand that it has been done before,' she retorted.

'You refer to Prinny's little escapade, I collect. That nearly ended in disaster and he had a coach behind him to act as a brake. He is also a prince of the realm and princes tend to be forgiven their foibles.'

'Are you saying it would not be seemly for me to follow his lead?'

'Not just unseemly, but quite shocking. If you value your reputation and that of your father, you should abandon this race. I cannot imagine how you ever agreed to such a foolhardy exploit.'

'I agreed because the proposal came from a person I thought trustworthy—someone you introduced me to,' she said bitingly.

'That does not absolve you from making sensible decisions. I reiterate, give up this race immediately!'

She bristled with annoyance at his words, but his tone was urgent and carried conviction. Astride a powerful black stallion, he looked magnificent. He also looked serious. She had never previously encountered him in such a severe mood and, though still smarting from his unwelcome interference, she was beginning

to take notice of what he said. But how on earth
had he come upon her here, miles from anywhere? And how did he know about the race?

'This morning's arrangements were secret,'
she protested, 'and I cannot understand how
you knew of them.'

'All of Brighton knows of them. The whole
town is buzzing with the scandal. There is even
a book being run.'

He saw her puzzlement. 'Wagers, Miss de
Silva, bets on who will win. Regretfully I have
to report that you are seen as an unlikely victor.'

His light tone did not disguise the gravity of
his news and she was appalled by the turn of
events.

'I don't understand how this is,' she faltered.
'How could the race have become common
knowledge?'

His gaze swept over her, at first sardonic and
then with something approaching sympathy.
'No, I imagine you don't.'

'We had an agreement,' she stammered. 'It
was to be just between the two of us.'

He was silent, but his face made plain that
he knew everything.

'And the duchess—surely she would not be a
part of anything openly scandalous?' Domino
was still groping her way through the dark, try-

ing to make sense of the morning's bewildering events.

'I doubt that she would,' he replied tight-lipped.

'But she is meeting me.'

'Yes?' He smiled derisively, his gold-flecked eyes glittering in the sunlight now flooding over the downland.

'I have an appointment with her at the cross-roads in just a few minutes.'

'Then allow me to keep it for you.'

She gasped. 'But—'

'My advice,' he interrupted roughly, 'is to turn around and ride back to Brighton immediately. Return to Marine Parade as fast as you can and say nothing to anyone about this day's doings. To the world, you never left your father's house.'

'But nobody will believe that, especially not the people who have placed bets.' Her voice wavered.

He looked at the long dark lashes downcast over soft cheeks, the full lips trembling despite all her efforts at control, and had a strong desire to punch someone.

'It was a joke, was it not?' he suggested encouragingly. 'A joke got up between you and the duchess. You never meant it seriously. Why would you willingly risk your life in such a foolhardy escapade?'

'And the duchess?'

'She will tell her own tale, no doubt.'

'But she will still be waiting for me.'

'I will undertake to put her mind at rest,' he said caustically. 'I will ride to the crossroads this instant and tell her that you have reconsidered the propriety of taking part in such a race.'

'I see you have it all pat.' Her fear and frustration came tumbling out.

'Don't be angry, Domino.' His voice softened and she felt herself once more caressed by velvet. 'You have been misled, but the situation is not irreparable. Allow me to be of some small service.'

His sincerity was evident and, battered by what she had just learned, she could only acquiesce. 'I thank you, sir,' she responded in a small voice.

She had no wish to be further indebted to Joshua Marchmain, yet he was offering her a way out of the morass into which she had plunged. How could she have been so stupid as to involve herself in something so evidently scandalous? How could the whole town have known of her intentions? Joshua had lodged no accusation, but it was clear that he believed Charlotte Severn to be the malign influence behind her troubles. If so, his intimacy with the woman made him the very man to deal with the problem.

She turned the horse to retrace her steps, all pleasure in the lovely morning gone. She had been foolish enough to believe Charlotte's repeated assurances that their race would remain secret and in her innocence had trusted the older woman to be sincere. She had been betrayed, but, if she were honest, she herself had contributed richly to that betrayal. She had been so intent on beating Charlotte, on avenging her humiliation at Steine House, her humiliation over Joshua, that she had lost all sense of perspective. She must never again make such a mistake. In the meantime all she could do was to rely on Joshua to stifle the gossip that must already be circulating.

As soon as he reached the crossroads, he saw Charlotte pacing irritably up and down, her horse grazing by the roadside. At the sound of his approach she wheeled around, her face startled at the sight of this unexpected visitor.

Joshua reined in beside her. 'Your Grace, how charming to see you out and about on such a fine morning. I trust you are enjoying your ride.' His voice was calm and gave no hint of his feelings.

The duchess's eyes narrowed. 'And why are you riding so early, Joshua? That is most unusual.'

'I can rise with the best of people if I have a reason.' His smile was ominous.

'And what would that be?' she enquired sweetly.

'Let us say, a little pre-emptive action.'

'I see. And since when have you played the shining knight?'

'Since I found myself wading through the festering garbage of a corrupt Court.' His eyes glittered.

She turned white and raised her whip hand in fury as though to strike.

Unperturbed, he continued, 'But don't let me detain you. For myself, I have friends to meet—I believe our rendezvous is Keere Street, somewhat singular, but one can never account for the whims of one's friends.'

And with that he rode off into Lewes, leaving the duchess furiously snatching at her horse's bridle.

A crowd of young bucks had already gathered at Keere Street and there were even a few grey heads among the crowd, Joshua noted. What people would do for a titbit of scandal in the hothouse environment the Regent created around him!

'Good morning, gentlemen,' he hailed them, relaxed as ever.

'Morning, Marchmain, come to see the fun?' asked one budding young dandy, almost muffled by a shirt collar whose starched points reached to his cheek bones.

'I fear not.'

'Why ever not?'

Joshua looked with distaste at the coarse-looking man who had spoken. His high colour signalled his partiality for claret. 'That Spanish filly—they say she's an out and outer on a horse, but I'm still backing the duchess. Tactics will win the day!' he rumbled floridly.

'Quite possibly, but not this day. Neither lady will be coming.'

'How can that be?' A sporting gentleman in a high-crowned beaver hat and a driving coat of many capes was indignant.

'It was all a joke, my dear fellows.' Joshua was at his negligent best. 'You cannot seriously imagine that two ladies of such impeccable virtue would engage in horse racing!'

'You mean the whole thing is a hum,' the dandy said disconsolately.

'The joke is on us, I am afraid. The ladies have proved that men will place a wager on just about anything.'

There were some disgruntled mutterings

among the group, but Joshua cut it short by suggesting that one of the present company might like to pick up the gauntlet themselves. As one they peered down the steep hill, watching it bump and curl on its way, finally to vanish in a dark pit of shadow.

Lord Wivenhoe summed up what they were all thinking.

'We'd have to be mad! Let's get a heavy wet—the Lewes Arms should be open by now.'

Chapter Five

Joshua rode slowly towards Brighton, well pleased with his morning's work. He was confident that he had managed to quash the torrent of gossip that might have poured unhindered if Domino had made an appearance at Keere Street. Now he'd had time to think, he could see Charlotte's strategy clearly. She would have delivered the girl into the lion's den, then stood back and protested her own innocence while the lions devoured the lamb. He smiled wryly. Domino was hardly a lamb. She had provoked him at every opportunity and by rights he should have left her to fend for herself; she had made no secret of the fact that she despised him, had even called him a rake to his face. So why put himself out? She was charming, but he had known far more beautiful women. She was interesting and intelligent, but she was also young and untried. So what was it? She was a challenge, perhaps, no simpering miss certainly. And though her impulsiveness led her into danger, it sprang from a fresh, unconstrained spirit. She still possessed a joy in life which he had long ago lost—whether she was dreaming by a quiet sea or walking windblown on the downs or taking up this ridiculous wager, fearing it, no doubt, but ready to brave her fortune. How long would that free spirit survive the bludgeoning of an arranged marriage?

She had begun to penetrate his heart, he realised, and that was troubling. When she was close he found himself captivated, unable to think or act the man he had been for so many years. He looked deep into those expressive eyes and wanted them to speak only to him, longed for them to sparkle with mischief just for him, to cloud with passion just for him. He must put an end to such feelings and make sure that she made no further inroads into his life. He had no wish to be drawn into the kind of intimacy that for years he'd been at pains to shun. It could only lead to disaster, and all-embracing disaster at that. Once upon a time he had been overpowered by youthful passion, had convinced himself that love had finally bloomed in a hitherto barren life. He had been heedless, inviting the spread of vicious scandal, piling further hurt on his despairing family and sacrificing the one friendship he had learned to treasure. That first and last wretched experience of love must surely be a lesson for life: never tangle with innocence. He was fairly sure that he need not fear Domino's attachment; this morning's events would have done nothing to change her attitude. He would still be a rake to her, a man to avoid.

Charlotte Severn would also avoid him. Their liaison had grown stale and unsavoury months ago, and this recent encounter was as good a way as any to draw a final line beneath it. He had suspected Charlotte to be venal, but had not realised before the depths to which she would stoop. He had mistrusted her intentions towards Domino since that evening of the soirée. Recently she and that cur, Moncaster, had had their heads together a little too often and when news of the race reached him, he had guessed that the two of them were involved. But why Charlotte should wish to destroy the young girl mystified him. Even less understandable was why Moncaster should be privy to the plot. He wondered if either of them would be waiting for him at the Pavilion—that would be an interesting conversation!

* * *

The duchess, though, had ridden straight to Steine House and found Leo Moncaster pacing up and down the pavement, his face wolfishly eager. She swept past him and up the steps to the open front door. They walked together into the drawing room and for the first time he had a clear view of her face and knew that something had gone badly amiss.

'She never came,' she said baldly. 'Marchmain must have intercepted her and persuaded her to return home.'

'And you let him!'

'What else could I do? She was already riding back when he met me at the crossroads. It was clear that he would expose my part in the plan if I did not also return to Brighton immediately.'

'And…?'

'And he must have ridden on to Keere Street and told the men there some tale to account for both our absences,' she concluded wearily.

Moncaster began his pacing once more, this time up and down the pale grey drawing-room carpet, leaving a dark tread in his wake. His face was thunderous and he bit his lip constantly, his agitation finally spilling over into words.

'It is hard to see how you could have managed this more badly,' he exploded.

'What do you mean?'

'You were the one who insisted that this would work. You would humiliate the girl, you said. Now look—she has humiliated you!'

'She has not. And let me remind you that you agreed to the plan; in fact, I recall that at the racecourse when we spoke of it you expressed complete confidence.'

'Clearly I was wrong to rely on your ability to bring this tiresome girl to account. From now onwards, I will be the one making decisions.'

'As you wish. I have no further interest in the matter.'

'You had sufficient interest until today.'

'It is unlikely that after this morning's events I will enjoy any kind of friendship with Joshua,' she said dully, 'and since that is so, I no longer care what happens to the girl.'

Moncaster moved towards her and took her hands. 'Do you not think, Your Grace,' he said courteously, his tone markedly different, 'that Mr Marchmain might still be persuaded back into the fold if this wretched girl were no longer around?'

The duchess remained silent, but broke free from his hold and walked towards the door.

'In any case, don't you want revenge?' he called after her retreating figure.

Charlotte stopped mid-room. Deep in thought, she beat a tattoo with her riding crop against the blue velvet of her modish ensemble.

'Can you deliver me revenge, Leo?' she asked slowly.

'I can. We have been too complicated. It needs something simple, something obvious.'

'You have an idea?'

'I have. Will you trust me with it?'

'As you have been at pains to point out,' she responded tartly, 'my plan has failed dismally, so what have I to lose?'

Domino was lucky to regain Marine Parade before any member of the household became aware of her absence, for it had taken time to return her horse to the stables and walk back to the seafront. Slipping into the house through the rear entrance, she heard muted sounds coming from the kitchen, but no servant appeared to embarrass her. She was still unhooking the last gold fastenings of her riding dress, when Flora knocked on the door with her morning chocolate. Seeing her maid's perplexed face, she gestured to the heavy gown she had just removed.

'I have changed my mind about riding this morning, Flora. I feel too tired to go far today.'

The girl looked concerned, but hung up the riding dress without comment and very soon left Domino to her thoughts.

Few of them were pleasant. The irony of the situation was crushing: she was relying on a man of dubious reputation to save her own. Joshua would save her, but why? She had not endeared herself to him. She had rejected all his advances and made clear that she found his presence odious. She need feel no guilt at the harsh treatment she'd meted out, for his behaviour had been intolerable. But not this morning. This morning his face had been grave, his tone abrupt and his words a million miles from seductive. There had been no trace of the reckless rake. Instead he had been stern and insistent; his rebuke over her conduct could have come from Richard himself. She thought she had discerned some sympathy in those gold-flecked eyes as he'd turned to go—maybe even a little tenderness. It seemed unlikely, but the thought made her feel slightly giddy. In her mind's eye she saw him again, handsome and unyielding. Seated on that large black horse, his caped greatcoat flung carelessly over his shoulders, he had looked superb, a master of the landscape. He had also looked like a man on whom she could depend, and so she had consigned her fate to his hands—or, rather, to his silver tongue. She could not imagine the tale he would tell those eager scandalmongers waiting at Keere Street, but she knew without doubt that he would make her safe.

It was to be some days before she set eyes on him again. For a while she had been watchful, keeping close to home, a little afraid of the gossip that might still be bandied around the town. But no startling news had reached her and she felt sure that if her name had become common currency, her father would have known of it. She had felt reassured, but strangely dull. Joshua's continued absence from her daily round was naturally to be welcomed. It could do her no good to be in the company of a known womaniser, but if she were honest, life without him was a little tedious.

Then the summons had come. Piqued by the success of the duchess's evening, the Prince Regent had been persuaded to hold a soirée of his own. He was well known as a devotee of music and was intent on outdoing Charlotte Severn's offering. Not just one Italian soprano, but three had been invited to perform on the following Saturday. Leo Moncaster's suggestion that the same audience be invited that had flocked to Steine House had appealed to George's vanity and his desire to stage a superior triumph.

Despite reservations over the Regent's lifestyle, the household at Marine Parade had been greatly excited at the prospect of an evening at the Pavilion. Even Carmela had taken to perusing fashion plates, a few years out of date to be sure, but with a view to having a new gown made swiftly for this very special event. On the Friday morning a large parcel bearing Domino's name arrived at the door—the eagerly awaited dress, promised by her father on the night of their own reception. She peeled back the layers of rustling tissue and pulled from the parcel an exquisite white-satin underdress and an overskirt of the palest pink gauze, together with new pink kid slippers and a fillet of tiny pink blossoms to be woven though her curls. Flora was entranced—such possibilities for dressing her lady!

Saturday came and Domino felt nervous. She doubted she would see Joshua at the Pavilion. If he knew that she had been invited, he would stay away. He seemed intent on keeping his promise not to importune her. Really, it was most disconcerting, but more worrisome was the strong possibility that one or both of her tormentors would be present at the Regent's entertainment. She made up her mind that she would not give them the satisfaction of knowing how much they had unnerved her. She would face them down. The prospect of exploring the unknown splendours within the palace was an incentive to bravery.

Punctually at eight o' clock the de Silva party drove through the Pavilion gardens and alighted from their carriage in the shelter of an illuminated portico, its design modelled on an Indian temple. Domino had often walked around the perimeter of the palace, looking with wonder at its oriental façade, and she could scarcely believe that she was now about to penetrate its mysteries. An impassive footman ushered them through the octagonal vestibule into the entrance hall, a square apartment lit by a Chinese lantern suspended from a tented roof.

'Papa,' she whispered amazed, 'those statues are wearing real robes!' She pointed to the lifesize Chinese mandarin figures, which stood in each corner of the room.

Carmela took in this abomination and pronounced her verdict, 'Ridiculous! And it is so very hot in here,' she grumbled. Despite it being July, a roaring fire filled the marble fireplace.

From the Inner Hall they made their way into the Long Gallery, which linked all the state rooms arranged along the east front of the building. There three further fireplaces threw out yet more heat and the atmosphere was already sultry. Domino was relieved that her dress was of the most delicate material and that both she and her cousin carried fans.

'Let us wait by the glass doors,' Alfredo advised. 'That should be the coolest spot in the room.'

They made their way towards the long windows, which looked out over lawns, still dappled by sunshine even at this late hour, and waited for their turn to be presented to the Regent. Domino looked around her in awe. The Gallery walls were covered with painted canvas, a peach-blossom background with rocks, trees, shrubs, birds and flowers pencilled in pale blue. The room was divided into five different sections and the Regent stood in its centre in order to welcome his guests. He caught Domino's eyes immediately, for he was dressed in the greatest of finery, but with little consideration for his bulk. She had leisure to study him and saw the lines of dissipation etched on his face, a testimony to his selfishness and excess. But when she advanced to meet him to make a nervous curtsy, she was disarmed by the kindness he showed in seeking to put her at her ease.

The hum of conversation was gradually abating and people began to move towards the vast mirrored doors at one end of the Gallery.

'Everyone is making for the Music Room,' her father said quietly. 'We should do the same.'

A blaze of red and gold oriental splendour made Domino gasp. If the Long Gallery had been superb, the Music Room was overwhelming. The ceiling was gilded, supported by pillars covered in gold leaf and decorated with carved dragons and serpents. A lamp made to resemble a huge water lily and coloured crimson, gold and white hung from the centre with gilded dragons clinging to its underside. More dragons embellished the crimson canopies of the four doorways leading out of the room and still more writhed above the blue-and-crimson window curtains. Large ottomans decorated with fluted silk and covered in enormous satin bolsters lined all the walls and an Axminster carpet of spectacular design flooded the floor: a riot of golden suns, stars, serpents and dragons on a pale blue ground.

'Utterly vulgar,' Carmela pronounced sharply, causing Alfredo to glance anxiously around in case his forthright relative had been overheard. But Carmela was unrepentant.

'To think of all the money wasted on such immoral foppery!' she exclaimed.

The ambassador made haste to usher her to one of the yellow satin covered seats that had been set out for the audience.

'I think we should have a good view of the musicians from here,' he said soothingly.

She made no reply, but noisily unfurled the fan she carried. The heat was even more oppressive than in the Gallery and many of the ladies were already cooling themselves vigorously.

The Prince's own private band of wind and string instruments, formed from the cream of Europe's musical talent, accompanied each of the three fabled sopranos. Domino once more set herself to sit stoically through the entertainment. She hoped her reward might be to explore further this strange and exotic building. Throughout the recital, the Regent, who had learned to play the violincello in his youth, beat time with his foot. When the last note had faded, an army of footmen whisked away the audience's small chairs and yet another army carried in tray after tray of refreshments. Domino, her cousin and her father began to walk around the room, taking in the expensive array of Chinese vases, pots, glasses and pot-pourris that decorated every available surface.

They had stopped in front of a particularly ugly ceramic jar when a modestly dressed, grey-haired man came to her father's side and whispered a message in his ear. Alfredo looked surprised, but immediately touched Domino on the arm and signalled that they should go with the retainer. Equally surprised, she followed and found herself confronting the Regent himself. The Prince, large and perfumed, smiled graciously down at her, seeming pleased with what he saw.

'Señor de Silva, lend me your daughter for a few minutes.' The Prince's languid tone did not disguise that this was a command rather than a request.

Alfredo was uncertain, particularly as a faint aroma of chartreuse hung in the air, mixed imperceptibly with the heady scent the Prince affected. The Regent seemed unimpaired, however, and the ambassador, mindful of his position, felt unable to quibble.

'I was wishful of speaking to you at greater length, my dear.' The Prince smiled archly down at her and offered his arm. She found herself returning his smile.

'I love to welcome foreigners to my modest little abode and I am most interested in how you are enjoying your stay in Brighton.'

'Very much, sir,' she responded politely. 'I

love living by the sea, for in Madrid we are landlocked.'

George looked gratified. 'I remember when I first came to Brighthelmstone—that was Brighton's original name, you know. It was a small fishing village then, but I was captivated. I simply had to build myself a little folly by the sea!'

She smiled again. 'It is very beautiful,' she concurred dutifully, though not at all sure that it was.

'Come, let me show you,' and Domino found herself once more walking around the Music Room while he described in detail every one of his purchases. She knew she should feel flattered, but the heat of the room, the proximity of the rotund prince and a slight, inexplicable feeling of panic made her wish that he would not be quite so gracious.

He steered her expertly into the Long Gallery, still talking smoothly about his possessions.

'This vase, you see, came from a most remote province of China. I had my envoy negotiate for months for it. Do you think it worth the effort?'

'Indeed, it is most striking, your Highness.'

He looked satisfied. 'How delightful to find a young woman of such discernment! So dif-

ferent from some of your countrymen...' The
sentence drifted away. 'But I have heard only
the very best things said of you and you have
more than proved them right.'

She was left little time to wonder what
exactly he had heard and who could have spoken of her. They had left the Gallery by this
time and traversed the library without stopping.
They were now in a room even hotter than anything she had so far experienced.

'The Yellow Drawing Room,' George announced. 'We can be private here.'

'Your Highness, should I not call my
cousin?' She was fearful of offending such an
important person, but becoming more anxious
by the minute.

'Your cousin is occupied,' the Prince returned cheerfully, 'and you have only to say
that you were with me for there to be no trouble.'

She felt doubtful on this point, but found it
difficult to rebuff a man who was old enough
to be her father and a royal prince to boot.

'These are my private rooms,' George repeated, 'and so much more pleasant than the
public areas, do you not think? So much more
tranquil.'

She had unfortunately to agree. As she
looked around, there was not another person

in sight. By now she had become accustomed to the assault on her senses and she took in the room's array of mirrors, Chinese pictures, flying dragons and white and gold pillars wreathed by serpents without a flicker of surprise. What was more disturbing was the sight of an open doorway leading to another room beyond. This was clearly the Prince's personal chamber; she was horrified by a glimpse of a huge bed in the far reaches of the room, massive and mahogany-panelled with at least five mattresses and crowded with satin bolsters and pillows.

The gnawing panic, which had been growing ever stronger, overcame her; but when she should have fled, she found herself transfixed. The light from a hundred candles bounced from mirror to mirror, reflection after reflection, disorientating her further and making her dizzyingly weak.

'I see you admiring yourself,' the Prince joked heavily as she turned this way and that to avoid the piercing light. 'And so you should. You are a taking little puss—my spies have not lied.'

Now thoroughly alarmed, she tried to extricate herself as diplomatically as she could, but the Prince was before her.

'I have brought you here to see some very special treasures,' he whispered hotly in her ear.

Her mind went into a tailspin at the thought of what treasures he meant. How was it that she seemed destined to fall from one scrape into another? She had little time to consider, for he was pulling out a series of drawers from a small chest that sat on the nearby table. The drawers contained the most brilliant collection of jewellery she had ever seen.

'What do you think?' he asked grandly.

Shaken, all she could utter was, 'Magnificent!'

'Which of these gems would you choose above all others?'

'It would be impossible to make such a choice. Every piece is exquisite.'

'Try,' he pressed.

To hasten her departure, she pointed to a small butterfly brooch studded in diamonds. 'This is very elegant, I think.'

He frowned; it was obviously the wrong choice. 'I agree, most elegant,' he said a little too heartily. 'But have you seen the other butterfly brooch? This one here.' He pointed to an item at the back of the drawer. 'Filigree, of course—not as expensive—but I would say far more fitting for a young girl.'

The Prince lifted the filigree butterfly from

its bed of satin. 'Here, my dear. Take this as a small token of my friendship.'

Domino had thought it could not get any worse, and yet it had. 'I am most grateful for your kindness,' she stuttered, 'but I cannot accept, your Highness.'

'Cannot?'

His frown deepened and his eyebrows rose haughtily. He looked an entirely different prince.

She was forced to reconsider. 'It is most kind of you,' she said faintly.

He beamed again. 'I am well known for my generosity, but you must think nothing of it. You are a delightful child and deserve to have pretty things. Now how about a little thanks?'

'Indeed, yes, I thank you very much,' she stammered, unsure of just how effusive she had to be.

'You can do better than that, surely!'

And with those words he lunged towards her, wrapping his arms around her in a bear-like clasp and pushing her towards the open door and the bed that lay beyond. The feel of his breath on her cheek and the overwhelming scent he wore repulsed her. She tried to struggle free, but the Regent was no lightweight and she was inexorably propelled towards danger.

'I like a little resistance, my dear. That is all

to the good. But not too much, you know, not too much,' he was saying.

She felt herself reeling and tried desperately hard not to faint. That was the last thing she must do; she had to keep control, but she was losing the struggle.

Then a toneless voice spoke from the door. 'Excuse me, sir, Signora Martinelli is about to leave and I know that you will want to thank her personally.'

Joshua Marchmain was dressed in the conventional dark coat, embroidered waistcoat and light-coloured satin breeches of a gentleman's evening attire, but to Domino he wore angels' wings.

The Regent stopped pawing at her and was annoyed, but soon recovered his composure and waved away the intruder.

'No, no, Marchmain, you must thank her for me. I am sure you will find just the right words. As you see, I am a little busy,' he finished irritably.

'I should mention perhaps, sir, that Miss de Silva's father is also waiting—he wishes to see his daughter.'

The Regent turned an angry red and finally released his captive.

'We will speak later, Marchmain,' he barked. 'Leave me now.'

'Certainly, sir,' Joshua said smoothly. 'Miss de Silva?' and he ushered her out of the room and towards the library. As the door closed behind them, she heard the Regent mutter quite distinctly, 'Drat Moncaster, telling me the chit was a likely romp.'

At the sound of that name, she stumbled and Joshua had to step quickly forwards to offer a supporting arm. She was shaking uncontrollably now. All the time she had been in the Regent's apartment she had managed to keep her nerve, but once rescue came, reaction set in.

For a moment she clung to his arm, then, drawing herself up straight, she said decisively, 'I cannot go back to the Gallery just now, Mr Marchmain, I need a few minutes alone.'

His gold-flecked eyes surprised her with their concern and when he spoke his voice lacked its usual mocking note. 'Will you allow me to escort you to my studio?' he asked gently. 'It is close by and I can promise solitude. You may be alone there for as long as you wish.'

She nodded agreement and he led her towards the western side of the Pavilion. It was not so lavishly furnished as the rooms she had previously seen but a great deal cooler. At the entrance to his studio, he paused and waved her through the doorway, motioning her to take a seat. She noticed that he kept the door ajar.

'I will leave you to your thoughts. But before I do, tell me about Moncaster.'

The request came out of the blue and she looked at him, startled.

'It's evident that he was behind that little unpleasantness just now. I heard the Regent's words as well as you.'

Her face was bright red, but she remained silent.

'Domino, answer me,' he said a little less gently. 'Why has Leo Moncaster been hawking you to the Prince as a likely lady-bird?'

She still said nothing.

'He was also behind the Keere Street race,' he continued inexorably. 'He seems to be trying to ruin you. Why?'

She supposed he deserved to know the truth since he had rescued her more than once from Moncaster's evil. But it was still painful to talk.

'I crossed him in the past and he is seeking revenge.'

'In what way did you cross him?'

'I met Lord Moncaster three years ago,' she began falteringly. 'It was when I came to England to stay with my aunt, Lady Blythe.'

'Yes,' he encouraged.

'I stupidly lost money to him at faro, money

I couldn't repay. He took my handkerchief as a token of payment. I didn't realise that it was a scandalous thing to do and when I tried to get it back, he blackmailed me.'

'That sounds like the man. But could you not have confessed your troubles to your aunt and asked her to pay the debt?'

'He would not take money,' she said without elaborating further.

Joshua looked grim. She imagined that he must know Moncaster well enough to guess the depths of his villainy.

Aloud he said, 'Would it be indelicate to enquire how you resolved your difficulties?'

'I eloped.'

'What!'

'Not exactly eloped,' she clarified. 'A friend helped me escape from England. The plan was to go to my father's friends in Paris and then on to Spain, but we only got as far as Dover.'

He seemed to smile at the innocence of this recital. 'What happened at Dover?' he prompted.

'Benedict's sister arrived and made us return to London.'

'Benedict?' A frown passed swiftly across his face.

'Yes, Benedict Tallis. Do you know him?'

'I have heard of him,' he said shortly.

'He got into immense trouble because of me and was sent back to Cornwall. But at least there was no scandal. And it turned out that as I was under age, Lord Moncaster could not insist on the debt and had no hold over me. My aunt paid him anyway.'

'You seem to have a lively ability to get into scrapes, Señorita de Silva.'

'I do, don't I?' And she looked so comically concerned that he burst out laughing.

'A girl after my own heart! Come, let us forget Prinny and his dastardly ways. Will you let me show you around my workroom or would you prefer to remain alone?'

'I would enjoy seeing your workroom,' she said a little shyly.

Though small by palace standards, the room was bright and airy. The last rays of the evening sun flooded through open doors, which led to the gardens beyond, and a breeze gently lifted delicate voile curtains hanging either side of the long windows. She breathed in the fresh air with relief, then walked slowly around the room, looking with interest at the pictures hung four deep on the walls and the several piles of canvases stacked against a large chest. A battered paint-splashed smock was thrown carelessly over an easel and to one side a tray held paint tubes of every conceivable hue.

'What do you think?'

'It is a genuine artist's studio,' she responded warmly.

'A studio at least—and I keep plenty of "genuine" art as a reminder of what I should be aiming for.'

She saw at a glance that the walls were hung with a plentiful display of works by the painter she had admired at the Grove Gallery. He was certainly a fine artist. She felt Joshua watching her as she wandered the room, every now and then pausing to look at a particular painting, viewing it from different angles until she was satisfied. He made no attempt to follow, but when she began to browse the canvases stacked against the corner chest, he moved swiftly towards her and placed a restraining hand on her wrist. In the companionable silence, she had regained much of her composure and his sudden prohibition jarred.

'They are mere daubings,' he explained smoothly, 'without interest and not good enough to frame.'

'This looks a little more than daubing…' she gestured to the canvas that fronted the stack '…it catches the light and the Sussex coast perfectly.'

'You are generous, but the rest are much the same and hardly worth your attention.' His tone admitted no disagreement. 'Can I get you some refreshment before we return to the Gallery?'

'A glass of wine would be welcome.'

She sounded politely neutral, but felt irritated that he had changed the subject so determinedly. It was strange that he was opposed to her viewing the remaining works. It was probably just vanity; no doubt the pictures deteriorated in quality the further you explored. But when he left her for a moment to pour the wine, she was sufficiently intrigued to defy his wishes and surreptitiously began to flick through them. He had been right about the similarity of the paintings; they were virtually all seascapes, the light clear, the atmosphere still and the meeting of sea and sky a hardly perceptible line. As she skimmed each canvas it seemed that their horizons grew more and more distant, attempting almost to span infinity. Something about them called to her, their sense of freedom perhaps, their suggestion of escape.

More and more seascapes, but then in the middle of the stack, a lone portrait. It was the image of a young girl. Dark eyes looked searchingly out at her, glossy raven curls tumbled on to soft shoulders and the creamy skin of arms and breast gleamed translucent in the dying light of the day. She gasped: she was looking at herself.

He turned at the sound, a glass in his hand, and stood motionless as her eyes travelled from the painting to his face.

'This is me!'

'I am glad that it is recognisable, at least.' The joke felt a little flat.

'But why have you painted me?'

'I take my inspiration where I find it.' His tone was negligent. 'Your face intrigued me—it's not an English face and I wanted to try to capture it.'

'It's very good,' she said slowly and looked back at the portrait.

The face was a study in radiance, the eyes sparkling with vitality, the curls glistening and tumbling with hidden life. Every line of the painting spoke feeling and she felt dazed at the thoughts that came unbidden to her mind. Was it possible that she stirred such emotions in him?

He cut her reverie short with a brusque enquiry. 'Your father mentioned that you would shortly be travelling to Spain. How long exactly are you fixed in Brighton?'

She ceased dreaming immediately. The return to her aunts had been temporarily forgotten, lost in more pressing concerns, but recurred now with unwelcome clarity.

'I'm not sure. For as long as my father thinks it worthwhile. I imagine that Papa will return to London when the Regent travels back to Carlton House.'

'And you will leave for Spain?' She found his questioning unsettling, but nodded a silent assent.

'Then be on your guard during the weeks you remain here. You have attracted the enmity of people in high places, the Duchess of Severn as well as Moncaster.'

'I cannot understand why I should have done so. Until I came to Brighton, I had never met the lady.'

'Charlotte Severn is a jealous woman,' he said obliquely.

She sipped at her wine, unsure of his meaning. Joshua enlightened her.

'It seems that Her Grace feels my interest in you is too great, hence her rather clumsy attempts at your social humiliation.'

A ready blush flew to her cheeks and she dared not look at him.

'She is mistaken, however. You are a piece of perfection, but I'm not in the market for *ingénues*. I leave that to the connoisseurs of Spain.'

His words were unexpectedly biting; he appeared to blame her for a future over which she had little control.

'I am sure the duchess will be delighted to hear the news,' she said witheringly. 'Perhaps you should tell her yourself and quickly. Then I might be spared any further "unpleasantness".'

Her indignation found vent in a swift walk up and down the room, her skirts swishing in noisy displeasure as she passed close to him.

'What the duchess knows or doesn't know is of no concern to me,' he said, equally withering. 'I am insulted that you believe me willing to consort with a woman capable of such base trickery.'

'Your friendship is at an end?' She could hardly believe her ears.

'It has been at an end for some time.'

'I did not know that.'

'Of course you did not,' he responded acidly. 'After all, I am the lowest form of masculine life, am I not?'

Her heart did a strange little dance. Whatever had tied him to the duchess, the knot was well and truly broken. It was time to call a truce.

'You have been good enough to rescue me,' she began with difficulty.

'On a number of occasions.'

'On a number of occasions,' she agreed. 'It

would be unbecoming in me not to acknowledge that.'

'It would—and so…?'

'And so I should apologise for calling you a rake.'

'You should not,' he said unexpectedly, 'for that is what I am.'

She let out a long breath. Really he was impossible.

'But,' he continued hurriedly, 'I give you my word that you will never find me other than an honourable man.'

A deeper flush spread across her soft cheeks, beckoning him closer. He resisted the invitation.

'Why do you always paint the sea?' she asked suddenly.

'I hardly know. Perhaps because the sea is ever changing and I am equally restless.'

She considered this for a moment, but before she could reply, he went on, 'Perhaps because the sea offers a constant promise.'

'And what does it promise?'

'Liberty, movement, transformation—all of these and more.'

She was intrigued. 'Why would you wish for such things?'

'Why not?'

'I can think of a dozen reasons. You already

have the liberty to be or do what you wish. You are wealthy, popular with those you live among, a favourite with the Regent. Why would you want to transform?'

His laugh rang hollow. 'Nothing in your list persuades me. The palace is a web of lies and popularity at Court is as transient as the gossip that it feeds upon. As for wealth, it's certainly better to have money than not, but that is the sum of its importance.'

For a moment she was taken aback until she recalled his words the very first day they'd met. She had wondered then why such an obviously successful man needed the solace of painting.

'It is always possible to change one's life,' she said tentatively, 'for a man, if not for a woman.'

'You think so? That is the innocence of youth talking. Once one's feet are set upon a path, Domino, they are generally doomed to tread it forever more.'

She was disconcerted by the weariness in his voice, but then he seemed to shrug off his depression and was studying her intently. 'Why do you think a woman is not able to change her world, if she has enough spirit? I cannot believe you to be wholly powerless in deciding the course of your life, for example.'

She flushed. 'There are circumstances,' she murmured faintly. 'It is not that easy.'

'Really? And what are those circumstances?'

She did not answer his challenge directly. She had no answer. Instead she took refuge in a timeworn phrase. 'I suppose that change may not necessarily be for the better.'

'Ah, yes, the old cliché. The trouble with truisms is that they are so often true. You're right, change isn't always good, the sea doesn't always deliver its promises.'

For a second only she glimpsed the deep well of disillusion beneath the surface calm.

'Does not your home in Norfolk hold any promise?' she said quickly. 'It would seem an ideal place in which to set up a permanent studio.'

'I have little interest in the house.' He had swiftly regained his nonchalance. 'I inherited Castle March from an uncle a few years back. It was not where I grew up; I hardly know the area.'

'Where did you grow up?'

'Oxfordshire.'

'Do you ever visit the county?' she was emboldened to ask.

'No. I no longer have ties there, or indeed anywhere.'

'But your family?'

'Yes?' The monosyllable should have warned her that she was approaching dangerous ground, but she pressed on. She wanted to know as much as she could about him.

'Your family is still in Oxfordshire?'

'I have a brother living there.' His voice lacked emotion. 'I hardly know him—he is ten years older than I. My parents have been dead these five years.'

'I am very sorry.' She felt bad now at having obliged him to offer information he evidently wished to keep to himself, but he seemed unperturbed.

'Don't be. We were not a close family.'

'They did not share your interest in art?'

'They did not share my interest in anything.' His laugh was laconic. 'I must confess to being an embarrassment to my family from the moment I was born. My parents were more than contented with one child and my arrival was inconvenient to say the least. And then I managed to continue the good work by being a permanent black sheep. Naturally my brother was the model son. I spent my youth breaking every known prohibition, so it's hardly surprising I was expelled from the family seat at an early age. Hence my wanderings.'

She looked stricken and he said in a rousing voice, 'There's no need for tears. I hated my home, whereas the time I spent travelling in Europe gave me lasting pleasure.'

'But you must have been very young when they sent you abroad,' she said sadly.

'Young enough, but I survived. Families have to be negotiated, do they not?' he asked slyly. 'Yours, for instance, seems intent on marrying you to a man you do not even know.'

'They are not forcing me,' she protested. 'I have agreed.'

'But why would you do so?' He sounded genuinely perplexed.

'I have to marry.'

'Then choose someone you love.'

'As you have?' she retorted.

'Learn from my mistakes. Life without love is hardly worth living.'

'I have loved,' she returned with dignity, 'but it was not sufficient.'

For the first time she found that she could openly acknowledge the hurt she had suffered; somehow the memory of Richard no longer felt so distressing.

'He must have been blind, deaf and insane to boot,' he said roughly, hearing the past pain in her words. Then, catching her hands in his, he demanded, 'Tell me his name and I will personally knock some sense into him!'

She smiled up at him, warmed by the sincerity of his voice and the glow from those leonine eyes.

'I fear you are too late', and she allowed herself a small gurgle of laughter. 'He has already made his decision and married another.'

'Then he deserves even more of a kicking.'

He let go of her hands to reach out for a stray tendril of hair and then curled it around his finger. Slowly he brought the curl to his lips. She stood motionless as his fingers moved from her hair to her face, lightly touching her cheek and then softly brushing her neck to come to rest on her bare shoulders. A breathless, slow heat began to uncurl within her. He was looking hungrily down at her, his eyes a molten brown flecked with that golden intensity. She felt herself mesmerised, falling into a vortex that was drawing her inexorably to his very centre; hardly knowing what she was doing, she brushed a flaxen strand of hair from his forehead and allowed it to drift through her fingers. The gesture seemed to unleash in him the passion he had so far restrained and he lowered his head and brought his mouth down on hers in a kiss of such aching pleasure that all rational thought vanished. She could think of nothing but the feel of him, the scent of him, the taste of him. He kissed her once more slowly and tenderly and then again, exploring, savouring and finally allowing the full force of his desire to wash over her. She was reduced to trembling sensation. When he lifted his lips it was to trail kisses down her neck, her shoulders and to settle whisperingly against the creamy swell of her bosom. A throbbing arrow of heat pierced her and she found her body arching, cleaving desperately to him. Somewhere in the distance she heard herself moan softly.

The sound seemed to bring him to his senses; in a moment he had stepped back from her, breathing heavily and looking considerably less polished. It was a while before he spoke and when he did his voice was still ragged with passion.

'You should keep your distance from me; I will only bring you distress.' Then, in a quieter tone, he continued, 'Forgive me, Domino. You are a beautiful girl in all senses of the word, but that does not excuse my breaking the promise I made—and so quickly.'

Still in a daze of desire, she managed to stammer a disclaimer. Neither felt able to say more and the silence between them was filled with unexpressed feeling until Joshua, in an attempt to make light of the situation, joked, 'As an experienced rake, I should advise you that now would be a good time to return to your family!'

As he spoke, he proffered his arm and she took it with as much dignity as she could muster, her head held high. Retracing their steps across the library and down the corridor, she saw them reflected in the many mirrors lining the walls. He may be dangerous, but what a comely couple we make, she thought. Almost respectable! She could have laughed aloud but for the mantra beating inside her head: she must never allow herself to lose control like that again. Her father must never know what had just occurred. He must never guess at the force of her desire. Nor Carmela and her aunts—certainly not—and as for the unknown Spanish husband, he must stay forever ignorant of such unmaidenly passion. And there was no reason that any of them should ever know. At least rakes did not kiss and tell or they would hardly be so successful.

Joshua caught sight of their reflection at the same time as she and smiled back at her. The scar on his cheek was hardly noticeable, but it gave him distinction, she thought softly. Not that he needed it, he was so beautifully made. Guiltily she caught herself up; from now on, such thoughts were taboo. She must focus on a very different future.

Once in the Long Gallery amid the noisy

buzz of chatter, he stopped and turned to her, a serious expression on his face.

'Remember my warning. There are those close by who wish you ill. If you need me, I am here.'

She saw her father rapidly approaching, a worried look on his face, and had no time to reply.

'We have been looking for you everywhere,' Alfredo fussed. 'Carmela is even now questioning every footman in the building.'

She was startled. 'Please stop her, Papa. As you see, I am well. Mr Marchmain was kind enough to offer me his escort from the Prince's apartments.'

It was Alfredo's turn to look startled. 'The Prince's apartments?'

'His drawing room, sir,' Joshua said soothingly. 'He wished to show Miss de Silva his magnificent collection of brooches.'

Her father's expression remained uneasy. 'I am sure his Highness was most gracious, but the time has come to leave.'

His tone was severe, and in a short while they had collected Carmela and were bowling down the driveway towards Marine Parade.

Joshua was left looking after the carriage, a prey to uncertainty. Domino was to be sacrificed on the altar of family duty—indeed, she was willing to be sacrificed—and there was little he could do. He was a disreputable man and could have no voice in her future. That kiss—those kisses, he corrected himself reminiscently—could only ever be an interlude, but what an interlude! It was ridiculous that his heart still sang. How many kisses had he known in his lifetime? Not like this, a small voice within him argued, not like this. She had been a revelation, all her youth and vitality poured into those moments of pleasure. He had known instinctively that she was a girl of strong emotion, that beneath her modest exterior lay a sleeping passion waiting to be roused, and he had been right. He had wanted to kiss her until she begged him never to stop, and she had wanted him to. She desired him as much as he desired her. Another conquest to add to the many, he thought acidly. All the more reason, then, to keep his distance. Otherwise he would hurt her, and hurt her badly. It was inevitable—for didn't he damage everything that became dear to him?

An unbearable restlessness seized him and he knew he had to get away from the chattering foolishness all around. He turned on his heel and strode back the way he had come. Once in his studio, he threw off his black evening jacket and shrugged himself into the spattered smock. A blank canvas was before him and he picked up his brush. In his mind's eye he saw her as she had stood just minutes before. His painting would capture that moment, would capture her lovely young face as he kissed her into mutual submission. It was as close as he would ever get to possessing her and with that he must be content. For her sake his heart must remain well defended: she was too young, too trusting, too innocent. For his own sake, too. The life he had fallen into was predictable, often unlovely, but always free from the pain of feeling; it was a life he intended to keep.

Chapter Six

It was a long time before Domino fell asleep that night. The visit to the Pavilion had proved a kaleidoscope of sights, sounds, happenings, that tossed and tumbled through her mind without settling. The strange architecture, the exotic furnishings, the overpowering heat, had all contributed to a strong sense of disorientation even before she had been assailed by the Regent's clumsy advances. For a while she had truly feared for her virtue; then came the sweet relief of rescue. It seemed it was her destiny to be saved from disaster by the one man who should have spelt the greatest danger to her.

Yet it was some time since Joshua had played the rake, if indeed he ever had. When she thought back to their first meeting on the beach, she had to acknowledge that it was her peace of mind that he'd threatened rather than her person. In fact, she had never felt seriously threatened in his company. Ruffled, irritated, occasionally shocked by his unconventional-ity, but never genuinely alarmed. He was sim-ply adept at provoking her. But this evening he hadn't provoked; he had seemed almost a different person. From the outset hints had sur-faced that more lay beneath the devil-may-care exterior than he cared to admit; but seeing him in his studio tonight, so much a part of his set-ting and among the things he valued, a serious and interesting man had assumed control. She'd felt a powerful connection to the paintings he loved and a powerful connection to him.

In her imagination she returned to his studio. She was flicking through the stack of canvases once more, then stopping abruptly. That picture of her! She saw it clearly in her mind's eye and pondered long over what it meant. He had said it was her foreignness that captured his interest, but the intimacy of the painting seemed to say far more. And the kisses that followed—what had they meant to him? They had certainly turned *her* life upside down. She had melted under their onslaught, every worldly consid-eration banished; all she had felt or known in those moments was him. She had never before experienced such emotion: her heart, her body, her whole being had shaken with the pulse of feeling.

Richard had never kissed her; if he had, she suspected that any kiss would have been but a poor reflection of what she had felt tonight. In retrospect her sentiments for Richard had been just what he had always said they were, a schoolgirl crush, painful and deep, but a mere rehearsal for the real thing. Was tonight the real thing? The thought scared her mightily, for if so it blew to pieces the future she had ordained for herself. She had left the Pavilion vowing never again to lose control, never again to succumb to her desires so shamelessly. She would block the moment from her mind as if it hadn't happened. Yet here she was thinking of it again and again, endlessly repeating those kisses, endlessly drowning in their delight.

After a restless night, she dragged herself from bed the next morning, feeling tired and dispirited. Doubts crowded out the euphoria of last night's lovemaking. She no longer knew what to think or how to behave. When she could label Joshua a rake, it had been easy to ignore the promptings of her heart. She could ignore them no longer and her heart lay exposed, raw and vulnerable. She tried to give it covering by dwelling on his past iniquities and telling herself how foolish it was to believe in his caresses, but the attempt was flimsy.

Without doubt he was a sexual buccaneer. It was not just his past relationship with the duchess: mistresses were a fact of life in the *ton*, never openly acknowledged, but discreetly tolerated. No, not just the duchess. His name had been linked to half a dozen others currently residing in Brighton; though she did not know the truth of these insinuations, the old adage of no smoke without fire came to mind. In short, he was a wholly unsuitable person to consort with. And how she had consorted! She had been utterly brazen.

With her mind torn this way and that, she was undecided whether to hide herself at home or fight the blue devils that threatened by venturing into town. Carmela made the decision for her. Her cousin was in a particularly disagreeable mood and it looked likely to last for hours.

'I do not understand why you felt it necessary to disappear last night,' she greeted Domino crossly as the latter took her seat at the breakfast table.

'The Regent wished to show me his collection of jewellery,' she replied in a tired voice. 'Papa knew where I was.'

'He did not, or else why would he have been looking for you everywhere?'

'But he took me himself to meet the Regent.'

'In the Music Room, Domino. You were to stay in the Music Room and not wander off to goodness knows where without a word.'

'The Prince wished to escort me to his drawing room. I could hardly refuse and there was no chance to let you know where I was going.' She thought it wise not to disclose that the Regent had resisted her plea to send for her cousin.

But Carmela had not yet finished her scolding. 'Your lack of thought caused both your father and I much worry and also a great deal of talk. What must people have thought when you left the room with the Regent and without a chaperon?'

'I imagine my absence would have gone unnoticed if you had not taken it upon yourself to alert every footman in the palace.' Domino's response was tart.

Her cousin bit back a retort, appearing to concede silently that she had been at fault in broadcasting Domino's truancy. But it was clear that she blamed her charge for the evening's troubles and for falling into one mischief after another. Doubtless she was counting the days until the family could leave Brighton and all its shocking attractions.

Domino left the breakfast table before her cousin could continue the harangue, but her father, encountered in the hall, proved no more benign. He was making his way to his office and the daily round of papers and, though he greeted her courteously enough, it was evident from his distant manner that he was far from happy. Her relatives appeared suspicious that she had conducted herself ill last night, but their suspicion fell squarely on the Regent. What would they think if they knew about Joshua?

The cloud that hung over Marine Parade spurred her to leave the house as soon as possible. In an effort to brighten a day which had started so badly, she slipped into the white figured muslin newly arrived from the dressmaker, and chose a charming gypsy straw bonnet, embellished with cherries and trailing matching ribbons. Flora, who was assisting her to dress, was delighted to learn that she was to accompany her mistress.

'It will be good to be on one of our adventures again, miss,' she squeaked excitedly.

Not much of an adventure, Domino reflected; a walk to the Level and back would have to suffice, but at least she would be in the

fresh air and safe from any further recrimina-
tions. And there would be plenty to see, for the
Level was a popular leisure area, frequented
by local people as much as by the members of
visiting London society. It was spacious and
grassed, with a variety of attractions, even a
cricket ground that had been laid out years before for the Regent when he was still Prince
of Wales. The broad avenue of elms, their
branches almost interlocking overhead, made
a soothing walk and she could imagine herself
in the country while the town thronged busily
around her.

Today they had hardly reached the beginning
of the walk when music came drifting to them
on the breeze.

'Oh, Miss Domino, do let's go and look.'
Flora was jigging up and down in her eagerness. 'It's the military, I'm sure. I can hear the
drums.'

The Prince's own regiment, the 10th Light
Dragoons, was based at the Church Street bar-
racks and, in the absence of another French
invasion, spent their time mounting guard on
the Prince's estate and occasionally taking part
in parades, grand reviews and mock battles as
part of the town's seasonal entertainments.

Domino felt a surge of interest. Italian opera

might leave her cold, but a military parade was another matter.

'I'm sure you're right, Flora,' she said happily. 'The soldiers must be practising for the Regent's birthday—it can only be days away now.'

'What do you think they're planning to do?' The maid screwed up her face in concentration, as though by sheer force of will she could conjure up the mystery entertainment.

'My father said there was to be the usual parade, but he thought something quite special too, possibly a re-enactment of the Battle of Waterloo.'

At this intelligence Flora could contain herself no longer and began tugging at her mistress's arm in a fashion which Carmela would instantly have decreed unseemly.

'Quick, miss, let's go and see!'

They hurried along the wide avenue until it suddenly opened on to a large clearing. Here a dazzling display of deep blue and gold met their eyes. The soldiers were a moving panorama, the brilliant gold braiding of their tight fitting jackets glowing in the morning sun and their ebony shakos sitting proudly atop their heads. Raised in the air, a cluster of curved swords gleamed wickedly. A band played nearby, the drum they had heard earlier beat-

ing out an insistent time as the soldiers moved
smartly first one way, then another, wheeling
and spinning in such orderly fashion that to the
dazed spectator they seemed not five hundred
single men, but one dashing entity.

'Ain't that just a sight, Miss Domino,' Flora
breathed, forgetting her acquired polish in a
moment of wonder.

'It certainly is,' said an amused voice a short
distance away. 'Flora, isn't it?' and a smiling
man doffed his high-crowned beaver hat in her
direction.

'Yes, sir.' She bobbed a nervous curtsy.

Joshua must have been at the far end of
the parade ground where officials from the
Prince's household were gathered and she
had not noticed him until he was nearly upon
them. As always the deep blue coat he wore
was moulded like a second skin to his powerful
shoulders. Beneath she glimpsed a paler blue,
ornamented Venetian waistcoat and the palest
and most close fitting of fawn pantaloons. On
his feet were glossy black Hessians with little
gold tassels, which swung jauntily as he came
towards them. Her eyes drank him in: he was
a pleasure to behold.

'And Miss de Silva,' he said, his voice coolly
welcoming. 'How delightful to see you here.'

She took her cue from him. They were to

meet as acquaintances, nothing more. Was this for Flora's benefit or was he refusing to acknowledge the kisses of a few hours ago?

'So what is to be—soldiers or sopranos?' His golden eyes, now laughing, smiled down at her.

'Soldiers, I fear.' Flora looked perplexed but Domino glowed inwardly. The mutual joke brought them closer.

'Why fear? They are a splendid sight, are they not? And so much easier on the ear!'

Laughter bubbled up. 'I doubt the *ton* would agree.'

'They would not, or at least they wouldn't admit to it. A preference for low pursuits denotes an instant loss of face. I seem to recall that when the circus visited town, opinions were most scathing!'

'When was that?' Her face lit up at the mention of a circus.

'It was a while before you arrived in Brighton, but I would place a heavy wager that if they were to return, you would be first in the queue.'

She was the most enchanting child, he thought, all youthful eagerness despite the womanly curves, which even now filled the figured muslin so becomingly.

'I would! I visited Astley's when I was in

London a few years ago and saw an equestrian ballet,' she added guilelessly.

'And you enjoyed it?'

'Immensely. It was an amazing spectacle.'

'I imagine it would be. I have never managed to visit Astley's myself, but I've heard legendary tales of their performances.'

Her cheeks flushed with remembered excitement. 'I think it was the very best event I ever attended.'

She was adorable, but he must keep a sharp watch on himself. He had painted through the night and emerged serene; all he need do now was to keep his distance.

'Did Lady Blythe take you?' he asked, disconcerting her for a minute. 'I would not have thought it to her taste.'

'Do you know my aunt?'

'Only very slightly,' he said smoothly. 'So who was brave enough to escort you?'

'Just a friend.'

Her tone was awkward and she seemed keen to change the subject. He wondered if it was the same friend who had spurned her youthful love and married elsewhere. She was a girl of great spirit, but also intensely vulnerable; he must tread very carefully.

'Flora and I were speculating', and she gestured towards the soldiers who had now come to a standstill and were awaiting commands from a scarlet-sashed officer. 'We thought the soldiers must be practising for the Regent's birthday celebrations. Do you know what they intend to present?'

'There will be the usual parade, of course, but I am not allowed to discuss the *pièce de résistance*—it's a state secret!'

She laughed out at him, her dark eyes alive with mischief, and he gazed back at her for as long as he dared; then, seeing Flora's enquiring expression, looked quickly away.

'Have you had a hand in this great surprise, Mr Marchmain?'

'I was dragged into the early planning and I am supposed to oversee rehearsals, but other than that I cannot claim to have taken a very active role. I enjoy the dash and colour of the military and that's about it. I am looking forward to seeing the final performance, though. It will mark a splendid end to the summer season.'

She looked at him questioningly and, when he responded, his voice was stripped of expression. 'Prinny is planning to leave Brighton the week after his birthday, you know. I am due to accompany him back to Carlton House and from there travel on to Norfolk.'

He saw the shadow skim her face and there

was a part of him that rejoiced. 'You will be leaving for Spain at the same time, I imagine.'

'I will.'

Silence fell. They stood side by side, looking blankly into the distance, hearing their own words, but not quite able to accept them.

'Our stay has passed very swiftly.' Her tone was wistful and her high colour betrayed her feelings. He pretended not to notice, and almost immediately she continued in a much brighter voice, 'I am surprised that you intend to visit Castle March so soon. I thought you would make a stay in London.'

'It's time I returned. I've been away too long, though I doubt I will be there many weeks. Just long enough to hang my da Vinci before the Norfolk weather drives me to warmer climes.'

'That is sad. Houses need to be loved, I think. But if you dislike the place so very much, why don't you sell and buy an estate you find more congenial?'

'It's true that I have little love for the house but, in gratitude to my great-uncle, I feel bound to keep it.'

'Because he made you his heir?'

'Because he left me Castle March at the right time.'

'And when was that?'

'When I'd grown tired of being a vagabond.

And a country seat is not to be sniffed at—a gentleman with a large estate always commands respect!'

While they were talking, Flora had sauntered away to mingle a little timidly with the soldiers who were now relaxing at the side of the parade ground. With her maid out of earshot, Domino seemed emboldened to ask a question he had no wish to answer.

'Could you not have found a home with your brother?'

His face assumed a darker expression and with a jagged motion he pushed back a strand of bright hair from his forehead.

'My brother and I have nothing in common,' he said, his tone verging on the curt. 'In any case, he has a family of his own to concern him and I can only ever be a discomfort.'

'But why?'

'He is convention made flesh. I was a constant thorn in his flesh while I was growing up, and once I hit town my conduct was unspeakable!'

'Whatever you did to make your family disown you is long past.'

Her sweet concern touched him, but the truth was brutal and he had no wish to hide behind pretence. 'For him, Domino, the scandal lives on. Believe me, it is for everybody's good that I keep away.'

'What did you do, exactly?' she asked shyly.

'I badly failed two people who were dear to me and who deserved better.'

She looked dismayed and he said tersely, 'It isn't a pretty tale and my parents were justified in packing me off to Europe as soon as they could. But I won't have you think me the victim. The family made sure I had a decent enough allowance.'

'But still…' Dismay had turned to bewilderment.

'My parents are dead, and I have regained a little respectability by inheriting Castle March. Life is easy for me; my brother can be forgiven for wishing to keep a hundred miles between us.'

He watched her closely to see the effect of his words. He had not wanted to have this conversation but, since they had, he hoped it would serve to push her away. She was already too close for his comfort. Last night had been a very bad mistake; he was damaged goods and his was a solitary future.

Despite that, he could not stop himself wanting, intensely, to see her again—and again and again. He found himself saying, 'What is this I hear about the Cunninghams' extravaganza on Thursday evening? Something quite out of the ordinary, I believe. Are you invited?'

Lady Cunningham was generally despised as an empty-headed woman who greedily extracted gifts from the Regent and flaunted them in public. But because of her influence over George and because of the opulent nature of the hospitality she provided, her parties were never short of guests. Domino had not liked Lady Cunningham when she met her, nor had she wished to be involved in her lavish preparations; the idea that ladies might perform on stage for their peers seemed of dubious propriety. But a combination of Carmela's horrified response to the invitation and her father's reassurance that these days the most respectable of ladies took part in such informal entertainments had persuaded her to accept.

Alfredo had convinced her that he knew the perfect role she could play. He had preserved a single dress of her mother's, a dress Elena had worn when she was not much older than her daughter, and Domino could appear in tableau as a grand Spanish lady. When she saw the dress for the first time, she had gasped. It was a dress as red as passion; a dress for flamenco. As soon as she'd put it on, she had felt its power. It had needed no alteration, fitting her curves to perfection, and no addition other than a scarlet flower for her hair and a pair of high-heeled black shoes. She had been feeling somewhat disquieted about wearing such a revealing costume, but the thought of Joshua being there made her face flame.

'Yes,' she assented as unconcernedly as possible, 'my father wishes us to attend.'

He chose to ignore the deep blush and replied easily, 'Then I shall see you there. Meanwhile I must report to the palace on the progress of the birthday plans', and, lifting his hat once more in salutation, he turned and walked away.

She was left prey to conflicting sensations: about him, about the party. His confession of wrongdoing had upset her. But so, too, had learning of his family's conduct towards him and his brother's determination to remain estranged. Whatever Joshua had done in his youth, the two were still flesh and blood. After all these years he must surely have expiated his crime. Was this brother so pure that he had done nothing wrong in his life? Joshua had failed those he loved, had not treated them as they deserved, but wasn't that true of many others? And she doubted that the case was as black and white as he'd made out. He'd declared his misdeed baldly and for a moment she'd felt dismay, but not for long. She was herself guilty of sufficiently bad things not to judge him: gambling illicitly, falling into debt, falsely eloping with Benedict when they were both minors— the list was worryingly long.

And now the Cunningham party was looming and bringing a new set of anxieties. The dress was magnificent and, wearing it, she was a warrior queen. But how warlike would she feel with Joshua in the audience? And Charlotte Severn and Moncaster, too? Their threat was always present to her, thrumming in the background. Joshua had warned her to be on her guard against them; if she drew attention to herself, what wickedness might that encourage? But unless she told her father of their continued persecution, she could not refuse to perform her part in the evening's entertainment. And to tell him would be to reveal the whole sorry business of her previous stay in England.

Her father had reassured her that all she would have to do was to walk across a small stage, a painted Spanish fan in one hand and a pair of castanets in the other. In general, he said, English people were woefully ignorant of other nations and even a simple appearance in traditional dress was sure to be greeted with interest.

But when the time came to leave on Thursday evening, she had worked herself up into a ball of terror. Reading the dread in her mistress's face, Flora ushered her quickly to the corner of the room and angled the cheval mirror.

'You should take a look, Miss Domino,' she said gently. 'Everyone will say you're all the crack!'

Her maid's attempt at *ton* slang made Domino smile faintly and she plucked up sufficient courage to look at herself properly in the mirror for the first time. The red taffeta of the dress fell in ruffled tiers to the floor. Each tier was ornamented with sparkling crystals and the final layer trailed alluringly behind her. The bodice was plain and modestly covered her bosom, but her arms were bare, framed by more ornamented frills. The dress moulded her figure so closely that every undulation, every softness, was accentuated. She caught her breath when she saw the stranger looking back at her. Could she really be this tantalising, sensual creature? She drew herself up to her full height, made prouder by the heeled shoes, and tossed the frilled skirt this way and that in sweeping gestures. Her dark eyes began to glow with anticipation, and when Flora placed a scarlet blossom in the ebony curls, now free from restraint and flowing to her shoulders, she smiled back at her reflection, captivated by the image she saw there. At her right hand, Flora gave a sigh of pure ecstasy.

'You don't look like yourself, miss. You look like...' and she struggled to put her feelings into words '...like a Spanish princess.'

'Dear Flora.' Domino hugged her. 'I fear that a genuine Spanish princess would be far too scandalised to wear such a gown!'

She ought to be scandalised as well, she thought, as the dress nipped at her curves and caressed the flowing lines of her young body. But she wasn't; instead, a strange exultation was rippling through her. She practised a few turns, swishing the deep frills of the gown from one side to another. Then holding the castanets aloft, she began to experiment with dance steps, gradually recalling the flamenco lessons she had taken without her aunts' knowledge. Another transgression! But it might serve her well this night. She wanted to perform splendidly and she knew why. She wanted to leave Joshua with a memory that he would never forget. She was not destined to be a part of his future, but she was determined to be a part of his history. All she needed was the courage to carry it through.

Once at the Cunninghams, Domino and her father were soon parted. He was ushered into a large salon, decorated in overpowering crimson, and filled with rows of delicate gilt chairs set out in a semi-circle. The first part of the evening's entertainment was to be the tableaux and mimes got up by the young ladies Sophia Cunningham had importuned. Later there would be an informal dance to the strains of a professional quartet. Before selecting his seat, Alfredo handed the musicians the gypsy music that would accompany his daughter across the stage. He felt relaxed. Knowing that the Regent had declined the Cunninghams' invitation, his fears were allayed that the Prince's recent conduct at the Pavilion might be repeated. There would be no danger from that quarter and taking part in something a little out of the ordinary would keep Domino busy and out of trouble.

Meanwhile she had been whisked to an adjoining room, already awash with nervous young ladies and their personal maids making last minute adjustments to what appeared to be highly elaborate ensembles. Domino herself had little to do but remove the black velvet cloak that covered her flamenco gown. She glanced around at the whirl of activity and was comforted by the sight of costumes a great deal more revealing than her own.

It seemed to be taking an inordinate amount of time for the gaggle of nervous girls to make ready, but at last they were being shepherded towards the rear part of the drawing room which had been curtained off to form the wings of an improvised stage. In no time what had initially appeared a large expanse had been flooded with a bevy of eager girls: Greek goddesses, Virgin Queens, Cinderellas, even Boadicea. Fussing and mingling around her, some of the groups looked askance at Domino's unfamiliar costume. That only made her hold her head a little higher.

As they waited for their turn to come, the girls could clearly hear from behind the curtain the ripples of polite applause that greeted most of the participants as they made their stately way across the stage, posing a while to enable the audience to absorb fully their finery, some of them embellishing their walk with a twirl, a curtsy or, even more daring, blowing a kiss to the audience. One Cinderella, clad in stylish rags and dolefully sweeping the floor with her birch broom, received a particularly rousing reception. Three girls dressed as Greek goddesses floated on to the stage and formed a small circle. For some minutes they danced fragrantly with each other, weaving a fragile pattern with their gauze robes. At their appearance a murmur of surprise, not all of it appreciative, had travelled around the room. One of the goddesses had been ill advised to wear a damped and transparent petticoat beneath her gauze and the more august members of the audience showed their disapproval of such flagrant exposure.

But it was Domino, far more robustly clad, who burst upon the audience with a thunderclap. She crossed the stage in one fluid movement, her heels already beginning to click and rap to the strong beat, her arms gesturing in dramatic flight and the castanets enforcing a compelling rhythm. The beat sounded at first slowly, then more rapidly, first quietly, then more loudly, alternating in tempo, but always there, throbbing, insistent. The musicians accompanying her threw themselves into the moment and music and dancer became one. Gradually the more forceful beat began to dominate, working its way to a crescendo while the dancer's feet stamped and twirled a mesmerising motif across the floor. Domino's supple, young body flexed and swayed in one direction while the red taffeta frills swished and coiled in another. The audience were silent, hardly daring to breathe. She had them wholly in her power, thrilled by the mastery of her dancing. At first the dance had appeared so daringly sensual that they could not believe they were watching it in a lady's drawing room, even

Lady Cunningham's. But as the black heels weaved their sinuous pattern across the stage and the lithe scarlet form twined and turned in sympathy with the music's yearning, they forgot where they were and gave themselves up to the fantasy.

Standing at the back of the room, Joshua forgot calm detachment. He was caught in the music's powerful rhythms, caught by the sensuous ebb and flow of Domino's body, so that he felt he was with her, moving with her, away from her, against her. He wanted to be there, he belonged there, but just when he felt he could not remain apart from her a second longer, the music reached its crescendo and with a last stamp of her heels, a last flourish of castanets, she was still. The applause was tumultuous. Emerging from her trance, Domino realised it was for her and smiled shyly back. Then, as quickly as she could, she left the stage.

After her performance there was little appetite for further tableaux and with one accord the guests began to move towards the dining room where a substantial buffet had been arranged. She felt unable to face her fellow guests immediately, but instead took shelter in a secluded corner of the salon. She had seen Joshua at the back of the room and she had danced for him. He had warned her away and she knew well that the kisses they'd shared would be the only kisses. They were treading separate paths; very soon they would say farewell for good. His future would be a procession of women, one after another, passing in and out of his life. He was sure to forget her, but she wanted so badly for him to remember. If they were destined never to meet again, she wanted him to hold this memory of her. She had danced to stun him, to leave him dumbfounded and dazed. Her cheeks flamed as she thought of the invitation she had offered, but she could not be sorry.

Almost as she thought of him, he was at her side. 'I won't ask you where you learned to dance like that,' he murmured slyly. 'I imagine your father knew nothing of your talent.'

She looked towards the doorway at Alfredo, still wearing a dazed expression, and inundated with extravagant compliments on his daughter's performance.

'Papa insisted I wore a flamenco costume,' she excused herself feebly.

'Then Papa got what he deserved!'

'I should not have danced,' she conceded shamefacedly. 'I was supposed only to walk across the stage. The dress was my mother's, you see, and Papa wanted to see it come alive again.'

'He certainly had his wish granted.' A wry smile lit Joshua's face.

'Yes, I fear he did,' she said quietly and then more emphatically, 'I really never meant to dance, but the music…'

'You have dance in your soul, Domino. You should not be sorry; you were magnificent!'

She peeped up at him. 'I *was* good, wasn't I?'

He laughed aloud. 'You *were* good, my little one. By God, you were good!'

Hearing his laugh as she entered the dining room, the Duchess of Severn glared in his direction.

'That chit seems to go from strength to strength,' she remarked acidly to Lord Moncaster, a few steps behind. 'She leads a charmed life.'

Leo handed his companion a glass of wine and said thoughtfully, 'She's a deal too close to Marchmain for her father's liking. Watch his face.'

They both glanced across at Señor de Silva. He was looking with some alarm at his daughter smiling softly at the exquisite figure beside her.

'Can we do nothing?' The duchess's voice was sharply edged, her frustration spilling out despite her best efforts at control. 'I despair of ever confounding the girl.'

'I understand she is to be married off to some Spanish grandee in the very near future. Marchmain will be history.'

'Before that happens it would be pleasant to torture her a little. I feel I deserve some small satisfaction.' The duchess's mouth twisted into an unpleasant grimace, surprising Moncaster by its ugliness.

'Hell hath no fury?'

'Not just for a woman scorned, Leo, but a man baulked of his prey,' she reminded him.

'It's true that I have not yet settled my score with the little upstart. But I have been giving it some thought.'

'Dare I say, it's about time? Since that débâcle with Prinny, you have been remarkably silent.'

'Marchmain skewed our pitch in that instance,' Moncaster began.

'Not just in that instance,' she interrupted bitterly.

'The joy of this plan, however, is that Marchmain cannot ride to the rescue. Indeed, he will be the very problem—we can use his name against her.'

The duchess looked sceptical and, stung by her lack of enthusiasm, he put down his glass on a side table and drew closer to his companion, almost whispering into her ear.

'I have a little knowledge of the señorita's past history that might serve our purpose.'

'Such as? I hesitate to remind you, Leo, but we have already employed your knowledge of her past and failed miserably.'

'We won't this time. She does not yet know the truth about our friend Marchmain. When she does, I am sure it will give her great pain. Her father, too—he will be most anxious to return her to Spain where she belongs.'

'Tell me!'

Moncaster readily obliged and the duchess's face was wreathed in an unholy smile.

'Excellent. But why now? We could have used this ammunition weeks ago.'

He gave an impatient shrug. 'Now that Marchmain has well and truly caught her, it will be so much more effective. Always keep your powder dry until you really need to use it, my dear.'

The duchess said nothing, but her smile broadened.

By this time a number of couples had been encouraged back into the salon where the chairs had been cleared and a small dance floor established. The musicians were striking up for a cotillion and Joshua, still by Domino's side, immediately offered his arm.

'Will you join us mere mortals?'

'Are you asking me to dance with you?'

'Yes, Domino, I'm asking you.'

The look in his gold-flecked eyes made her body turn to water. She stood gazing wonderingly up at him until light pressure on her arm encouraged her forwards and they joined the lively procession of couples already assembled. Her first dance with Joshua would forever stay in her memory. It was as though she moved through it in slow motion, every moment etched indelibly into her soul. The feel of solid muscle beneath her hand, the musky male scent filling her breath and the heat of his body as he drew close to her, their figures touching and parting in the graceful movements of the cotillion.

The dance meant they were separated for long periods, but always eventually they came together, their limbs warm and eager, their hands caressing fleetingly. For Joshua it was torment. Each time they were forced apart by the pattern of the dance, a voice screamed through his head that this was the stupidest thing he had ever done, but then—the wonderful moments when they came together again, the voice obliterated and his body touching hers, lightly, gently, promising delights he must not think of.

Eventually the music stopped and partners were bowing graciously to each other, but they stood motionless and silent, in thrall to the spell that encircled them. It was Joshua who gathered his wandering wits and realised the spectacle they were creating. Hastily he ushered Domino from the dance floor. By now, the room was very hot; he led her towards one of the curtained windows overlooking the wide spaces of the Steine. Its bay formed a small enclave and, as they entered, the crimson and velvet curtains closed behind them, cutting them off from the rest of the room.

'The temperature must rival that of the Pavilion,' he managed to joke, pushing the casement doors wide open so they were able to walk out on to the small ironwork balcony.

She smiled a little shakily. After the intimacy of their dance, her knees felt ready to buckle. He was feet away, though, and seemed intent on keeping a distance between them.

'Domino,' he began and then he was beside her and she had walked into his arms. His lips were on her hair, brushing the stray tendrils aside and then gently trailing kisses down the line of her cheek until his mouth found hers. As though in a dream she reached up and buried her hands in his hair, destroying its modish style in an instant, pulling him ever closer. Her eyes darkened with pleasure and her lips parted invitingly. Again and again his mouth found hers, kissing her long and hard, his tongue gently exploring at first, then growing more urgent, until she tasted him to the full. He undid the small crystal fastenings of her bodice, slowly and carefully, and his lips on her bare skin flickered fire through every nerve, every fibre. His hands cradled the gentle swell of her bosom and then his tongue was there, teasing the dress aside, closing over her breasts, bringing her aching flesh to an ecstatic hardness. She closed her eyes and gave herself up to rapture.

Once again, he was the first to come to his senses. What madness! In the middle of the Cunninghams' drawing room with a hundred people just a curtain's thickness away. And after he had sworn never to touch her again! Her dancing had aroused an elemental passion in him and, once they were close and alone, he had felt himself powerless: powerless to stop his arms from enfolding her, powerless to keep his lips from her mouth and from her body. It was ridiculous. A man of his experience, to be overwhelmed by emotions he could not control. He had to fight this insane desire or he would wreck her on the rock of scandal. For himself, the gossip mattered not a jot. The whole world knew him for a rake; people would simply shake their heads and say what else could you expect? For Domino, though, it could mean utter ruin.

But the more he saw her, the more he wanted her, and this after years of indifference, years of ensuring that he felt nothing. With every encounter his emotions deepened and he knew, even if she did not, where it would inevitably lead. He must stop. While she remained in Brighton, he must remain her friend, and nothing more. Yet he had never before felt such raw hunger as when she'd pressed her slender body into his and offered herself to him. Blame the dress for that, he muttered silently to himself, but he knew it to be a poor excuse.

He led her back into the drawing room as discreetly as he could and went to procure drinks, but her father was before him. Alfredo had been unnerved by the sensuality of his daughter's dancing; watching her disappear into the window embrasure with Joshua Marchmain, he became thoroughly fearful. He had been on the point of following the couple when they emerged from their shelter. He noted the tell-tale flush on Domino's face and Joshua's dishevelled hair, and suspected the worst. He must remove her from Brighton immediately. First that unpleasantness with the Prince Regent and now this man—less exalted, perhaps—but still of questionable morals. He knew enough of Marchmain to fear for his daughter's reputation. The aunts had been right. He had been too indulgent. Carmela had been right. She had been warning him of just such a disaster for weeks, but he had refused to believe her. Now he had seen the truth with his own eyes. Domino must leave for Spain immediately.

Joshua, returning with glasses of fruit punch, was in time only to receive a hurried curtsy from Domino and a curt nod from her father. In a moment they had bid Lady Cunningham goodbye and were on their way home.

The thunderous look on Señor de Silva's face meant only one thing, Joshua decided. Domino would be shipped back to Spain before she had time even to pack her wardrobe. In a day she could be gone and he would never see her again. He quickly downed the punch and as swiftly bid his hosts a gracious farewell. In a moment he was in the Steine and strolling towards the sea. He wanted fresh air and he wanted space. The evening was closing in, but the heat of the day had not yet disappeared. Lightly clad couples were hastening to and from the different entertainments on offer and the town had a subdued hum.

He needed to think. He had to see Domino again before she left, had to tell her...what, exactly? He hardly knew. Only that her kisses had marked him enduringly, that their love-making had mattered to him. He stood stock still, an arrested expression on his face, neither seeing nor hearing the constant murmur of water as it greeted the pebbled shore. It *had* mattered, truly mattered!

He'd been charmed from the start by her youthful beauty and intrigued by her boldness of spirit. She was fascinating but nothing more than a passing whim, he'd thought, and he had known plenty of those. He had sparred with her, flirted with her, but always made sure to keep his distance. Until that moment in the studio. Afterwards he'd convinced himself that their kisses had simply been a reaction to the drama with Prinny, a fragile moment to treasure, which would soon be forgotten. But tonight? How was he to explain that?

Was it possible that he was falling in love with her? He hardly dared think it; he could not, must not, lose his heart. He had loved before, just once, and the affair had ended in catastrophe. She, too, had been young and passionate and given herself willingly. Together they had broken every rule in the book and made themselves pariahs, cut dead in the street by friends and enemies alike. They had lost reputation, lost the world they knew, and broken their parents' hearts. And for what? A few months of madness, for he had not the guts to see it through. He had betrayed his best friend, provoked social mayhem, but finally lacked courage; he had left his lover to face the music alone. After that, how could he live with himself? The answer, of course, was that he could not. He had become a different person and lived with him instead. And now, after he'd deliberately suppressed every painful memory of that time, had thought himself forever incapable of tenderness, indeed hoped that it was so, he found himself in danger of loving this enchanting child.

It was foolish to imagine that allowing his feelings the licence they craved would change his world in any way. His reckless, empty life would continue; Domino's youthful innocence was not his to spoil. She would never be a mistress and he would never be a husband. The man she married should be as carefree and innocent as she. He knew himself well enough to recognise that he would not stop wanting other women once Domino was no longer with him. He thought cynically of all the females who had literally passed through his hands. No, his life would continue along the self-same path. But he would never again feel untrammelled pleasure, for Domino's sweet face would always be before him and her firm, young body always entwined with his.

Dusk had fallen and the lights of the small boats anchored just offshore winked out at him. The gentlest of breezes had whispered itself to a stop. But he made no attempt to move. Instead his hands began to drum against the promenade railings in an impatient tattoo as his mind beat in unison. Whatever she might feel for him, she was still willing to return to Spain to marry a man she did not know. He would not try to persuade her otherwise, for he could offer her nothing but the shell of the man he had once been. They were destined to play roles already determined for them and there was to be no deviating from the script. Nevertheless, he had to see her again, if only to bid her a final farewell.

Chapter Seven

Domino cast a concerned look at her father as the carriage rolled its way homewards to Marine Parade. His face was impassive. She wished he would say something, anything, but he remained mute. It was clear that he judged her conduct unbecoming, but his refusal to discuss her crime meant she could not defend herself against the charge he was silently bringing. He might not say anything, but she was sure that he would act: her return to Spain appeared imminent.

And what exactly was her crime? The answer was simple: she had fallen in love with a rake. She was in love with Joshua and that was improper. Stupid, too. It didn't feel so—it felt warm and wonderful. Naturally it would, she counselled herself. Rakes don't become rakes by not giving pleasure. They don't become rakes by not being able to kiss. And he could certainly kiss. Moments ago she had burnt in a firestorm of passion and she had wanted more, much more. She had wanted to throw reputation to the winds and satisfy that fierce consuming desire. And she still did. She could no longer marry the nameless husband; she could no longer marry anyone.

Hunger for Joshua must remain unfulfilled, but anything less was now unbearable. In retrospect the love she'd had for Richard had been mere baby steps on the pathway to maturity. This was what it felt like to belong to a man, body and soul. Joshua would not change. He would remain the restless, untamed creature he had always been. He would never wish to marry, but that made little difference. She could not wed another. On the morrow she would go to her father and tell him she would not be returning to Madrid to choose a bridegroom.

When the morning arrived, however, it brought two surprises. A letter had been delivered the previous evening and sat waiting for her on the hall table. Neither she nor her father had noticed the envelope on their return from the Pavilion, for they had been too absorbed in their own thoughts. But this morning it was the subject of animated discussion between Flora and the upper housemaid. Such personal missives were rare in what was an official residence. Flora placed the letter carefully on a tray alongside her mistress's hot chocolate and made haste to the bedroom, eager to hear its contents. But Domino was not in a confiding mood. She thanked her maid prettily and, ignoring Flora's evident disappointment, told her she might go.

Once alone she examined the envelope with curiosity. The handwriting was vaguely familiar, but it was not until she had extracted the two sheets of stiff paper and spread them flat on her lap that she realised the identity of her correspondent. The charming note had travelled the long distance from Cornwall and brought unexpected news of Lady Christabel Veryan. Since Christabel's marriage to Richard, Domino had communicated with her from time to time, although never easily. Three years ago she had been the one to bring the couple together; she had known even before Richard himself that his happiness lay with Christabel and she had wanted him to be happy. But her own rejection at his hands had remained raw and she had resolutely refused all invitations to Madron Abbey, contenting herself with the occasional letter addressed to Christabel alone.

Now all sense of strain had miraculously disappeared. Her feelings for Richard had faded into insignificance and she re-read the letter with genuine pleasure. Lady Veryan, it seemed, was in an interesting condition and her husband and family were most anxious for her to consult a doctor in London's Harley Street. Her father would accompany her to Brighton, she wrote, and she hoped that her dear friend, Domino, would lend her support for the short journey up to the capital. Before that it would be a great treat to spend a few days in the Regent's seaside paradise.

For the first time in their acquaintance, Domino felt that she could meet Lady Veryan without pretence and make a true friend of her. She badly needed to confide in someone and Christabel, a seasoned married woman, would be the very best confidante. She wanted to tell her about Joshua.

When, later, she knocked at the door to her father's office, it was not to tell him that she no longer wished to marry a man of her aunts' choosing, but to request that she entertain a friend she had made during her previous stay in England. For a brief moment her father looked nonplussed. Overnight he had perfected a plan to despatch his daughter immediately to Spain and had been on the point of sending a courier to warn the aunts of her arrival. But he could not be inhospitable. It was an annoying hiccup, but when he thought more about it, he could see advantages to the visit. Lady Veryan was a mature and experienced woman, and a pregnant one at that. She was likely to offer sensible advice to her younger friend and their time together would be spent largely within the confines of Marine Parade and not on the dangerous territory beyond its doors.

It would be beneficial for his daughter to enjoy new company: Carmela was hardly the most joyous presence, nor was a middle-aged parent who had too much work. The lack of suitable companionship, he reflected, might be one of the reasons that Domino had gone a little astray. A woman nearer her own age, but sensibly married, might be just what was needed. Lady Veryan could help prepare the girl for the wifely role that lay in front of her. If she were able to bring Domino to a more rational frame of mind, he might never have to raise the distasteful subject of her conduct last night. He would infinitely prefer to forget the whole disturbing series of events that had culminated in their tense ride home together.

Feeling happier than he had for days, he made his way to Raggett's, the town's most prestigious gentleman's club, and a useful place for garnering the latest political gossip. Equally happy, Domino returned to her bedroom to reply to Christabel's letter. How fortunate that Carmela was laid up with a chill and that the invitation could be issued and accepted before she was up and about again. She would almost certainly object to any unknown guest.

Domino had just laid down her pen when the second surprise of the morning arrived. A scratch at her door revealed Marston, looking perplexed.

'A caller is below, Miss Domino.'

'A caller?'

'He asked particularly for you, miss.' She noted the reproachful expression that the butler could not quite conceal.

'And does this caller have a name?'

'He is Mr Joshua Marchmain.' The voice was expressionless, but she knew that very little went unnoticed by Marston; he would be well aware that Joshua was not a welcome visitor.

Without wasting further words, she slipped past the butler and tripped lightly down the stairs, her heart beating a little too loudly. But when she reached the hall, it was empty. The front door was open to the sound of a booming sea and she crossed quickly to the doorway and looked along Marine Parade. Sure enough, there he was at the corner of Chapel Street and about to retrace his steps. He was leading two horses, walking them up and down to prevent them taking cold, for the day was sunless and there was a chill in the air.

In that instant he saw her and waved cheerfully. 'I'm glad to find you at home. I took a chance in hiring a horse for you. See, it's the pretty mare that you rode before.'

She blushed slightly at his reference to the ill-fated race, but there were more important concerns. She was bemused by his presence and needed some answers.

'What are you doing here? And with horses?'

'Riding! I thought you might appreciate a morning on the Downs. It should blow the cobwebs away.'

'But I'm not dressed for it,' she said weakly, indicating the simple dress of jaconet muslin that she had donned in anticipation of a day at home.

'I will walk the horses for ten minutes—I'm sure you and Flora can work wonders in that time.'

Aware of a disapproving Marston in the shadows, she ignored this sally and sought a further pretext. 'My father is away from home and I should not leave the house without his knowledge.' It was convenient to forget all the times she had done just that.

'We won't be gone long,' he said encouragingly. 'And no one will be around to tell tales—it's too early for most people. We might even manage a gallop!' She wavered. After her father's severity last night, it would be prudent to ask his permission, but he was not in the house and Joshua was on the front steps. He saw her hesitation and pressed home his case.

'It's a morning for being out of town, Domino, and I wish very much to talk to you. Where could be better?'

The prospect of a private conversation was too tempting to refuse and she flew up to her room, calling to Flora on the way. Together they managed the change into riding dress in record time. Domino's costume of pomona-green velvet ornamented with gold epaulettes was tailored to mould itself to her lithe young form. She watched Joshua's eyes warm with appreciation as she came down the steps to meet him, but she was glad that he offered her no compliments. She could pretend that the ride was simply a meeting between old friends and that the absence of a chaperon was unimportant.

The chill in the air had turned the sky slate grey and made the promise of an energetic gallop even more enticing. They soon left the town behind, riding single file along one of the narrow chalk paths that led upwards to the smooth contours of downland. The wind was in abeyance and the white gulls dipping and calling seemed almost to hang in the air. Once they reached the expanse of open grass, their genteel trot was abandoned for a headlong gallop. Both riders launched themselves forwards and sprinted in harmony across the turf, Domino's ringlets loosening from their hold and streaming behind her like a soft, waving banner. On and on for miles until, exhausted, the horses came to a halt at the top of a particularly steep rise in the ground. Below, the town of Brighton stretched itself lazily towards a dreaming sea, not a breath of wind ruckling the water's surface.

They sat for a moment, taking in the sweep of grey stone and white cliffs while they regained their breath. Then Joshua slid easily from the saddle and secured his reins on the branch of a solitary tree. As he did so, a shaft of sunlight broke through the leaden sky, catching them in an illuminated circle. She smiled down at him, her face radiant with pleasure and her unforced joy in the ride evoking an answering smile. Before she could join him, he had turned aside and picked a small bouquet of wild daisies and cowslips and presented them to her with a courtly bow.

'Does Spain have its own language of flowers? Here the daisy means innocence and the cowslip winning grace—what could be more apt?'

She blushed at the extravagant compliment, but said lightly, 'I think the language of flowers is universal, is it not?'

He reached up to help her dismount. 'Shall we rest the horses and walk a little?'

She nodded agreement and took his proffered arm. They strolled in companionable silence over the springy turf, wending their way along the ridge of the hill. When he spoke at last, there was some hesitation in his voice.

'I was hoping you would accept my invitation this morning. I wanted to apologise for ending your evening so badly.'

When she looked bemused, he added, 'I imagine your ride home wasn't the most pleasant you've ever taken.'

She coloured. 'There's no need for you to apologise. I was as much to blame for...' she was looking straight ahead, her cheeks now bright red '...for the incident.' Despite her embarrassment, she wasn't quite able to repress the smallest of giggles. 'You should know that my scandalous conduct went unremarked!'

'I am relieved to hear it. I was worried that you might already be on your way back to Spain. But your father seems a most level-headed gentleman. You are fortunate: families are not always so sensible.'

'You are thinking of your own?'

When he didn't respond, she said gently, 'I can understand why you should. They appear to have been very quick to judge you.'

'They had past history on their side.'

'Then you must have been in some very bad scrapes while you were growing up.'

His smile did not quite reach his mouth. 'I was.'

'But why?'

'Why? That's a strange question.'

'Not really. Boys are naturally a little wild, but why were you so very wild?'

They continued to walk in a leisurely fashion along the narrow chalk path, but she felt his figure tense beside her.

At length, he said, 'Perhaps because no one was paying me too much attention. I wasn't much use, you see. My parents already had a perfectly satisfactory heir—indeed, a paragon of an heir. And then ten years later another son came along at a time when I imagine they must have thought themselves clear of child rearing.'

He had never before revealed so much of

what was evidently still hurtful. She unlinked her arm from his and took his hand in a warm clasp. 'You're saying that you were unwanted.'

'I'm saying there was no point to me,' he said in a deliberately light tone. 'It didn't seem to matter what I did. So I suppose that goaded me into exploits that became more and more outrageous.'

'Including breaking faith with those dear to you?' She knew she was venturing into dangerous territory, but it seemed important to know all there was to know.

'That was the final icing on the cake.' The light tone had vanished and his voice was riven with bitterness. 'My perfidy ensured my parents disowned me. My brother, too—the scandal I caused jeopardised his betrothal to an earl's daughter.'

'But the marriage went ahead?'

'Yes, he married. But the bride's family made it clear that the wedding would only happen if I disappeared for good.'

'And so you went abroad.'

'And so I was sent abroad. It was the perfect solution. I'd ruined my parents—I was responsible for their early demise, or so my brother always maintained. I'd badly injured my sibling, my best friend and my first love. Going to Europe and staying there was the best thing I could do.'

The atmosphere had become heavy with the bleakness of the memory and, in an attempt to break through the grey cloud, he said in a falsely cheerful voice, 'I imagine it won't be long before you'll be on *your* way to Europe, too.'

She said nothing, but her silence told him he was right. 'Before you leave, Domino, there's something I need to say.'

She felt apprehensive, but also strangely excited. After last night's heated encounter she had come to see the impossibility of following her family's wishes, but she had also been forced to swallow the bitter knowledge that a solitary life awaited her. The only man she could ever marry was walking here by her side and there was to be no future with Joshua. He was not looking for a wife; she doubted if he was looking for a permanent liaison of any kind. Yet this morning he had sought her out and brought her to this deserted spot in order to have private conversation. Could it be that he cared enough to prevent her return to Spain? Was the bleak future she had envisaged about to vanish? She hardly dared think it. That was just as well, since the very faint hope was instantly extinguished.

'I respect your decision to return to Madrid and to your aunts' protection,' he was saying, 'even though I may not agree with it.'

He put up his hand as she tried to interrupt and repeated quietly, 'I respect your decision, Domino. But before you leave I need you to know one thing.'

'Yes?'

'I need you to know that I meant every one of those kisses last night.'

She felt baffled. What was he saying? That he was happy to see her go as long as she realised that his feelings had been honourable? Her silence seemed to urge him to another attempt.

'I have not led the most creditable of lives, but in all my dealings with you, I have been honest—unusually so. I realise that it makes little difference to either of our futures, but it matters very much to me that you know my lovemaking has been sincere.'

She was still uncertain whether her heart should be leaping skywards or plummeting to earth. To gain time she repeated, 'Sincere?'

'Genuine. A difficult word for me—I am a rake, after all!' His tone was jesting, but when he spoke again, there was a new heat to it. 'I *meant* those kisses.'

And then swiftly, before she could respond,

'You must not worry. I won't disturb your life further, but I could not allow you to leave England without confessing what knowing you has meant to me.'

She turned to face him, grasping his hands in an impulsive movement.

'You may disturb my life as much as you wish, Joshua. Should I return to Spain, it will not be to live with my aunts.'

It was his turn to look baffled. 'When did you make *that* decision?'

'Last night,' she murmured shyly.

She could not bring herself to confess the whole truth of her feelings. Some small vestige of doubt held her back. The memory of Richard's rejection still played through her mind and she did not know if she could bear the far worse pain of Joshua's dismissal.

'Why have you decided this?' he was asking.

She prevaricated. 'My aunts are insistent that I wed a man of their choosing, but I can no longer contemplate an arranged marriage.'

'And why is that?' His amber eyes seemed to probe deep into her heart.

'There are reasons.'

He was looking at her in a way that made her stomach tie itself into the severest of knots, but some distant warning voice kept her from saying more.

'And I am not to know those reasons?' he asked softly.

'They are not important.' She must continue to hide her secret. Joshua would not want to hear words of love, words he could not reciprocate. But though she could not speak the truth, her body was pushing her to be honest. She reached up to touch his face and her finger lovingly traced the scar on his cheek.

He stood stock still for a moment, hardly believing the touch of her hand; then, in a sudden movement, he pulled her roughly into his arms, showering her hair and face with a torrent of kisses, until they were both breathless and forced to stop. For a moment they stood immobile, holding hands and laughing foolishly at each other. Then he wrapped his arms around her once more and kissed her again, this time slowly, tenderly, savouring every touch and taste of her. She breathed in his familiar scent and closed her eyes. The memory of last night's kisses still lingered on her body and she wanted his lips back where they belonged. Soon she had her wish. His mouth began to trail slow kisses down her neck. Then, expertly unbuttoning her riding dress, he raised the satin skin of her breasts to his lips. She gasped with pleasure and fell back against the tree they had stopped beneath. He teased her with his tongue and she pressed into him, moulding herself like a second skin, her soft warmth cleaving to his hardness. They paused for a moment, shaken by the intensity of their feelings, but an irresistible force made them greedy for more.

He picked her up in his arms and laid her down on the soft turf, then he was beside her, drawing her towards him, fitting his body to hers. Whirls of shocked pleasure eddied through her. The gold-flecked eyes were dark as he hungrily sought her lips once more, bruising them in his need. She reached out and unbuttoned his shirt, imprinting her kiss on his chest and burying her face against his muscular frame. With a tender delicacy he began to undress her and her bare skin flamed with desire. Each item of clothing was hastily discarded, each part of her body caressed, gently at first and then more and more urgently. There was a burning coal in her stomach and its fire was spreading outwards and outwards until the very tips of her body were consumed by its heat. She tugged urgently at his shirt; she had to feel his naked skin on hers and in response he threw shirt and breeches roughly to one side. His fingers were thrilling her in ways she could not have imagined and when she felt she could bear it no longer, his mouth followed where his hands had led, melting her into an ecstasy that had to be fulfilled. In one swift movement he pulled her beneath him, covering her with his body. She felt him moving slowly against her, hard and ready.

'Love me,' she whispered.

But suddenly he was disengaging himself, setting their dress to rights, pulling them both to their feet. He met her bewildered gaze directly, but when he spoke it was as though the words were being dragged from him.

'I must not. We must not…' His voice trailed away.

She looked at him uncomprehendingly. Was this the cruellest twist of all, was this the way rakes disencumbered themselves from the women they no longer wanted? By bringing them to a frenzy of desire and then walking away? A minute ago, a second ago, she had shown him as plainly as any woman could that she needed his love in all its fullness. As any immodest woman could, she corrected herself flinching. She felt humiliated and desperate.

He turned away and gazed blindly into the distance. She heard his breath coming short and harsh. Then he swung round to face her, grabbing her hands and pulling her towards their waiting horses. Without a word he tossed her into the saddle and turned his mount towards the town. They rode in silence until they were once more outside the house in Marine Parade. He dismounted swiftly, springing up the front steps to summon Marston to the door. Ashen faced, Domino slid from her saddle and brushed past him into the open hallway. With a brief bow, he turned and led both horses away.

Once in the privacy of her bedroom, she allowed the tears to flow. How could this happen? Walking together this morning, she had felt closer to Joshua than ever before. He had never hidden his dislike of his family, but today she had realised for the first time the powerful hold the past still had on him. He had let down his guard and confided in her. She'd felt sad and distressed at the story. Angry, too, at his parents, at his brother, even at the friends he'd betrayed. None of them, it seemed, had really loved him, not enough to save him from himself. She had even begun to understand why, after that last catastrophic event, he had fallen into a rakish life. He must have thought himself permanently tainted, a danger, a bad omen for anyone unwise enough to get too close. But after all these years, he *had* allowed himself to get close—to her.

He'd sworn that the kisses they'd exchanged meant more to him than simple physical pleasure and she had gloried in the feeling of being wanted by the man she loved, even though their futures would remain separate and unchanged. She had given herself up to his lovemaking with such joy, such abandon—only to be made a fool of. How could he take her so far, only to spurn her? It could only be that he was playing with her. His fine words had been meaningless, spoken only to lure her into believing that she mattered to him, a notion destroyed forever by his rejection at the very moment they were to seal their love. It was a brutal but effective ploy. Their passionate encounters must have scared him. He had needed to rid himself of a clinging woman, make sure she would not importune him in future. Well, she too would do some ridding. She would smother her feelings; more, she would destroy them utterly, cut them off at their very roots and never ever let them bloom again.

Joshua slammed the door of his studio shut. He had no intention of painting, but he had to be alone, and this was the only room in the palace in which he could be sure of privacy. He had to be alone, he had to try to make sense of the morning's events. Methodically he began to sort through a stack of old canvases which he intended to reuse; the tedium of the task allowed his mind to wander. The news that

Domino did not intend to return to her aunts' chaperonage had fallen on him like a lightning bolt. He was still trying to absorb its import when she was in his arms and asking to be loved. She was not going ahead with the arranged marriage because she could no longer wed a man for whom she had no feeling. That meant only one thing: she loved elsewhere. He'd known that he was the man she loved; it could not have been plainer. He had been carried away by the sheer physical delight of wanting her, but when she had breathed that command, when she had asked him to love her totally, the reality of the situation had hit him and hit him hard. He had paused long enough to realise that what they were doing was madness. She was in love with him and she was willing to give herself, without thought for the future, but he could not let her. It was too great a sacrifice; no longer a virgin, she would be consigned forever to spinsterhood—and, even worse, she would be cast out from society. He had pulled back instantly. He cared too much for her.

But now in the quiet of his room, with time to think and think deeply, he grew certain that in pulling back from the path on which they'd embarked, he was already too late: she had already sacrificed herself. He knew little of

Spanish society, but enough to realise that in its eyes she had committed a grave sin. Whether she were a virgin or not was doubtless irrelevant; she had lain naked with a man and that in itself would place her beyond the pale. She would no longer be considered a suitable wife for any decent man. He could not believe he had done this to her. How could he have been so stupid as not to realise the true import of his actions? She had not realised either, he was sure, but she was young, trusting, blinded by love. It had been his responsibility to keep her safe and he had failed miserably. She would say that she did not care, that she had no wish to marry any man, but he knew from long experience of women that such vows rarely held. There would come a time when she did want to marry and she would have to confess to her intended husband something at least of her past. He was quite certain that, however mild the confession, it would damn her irrevocably. He had quite simply ruined her young life and could offer her no recompense.

Swept with remorse, he angrily tossed the pictures aside and walked to the open windows. An unkempt profusion of honeysuckle and dogwood looked back at him. How could he ever make it up to her? It was impossible, except...

The mad notion of asking her to be his wife

flitted through his mind and was immediately dismissed. He spelt disaster for anyone who came too close. He could not possibly ask her to marry him. The old Joshua would have plunged in fearlessly, but not this one, not the man he had become. As long as he remained at a distance, he could not be responsible for another's suffering. It was the only way to get through life. He could never return to the old Joshua.

Or could he? He paced up and down the floor, wooden boards creaking and cracking as he went. Dared he embrace a different kind of life, a life where he was no longer in control, one which held unknown pitfalls and sorrows? To live as he had these last six years was undemanding and free of pain. But she was in trouble. She needed him. Was he such a coward he could not step up to that challenge? Because of him, she had turned away from the future she'd envisaged—and to what? A wasteland. There was no longer any future for her. He might have burned his fingers, but he had burned hers, too. He had to put it right. He had to step right into the fire, there was no other way. He had to marry her.

Domino's resolve to obliterate Joshua Marchmain from her world was put to the test almost immediately. She had slept little and was making her way bleary-eyed to the breakfast table the next morning when a disapproving Marston put a small posy of wild flowers into her hand: blue bellflowers and pink eglantine roses interweaved with strands of ivy. She carried them into her small downstairs parlour and sat staring at them for what seemed an age. There was no note, but she knew from whom they came. Reluctantly, she took down the dictionary of flowers from its resting place and flicked through the pages. Here they all were: bellflowers for thinking of you, the roses for a wound to heal and the ivy for friendship. And this was his response to her complete humiliation! She threw the book on to the table and strode into the hall, grabbing the posy on the way. One of the undermaids was busy dusting a console table and bobbed a small curtsy as she saw Domino approach.

'Lizzie, isn't it?' The maid nodded nervously, wondering if her dusting was at fault. It was usually Miss Carmela who took her to task.

'I'd like you to have these, Lizzie. They will cheer your bedroom.'

The maid gaped and Domino said in a voice that brooked no argument, 'You will need to put them in water—now.'

The hall clock was striking eleven as the

maid scurried away and Domino, still trembling slightly, walked back into the parlour. Almost immediately she spied his figure through the small square panes of its window; in the distance Joshua walking slowly back and forth along the promenade. He was waiting for her, she knew. Her anger had begun to cool and in its place the impulse to run to him was gathering strength. Determinedly she beat it back, but it cost her dear and she thought it wise to retreat to her bedroom, which faced the opposite direction. An hour later, she returned to the parlour and saw that he was gone. She felt empty and aching but knew that she had done the right thing. Twenty-four hours dragged by and brought with them another bouquet. This time Marston could hardly bring himself to hand the posy to his mistress. She ignored the servant's deep frown and took them in silence. But her anger was reignited and she stomped through to the back kitchen and plunged the flowers unceremoniously into the rubbish bin. She had no idea what Joshua's intentions were, but if he thought that two bunches of wild flowers would erase the pain he had caused, then he was more arrogant than she had ever believed. She felt proud that she had ignored his siren call and marvelled at her resolve, but a small, hard nut of anguish had settled itself firmly within her and she knew it would be her companion for years to come.

For three days she dared not venture beyond the front door for fear of being waylaid, but when no further offerings arrived and Joshua's figure no longer strolled the seafront, she thought it safe to leave the house. A travelling fair had come to Bartholomews and Flora was mad to attend. The fair's unsophisticated pleasures were unlikely to soothe Domino's anguish, but she knew that she could not stay indoors forever. After the ravages of recent days, modish clothes had ceased to be important and she donned an inexpensive sprig muslin and a plain straw bonnet for the outing. With Flora chattering by her side, they began the walk along Marine Parade towards the Steine. They had barely walked fifty paces when, at the corner of Chapel Street, an immaculately attired Joshua stepped across their path and forced them to a halt.

He could not have known we would be walking here today, Domino thought. He must have been waiting nearby for days. He bowed deeply and she nodded briefly in response, edging around him in an effort to continue her journey. Already she could feel her traitorous body working against her.

'Would you do me the honour of allowing me to escort you this morning, Miss de Silva?' he enquired formally.

'Thank you, Mr Marchmain, but as you see I have my maid with me and she is all the protection I need,' she was glad to be able to reply with equal formality.

He bowed again and she could see him looking searchingly at her face. She hoped he would not remark her pallor and the dark circles beneath her eyes. The longer he stood there, the harder it was to avert her gaze from his beautiful person. And she needed to.

'We are a trifle short of time this morning, sir. If you would excuse us...' and she edged even further ahead.

'So short of time that you cannot spare five minutes?'

There was something in his voice that made Domino pause. He was dressed in his usual elegant fashion, his skin lightly tanned and his hair glinting gold in the late summer sun; as ever he looked the perfect man. Yet there was something different, she felt. Could it be that he was nervous? Surely not!

During their interchange Flora had been looking from one to the other, her mouth opening and closing like a fish searching for water. She was evidently confused and now the flush on her cheeks signalled her annoyance at the unwanted intrusion on her mistress. She looked likely to find her tongue at any moment.

Domino made a swift decision. 'Go ahead, Flora, I will catch you up.'

'But will you be all right, Miss Domino?'

'Perfectly. I shall be with you in an instant.'

They watched the maid walk unwillingly towards the town before Joshua spoke.

'I sent you flowers.'

She said nothing.

'I hoped you would understand their message.'

'I understood.'

'Then why did you not respond?'

She would have liked to harangue him with her opinion of his message, but instead she settled for scorn. 'Since when have I had to account to you for my actions?' Her voice trembled only slightly.

He wasn't deterred. 'I wanted to speak to you, Domino—badly.'

She raised her eyebrows and he continued hurriedly, 'I've been a fool. I was a fool on our ride. Not because I escorted you home—that was the right thing to do—but because I should have told you...' he paused uncertainly '...told you what I am about to say.'

Her eyebrows climbed higher. She had no

idea what he was about. All she knew was that she must not look at him, but concentrate very hard on what he was saying.

'You are no longer willing to accept an arranged marriage?'

She nodded mutely, wondering where this was leading.

'So you are free to make your own choice of husband?' he was saying. Then the bombshell. 'I think your choice should be me.'

'What!' She was stunned.

'I think you should marry me.'

'Is this some kind of perverted joke?'

'I can't blame you for judging me harshly. But it's no joke, though it may seem so. In truth, marriage to a rake is unlikely to advance your social standing.'

She was incensed and hurt in equal measure. His false proposal was yet another dagger to her heart.

'I do not deserve your mocking, sir. If this is no joke, then it is a Banbury story. If I were foolish enough to accept your offer—which, rest assured, I am not—you would be sure to decide that your proposal was after all an unfortunate mistake.'

'However much to the contrary it may appear, I was sincere in our lovemaking, Domino, and I am sincere now.'

She was still recovering from the first shock of his announcement and could hardly take in what he was saying. Bewilderment made her cutting. 'You would not know the meaning of the word.'

'Please believe that I have always had your best interests at heart.'

'And now you have my best interests at heart by asking me to marry you? Forgive me if I am very slightly sceptical.'

'Your feelings are understandable. But I have done a good deal of thinking over these last few days and I know this is right.'

'And when did this improbable revelation visit you exactly?'

'I've made you angry. I'm sorry for that. You see, I never wished to disrupt your life and I didn't think I was the one to make you happy: I carry too much of the past with me. I should have kept away, but somehow I couldn't, and now that you've given up all idea of marrying to please your family, I'm asking you to marry to please me.'

Seeing her desperately trying to make sense of his words, he pressed home his case. 'Please believe me when I say that I don't ask you this lightly. I know that I want to live with you, to make a home with you—if you will have me.'

She was weakening. He sounded so earnest,

but this change of fortunes was too much to swallow. 'It's not possible. Joshua, you cannot want to marry!'

He looked at her so fiercely that she was almost afraid. 'But I do.' Then, in a weak attempt to return to the Joshua she knew, 'If we marry, I may even allow you to hang my precious da Vinci!'

The quip faded and his expression took on a rare seriousness, 'You should know, Domino, that if you take me as a husband, you will do yourself little good socially and are sure to upset a great many people. Marriage to me may be a step too far.'

'It is a step I never thought to take,' she said slowly, but her face had gained colour, the olive skin of her cheeks lit by a slowly spreading inner glow. This morning has brought a miracle, she told herself, and like any miracle it had to be believed rather than reasoned. She could not understand how he had come to this decision, but it was clear that he meant every word he spoke. This was no cruel jest, no mocking overture. He had asked her to marry and all she had to do was say yes.

'You have turned my life upside down—but you are the only man I could ever wed.'

'And...?'

'And if you are truly honest, you have my answer!'

He held out his arms and she walked into his embrace. For long minutes they remained nestled in each other's arms while the waves lapped gently in the distance. But then the unwelcome thoughts began arriving.

'What about my father?'

'You haven't told him that you are not returning to your aunts?'

'No, not yet. That would have been difficult enough, but now this!'

He stroked her arm to still her agitation. 'It's easy—we'll see him together and tell him that we are wishful of marrying.'

'If only it were that simple.' She hesitated, unsure of how to phrase the unpalatable. 'Papa is aware of Court gossip. He holds some strong opinions.'

'Don't let's sham it. He knows me for a rake and will be horrified that his beloved daughter has chosen to throw her lot in with such a loose fish.'

'So…'

'So I will have to prove him wrong, prove that my inglorious career belongs to the past— that you are now my future.'

'That could take some time.'

He pulled her towards him again, burying

his hands in the tangle of silken curls and lifting her face to his.

'Another year is neither here nor there, my darling.'

'A year!'

'Have patience. Before the time is out my charm offensive will have him begging me to marry you.'

She smiled a little wanly, a furrow still creasing her brow. 'There are my aunts, too—they will be completely opposed.'

'Aunts are no problem. I can deal with any number of aunts,' he said easily.

'You will be very busy, then.' A smile flitted across her face at the thought of Joshua 'dealing' with those fearsome matriarchs. 'They will do anything to protect my fortune.'

'I have a fortune, too,' he pointed out. 'Not, I imagine, of the same magnitude, but still a cool ten thousand a year. Who could want more? You can sign your inheritance over to the aunts and never have a thing to do with it.'

'That still won't make them happy with the match; I fear they will make sure my father refuses his consent.'

'But if we wait until you are twenty-one, you can marry where you wish.'

'I don't want to upset Papa,' she said miserably.

He hugged her even more tightly, 'Don't despair, darling Domino. Let me talk to him, get to know him. Make him see I will look after his little girl.'

She looked dubious, but Joshua was encouraging. 'I will invite him to dinner and then the theatre—just the three of us, if you can bear to leave your duenna behind—so that we can at least break the ice.'

'However will you get him to agree?'

She doubted if anyone could persuade her father to spend an evening with Joshua Marchmain, let alone include his daughter in the arrangement. Yet persuade him Joshua did.

The following Thursday on the stroke of eight, he arrived at Marine Parade in a carriage hired for the evening. As always he looked complete to a shade, satin knee breeches and black tailcoat throwing into relief the dazzling snow of ruffled shirt and cravat, the latter arranged in precise and intricate folds. A silk-lined cloak completed a picture of refinement. But Domino's choice of dress more than matched his style. A cloud of jonquil gauze over a white satin robe furnished a perfect foil for the ebony curls that framed her lovely young face.

Her father greeted his host with a stiff little

bow, but she curtsied shyly to her lover, giving him her hand with the most mischievous of smiles.

They were to dine at the Old Ship, the oldest hostelry in Brighton, and one that frequently accommodated the Regent's guests. Domino had attended a ball at the Ship's magnificent assembly rooms the previous month and marvelled at the ninety-foot-long ballroom with its spectators' and musicians' galleries. But tonight Joshua had bespoken a private parlour, equally luxurious, but a good deal more intimate. He had obviously gone to a great deal of trouble, Domino thought, in planning this evening. Not only was the room he had chosen a perfect backdrop for a congenial dinner, but the meal itself had been carefully ordered to appeal to the tastes of a middle-aged Latin gentleman.

A modest but delicious repast ensued, beginning with a turtle soup served alongside a series of entrées including the omelettes her father loved. He ate well, but remained chilly and aloof. For a while the talk was general: the beauty of the Sussex landscape, the benefits of sea air, the numbers of dandies parading Brighton's seafront with their ridiculously padded shoulders and collars so high they were unable to turn their heads. It was not until the serving of a second course of goose, lobster and a braised ham alongside chafing dishes of French beans, peas and asparagus that Señor de Silva made mention of his unexpected invitation.

He lay back against his chair, sipping a second glass of wine with undoubted pleasure. 'I must thank you, Mr Marchmain, for a superlative dinner.'

'I am very glad the meal has met with your approval, sir,' Joshua responded politely. 'It is always hazardous to order for another at whose tastes you can only guess.'

'Indeed. Would it be discourteous of me to ask why my particular tastes interest you? Why, in fact, you have invited me to accompany you this evening?'

'Not discourteous at all. On the contrary, I find it understandable and very simple to explain. I wish to marry your daughter.'

The announcement, quiet and measured as it was, did not prevent Alfredo choking violently on his wine. When he recovered sufficiently to speak, his voice seemed not to belong to him.

'You wish to marry Miss de Silva?'

'I do. I am hopeful of winning your consent and thought it right that we should further our acquaintance as soon as possible.'

'Marry!' her father repeated. Then, turning

to Domino, he said in a voice barely above a whisper, 'Can this be right, my child?'

'Yes, Papa. I love Joshua. He is the only man who will make me happy.'

'But—'

'I am aware of the misgivings you must have,' Joshua interrupted smoothly, 'and naturally I am happy to give, in private, whatever reassurances you need, but Domino and I are quite resolved. We will marry—whether it's next month or next year.'

Her father drew himself up proudly, looking every inch the Spanish noble.

'You may not realise it, Mr Marchmain,' he pronounced haughtily, 'but my daughter's choice of husband is of the greatest significance. Through her mother's family, she will inherit a very large estate when she reaches the age of twenty-one. That may influence your decision.'

'I cannot see how.'

'You would not, I am sure, wish to be seen as a fortune hunter.'

'Papa!'

'You are right, Señor de Silva. I would not. But since Domino's fortune is neither here nor there, I think it unlikely. I have a considerable inheritance of my own and am more than happy to share it.'

His cheerful insouciance stung Alfredo. 'When I said a very large fortune, I doubt you have any idea of its size.'

'Papa, don't you see?' Domino felt incensed by her father's wilful lack of understanding. 'Neither of us is concerned with my inheritance. Joshua has a splendid country estate of his own and enough money to keep us both in comfort.'

'Not concerned with a massive fortune? What nonsense is this?' her father spluttered.

She leaned towards him, her tone placating. 'Could not my aunts devise a new plan for how best to use the money? I know them to be involved in any number of charitable causes and my fortune would be well spent.'

Alfredo struggled to digest this heresy and there was an uncomfortable silence.

'Papa, dear Papa', and Domino reached across the table and took his hand in hers. 'I love Joshua. That is surely what is most important.'

'And I will look after her, you can be sure,' Joshua put in. 'Who better, after all, than a reformed rake?'

Domino gave him a sharp glance, feeling that her lover's intervention was hardly helpful. But Joshua's words had set Alfredo thinking. This match was the very last thing he desired for his daughter; his instinct had been to grab her by the hand and incarcerate her immediately within the confines of Marine Parade until arrangements could be made for her travel to Spain. Lady Veryan, when she arrived, would have to get on as best she could without her young friend. But what Marchmain said made a kind of sense. Who better to look after a young and naïve girl than a man who was thoroughly experienced in the wiles of the world? If she was compelled to marry a man she did not love—not that he would insist on such a thing, but the aunts could be very forceful when they chose—well, what kind of trouble might result? He had seen, with his own eyes, the power of his daughter's budding sexuality. He shuddered to think of the likely outcome of an unsuccessful marriage. And as for the fortune she would inherit, Marchmain seemed genuinely unmindful; no doubt the marriage settlements could ensure the rightful disposition of such a large estate.

The third course of creams, jellies and a basket of pastries had been virtually untouched, but the mood was mellow as they made their way to the Theatre Royal where Charles Kemble was once more the star of the stage. Fifteen years ago the actor had launched the new theatre with a stunning performance of *Hamlet*, but this evening he was playing comedy at which, it was universally agreed, he excelled. The box Joshua had reserved ensured them an extensive view of the auditorium. Domino surveyed the gold and glitter of the fabulous building with pleasure, its elaborate decoration scintillating in the sparkle of newly installed gas light. An ocean of faces and a thrum of excited chatter filled the entire space, from the Royal Box, housing members of the palace household, to the cheapest seats in the furthest recesses of the theatre. She had never before attended a performance at the Theatre Royal, since Carmela naturally dismissed acting as a pretext for sin. To do so this evening, and beside the man she loved, was a double enchantment.

The squabbles of Beatrice and Benedick were soon filling the auditorium as *Much Ado about Nothing* unfolded the foolishness of its hero and heroine. Sitting close by on a matching gilt chair, Joshua stole glances at his betrothed whenever he thought himself unobserved. The perfectly sculpted cheeks, petal soft, beckoned him to touch, but the presence of her father forced him to observe the proprieties. She was enthralled by the play, face alight and hands clasped together in excited pleasure. *She has forgotten that I exist*, he thought wryly. Then she took her eyes from the stage and looked across at him with a smile so radiant that his heart almost stopped. The doubts that had plagued him momentarily disappeared. He had done the right thing. He smiled back at her and a wave of emotion rippled towards him.

As if sensing a disturbance in the air, her father shifted his position, rearranging the red velvet cushions better to support his back, for this latter part of the evening was proving something of a trial and he was barely managing to keep his eyes open. When the curtain came down for a short interval he was more than willing to stretch his legs alongside his host in the galleries behind the auditorium. Domino declined the offer to accompany them, realising her lover intended to use the opportunity to advance his acquaintance with the man he hoped to make his father-in-law. Instead she set herself to study her theatre programme.

She was not long to be left in peace. Almost as soon as the door closed behind Joshua, it opened again to reveal a female figure rustling forwards in stiff taffetas and emanating a powerful, musky perfume. Domino looked up in surprise.

'My dear,' the duchess cooed, 'forgive me for disturbing you, but I was sure you would not mind. It's high time we renewed our acquaintance.'

With Joshua's warning ringing in her ears, Domino smiled politely, but said nothing. She would like to believe Charlotte innocent of plotting against her, but common sense told her otherwise. Joshua had made clear to this woman that he wanted nothing more to do with her. At the same time he had also made clear that he wanted a great deal to do with Domino. That was hardly conducive to friendship.

'I haven't spoken to you for such a long time,' the older woman mouthed, echoing the girl's thoughts. 'We seem to have become almost estranged, but that is certainly not my wish.'

She slid smoothly into one of the vacated chairs and continued to flatter.

'You look so beautiful tonight, my dear, so young and vital, it makes me feel almost sad.'

Domino closed her ears. Did the duchess really think her compliments would renew trust?

'It is such a shame.'

This time the words penetrated and the young woman became alert.

'A shame?'

'Yes, my dear, a dreadful shame. That's why I am here, you see.'

'I am afraid I don't, Your Grace.' She felt a gnawing anxiety begin to take hold.

'Charlotte, my dear, do call me Charlotte. We know each other better than to stand on ceremony, I hope.'

Domino was silent. Whatever Charlotte had to say, she was not going to help her.

'Yes, a shame,' the duchess repeated meditatively, 'but you are still very young and I am certain that you will rise above these problems.'

Domino could not stop her brow furrowing. The cat-and-mouse game the duchess was playing was beginning to find its mark.

'If I did not think you would recover easily,' the woman continued silkily, 'I would say nothing, even though I feel you are entitled to know what might be vital for your future happiness.'

The duchess's voice had assumed the cloying sweetness that always made Domino feel slightly sick. She sat mute, perched rigidly on her chair, and waited for whatever blow might fall.

'Of course, it may not *be* a problem,' the older woman was saying. 'The man may mean nothing to you. But I cannot take that chance. You are too precious!'

If only Joshua and her father would open the door this moment and put an end to this dreadful interview.

'If you care nothing for him, then all will be well, but otherwise...' The duchess allowed her voice to fall away in mock concern.

'Who are we talking about?' Domino managed, barely above a whisper. As if she did not know.

'Who? Why, Mr Marchmain, naturally.'

'And why should that interest me?'

'Would it be foolish to point out that you are here this evening with him?' Charlotte queried archly.

'I am here with my father. We are both Mr Marchmain's guests.'

'How very civilised. I should not disturb what is so obviously a delightful evening.' And she got up to leave, her skirts rustling noisily behind her.

Domino wanted to scream, *What is it? What do you know that is so bad?*, but she managed to maintain a posture of indifference. The duchess's hand was on the door handle when she turned back to face her quarry.

'I understand that you have a dear friend who now lives in Cornwall—or perhaps we should say a *former* dear friend.'

Christabel? What on earth did Christabel have to do with anything? Her mind was skittering in confusion, but she willed herself to maintain an impassive face.

'Her name is Christabel Tallis, although she is now a Veryan. But of course, you know her name,' Charlotte purred, 'after all, how many dear friends would you have in Cornwall?'

'What of Lady Veryan?'

'An extraordinarily beautiful woman, I believe, and one with an unusual past. A little colourful, shall we say?'

'I fail to see what such tittle-tattle has to do with me.' Domino's voice was glacial. Whatever this woman was engaged in, it was tawdry.

'Let us see, shall we?' Charlotte Severn let go of the door handle and walked back a few paces into the room. She looked Domino in the eyes and a derisive smile lit her face.

'When Christabel Tallis was engaged to the man who is now her husband, she allowed herself to go just a little astray.' And the duchess drew out the 'little' in a mocking fashion. 'And who could blame her, faced with so particularly charming a temptation? Thank goodness it ended well. But the man who enticed the ravishing Christabel from her fiancé and who—I blush to mention this in a young girl's hearing—who seduced her and then left her amid a mountain of scandal, was the man you have made your particular friend. In fact, *our* particular friend: Mr Joshua Marchmain.'

It seemed that the theatre walls were closing

in on Domino; the ceiling hovered lower, its beams heavy and threatening; crystal chandeliers rocked and the wall sconces with their bright, bright gas jets ripped themselves adrift from their moorings and crashed down on her. A huge weight seemed to be breaking her body in two. Yet she knew she must respond to this wicked woman. After what seemed an age she managed to speak, although how she never knew. She kept her face blank and her voice steady by sheer overpowering force of will.

'You are misinformed, Your Grace. Mr Marchmain is not a particular friend of mine. The tale you tell is indeed sad, but is of no interest to me.'

'I am delighted to hear it,' the duchess returned and, with one last false smile of condolence, whisked herself through the door.

Domino hardly realised her visitor had left. She was staring into an abyss, a black nothingness. She felt herself hardly able to breathe. She had to get away. She had to get out of this place. She jumped to her feet, upsetting the delicate gold chair, and stumbled out into the gallery. Her father and Joshua were making their way back to the box, ready to resume their seats. She saw, but didn't see their startled expressions; she was looking through them, falling down into a dark and endless void. She had to get away, get away, get away.

'Domino?' Her father approached her uncertainly.

But she rushed past him along the gallery, down the sweeping staircase and out of the front door. Carriages had not yet been called for and New Road lay peaceful in its solitude. A moon rode high in the sky, only occasionally obscured by tattered fragments of cloud. She looked on the scene blindly; the world no longer existed. In the ghostly silver light she ran for shelter like a frightened mouse. Marine Parade was reached in minutes and a surprised Marston summoned to the door. Not a word did he get from his young mistress. At the sounds of arrival, Carmela appeared from the drawing room, her embroidery still in her hand. She called something to Domino, but Domino neither saw nor heard. Up the stairs, past a dozing Flora on the landing, and finally to sanctuary. Only now could she rest, here at the bottom of this dark, dark pit that had swallowed her whole.

She fell on the bed, dry eyed, too stricken to cry.

How long she lay there she had no idea, minutes perhaps, hours even, before Alfredo's anxious face appeared in the doorway.

'*Querida*, what on earth is the matter?'

'I am sorry, Papa,' she whispered hoarsely, 'I felt most unwell and had to get home.'

'But why did you not tell us? Mr Marchmain would have ordered the carriage immediately. He is most worried about you.'

She could no longer bear even to hear his name.

'Papa, you will forgive me, but I feel too ill to talk this evening.'

Her father looked stern. 'How can this be? We left you perfectly well and out of nowhere you become so ill that you behave with the utmost discourtesy. I demand to know what has happened, Domino.'

'Nothing has happened, Papa. I am simply unwell,' she repeated in a failing voice.

'But to rush off like that—what will Mr Marchmain think?'

'I no longer care what Mr Marchmain thinks,' she said in a much stronger voice.

Alfredo's face expressed surprise, but he did not press the matter.

'At least allow Flora to help you undress.'

She agreed, hoping that, in doing so, she would be left alone. But the misery of the evening was not yet finished, for her father was the bearer of more unwelcome news.

'Did Carmela tell you that while we were at dinner, Lady Veryan arrived?'

'Lady Veryan?' Her voice shook.

'The friend you very much wished to see.' Her father's tone was unusually tart.

'But she is not due for another day.'

'That, too, was my understanding. It seems she decided not to stay in Winchester overnight, but continued instead to Brighton. Her father is already on his return to Cornwall; he did not wish to be long away, I believe.'

'Christabel is here!' and her voice broke with wretchedness.

'She is, my dear, so whatever ails you, it would be wise to find a swift cure. Carmela reports that Lady Veryan was tired from the journey and decided on an early bedtime. But she is looking forward to seeing you on the morrow, for she has a good deal to tell you and is sure that you will have much to tell her.'

And with that, her father called Flora into the room with instructions to help her young mistress into bed immediately. Domino was hardly aware of the maid's presence and mechanically permitted herself to be undressed and slipped between the covers. Left alone, she lay prone, her newly brushed hair streaming wildly across the pillow and her eyes staring blankly ahead. Where once there had been colour and light and the sounds of pleasure, now there was nothing. She felt nothing, her whole body had retreated into a pitiless limbo. She pinched herself and it did not hurt. That should scare her, but it didn't. Nothing scared her, nothing touched her, nothing ever could touch her again. Three years ago she had lost the man she loved to Christabel. It did not matter that Richard had never returned her love, did not matter that her love now seemed juvenile. It had hurt so badly then, cut her into little tiny ribbons until she had thought she would never be whole again. But over the years she had remade herself. And finally she had found the man she thought would fill the rest of her life. Now he was gone also: another love lost, but this so much greater than the first. This time she would not be able to stick the pieces together again. And how had she lost this man, this man who was to crown her life with romance and adventure and love and joy? Why, she had lost him to the very same woman, indirectly perhaps, but indisputably she had lost her love to Christabel once more. Such bitter irony!

Chapter Eight

Flora brought her the message while she was still abed. Her chocolate had grown cold on the bedside chest and the hot water for bathing had cooled in its basin. But she had not stirred. She had no wish ever to leave this room, no wish ever to move again.

'I think you should read it, Miss Domino,' the maid dared to suggest, aware that something dreadful had happened, but able only to guess at what the cause might be. It was a man, she reasoned, no doubt the same man that had been sniffing around her mistress for weeks. The one who had stopped them in their tracks just a few days ago, then come to the house very early this morning and personally handed her an envelope with strict instructions to place it only in her mistress's hands. She tried again, this time folding the envelope into Domino's listless grasp. Then she withdrew, sighing heavily to herself.

Left alone, Domino glanced indifferently at the message. She knew its author and she knew that she did not want to read it. But something still impelled her to rip the seal open and scan the few words within.

It was brief and to the point.

Whatever has gone wrong, I need to know, he wrote. *I hope you will feel able to tell me in person. I shall be by the groyne directly opposite your house at noon today. Please meet me there.*

It was signed simply *Joshua*.

He had named the very place they had first met all those months ago. Two months ago, to be precise—was it only that long? She felt that she had lived a lifetime since then. She recalled her feelings at their very first meeting. There had been an undercurrent of excitement, but also a distinct unease. He had been mockingly persistent, caring little for her discomfort. Surely that had been an omen for the future. He'd behaved in much the same fashion more than once. But deceiving her so wretchedly about his past was of a different order; he had destroyed her trust, her belief in herself, and left her vulnerable to the cruelties of a woman like Charlotte Severn.

But it made no sense. Hadn't Joshua also rescued her from the same woman's clutches, protecting her, defeating attempts to wound her, not just once, but again and again? He'd warned her to be on her guard against the duchess and Moncaster. So why, last night, had she not been? Why had she chosen to believe Charlotte? The frailest whisper of hope began to bloom. The duchess had lied before and proved unscrupulous, even malicious. The tale she'd told at the theatre could be another attempt to destroy, a fabrication concocted out of desperation when every other of her despicable plans had failed. The more Domino thought of it, the more likely it seemed. It was such a far-fetched story.

True, Joshua had lived a rakish existence— she was well aware of that—and she knew that as a young man he'd failed his friends badly and been exiled for his wrongdoing. But it would have to be the most diabolical coincidence that the friends were Christabel and Richard. Why had she been so willing to believe the worst? Was it that her earlier unease had never quite disappeared, that she'd never quite believed the rake had reformed? Or, more honestly, that she'd been the woman who could reform him? When he'd asked her to marry him, she had thought at first it was a cruel joke, then she'd settled on it being a miracle. She had not believed she was that special. After all, Richard had rejected her—why should this man, with even more worldly experience, choose to change his life completely because of her?

She had been foolish! Joshua's feelings were genuine; he loved her. Of all the women he'd known, he had asked *her* to marry him. She *was* special! And what had been his reward? To have his chosen bride believe a scurrilous story from a corrupt woman.

She started out of bed. She could see now that she had behaved very stupidly. She must go to him and make an immediate apology. Their meeting would give him the chance to deny the duchess's evil words; his answer to a simple question would set everything to rights. She pulled the first gown she could find from the wardrobe and dressed quickly, her face a pale oval against the gown's drab olive.

Slipping unseen from the house, she made her way swiftly towards the groyne. The sky was overcast, all trace of summer having for the moment disappeared, but only a light breeze blew and the water was unnaturally calm. She clambered down the sea-stained steps to the lower promenade. Then she saw him. Suddenly, out of nowhere, the night's harrowing events were back and landing with a sickening thud. Her stomach was aflutter, but she continued to pick her way stone by stone across the beach until she stood only a few feet from him.

'I cannot stay long.' It was nerves that made her brusque. The certainty she'd felt minutes ago in her bedroom was deserting her.

'Then I must be grateful for the few minutes you can vouchsafe me.' He spoke lightly, but his eyes wore a puzzled expression.

It was better to ask the dreadful question at once, she decided; then they could clear the air and be comfortable together once more. But her voice when she spoke was hesitant. 'Please accept my apologies for the way I behaved last night. I heard a disturbing story and it upset me greatly.'

He was still looking baffled. 'Last night, Domino, we were at the play and enjoying ourselves, as I thought. What could possibly have disturbed you?'

'The Duchess of Severn,' she said baldly. 'She visited in the interval.'

'Dear Charlotte—and what now have I to thank her for?'

His tone was so much one of levity that

Domino was convinced in that instant that the duchess's spiteful story had been a complete falsehood. There was not the smallest shadow of guilt in Joshua's face. Instead he was smiling gently at her, waiting it seemed for her to come to her senses.

In the face of his good nature, she was finding it difficult to continue and her words came haltingly. 'The tale she told was most dreadful—and it concerned you.'

His look was still one of bland enquiry. She tried again, her words so quiet they were hardly audible against the soft swell of the tide. 'Some years ago, she said, you seduced a young woman on the eve of her wedding; you were the bridegroom's best friend.'

She was watching him closely as she spoke and saw his eyes narrow. A terrible premonition began to burn through her that he knew the rest of the story and she turned as white as the chalk cliffs that rose in the distance.

'Say something, Joshua,' she pleaded. 'Say that it is not true—surely it is not true.'

'Alas, my dear, for once the duchess is telling the truth. But it is an old story and I wonder how she came by it. No doubt Moncaster could tell us.'

She was speechless. Her rekindled trust in his innocence shattered in one savage stab. She had mentioned no names, but still she knew that her worst fears were confirmed. He had confessed, yet he was shaking it off as if it meant nothing. The vision she held of him crumbled into dust. He was no longer the man she had thought him. A different person stood in his place, a person that she could neither trust nor revere. She felt the dark abyss opening again beneath her feet, but this time she did not turn tail and run.

Gathering every ounce of resolution she possessed, and with a voice hardly wavering, she said, 'Mr Marchmain, I regret that I cannot marry you.'

'What! What are you saying?'

'I cannot marry you,' she repeated dully.

'This is a nonsense, Domino. Last night we were to wed. Last night you were eager to persuade your father that I would make an excellent husband!'

'Last night I also learned of your past. And it is a past I cannot forgive.'

His head was shaking in disbelief and he began to stride back and forth, crunching the pebbles beneath his boots. After some moments he came to a halt in front of her, his gold-flecked eyes keen and lacking any trace of his usual lazy amusement.

'My dear', and he made to move towards her,

but she stepped nimbly to one side, evading his touch.

His expression clouded, but he continued calmly, 'My dear, you knew of my past, if not its details. I am too old and have wandered the world too long not to have a history. But that's all done with. You are my only concern now, the only woman I have need or desire for.'

'This has not to do with *your* desires, but everything to do with mine. I cannot marry a man for whom I feel contempt.'

It was a most terrible thing to say. Had she meant it? She must have done, since the blurted words had come instinctively, involuntarily. They had their effect. Joshua appeared thoroughly shaken. His face darkened into a scowl and when he spoke his voice was edged with anger.

'I am not proud of my past. But, tell me, what exactly has earned your contempt?'

'The people you hurt were dear friends of mine, and you hurt them not by accident, but purely to pursue your own pleasure. Her name was Christabel Tallis and the man she was to marry was…was Richard Veryan.' Her face coloured with a suddenness that caught his attention.

'Christabel and Richard Veryan!' His brow furrowed for a moment, then she saw a dawning comprehension. 'And was Richard the man you loved so hopelessly?'

He was mocking her, but she ignored the provocation. 'It matters not. He was your friend and you betrayed him. Then you betrayed Christabel.'

'I repeat, I am not proud of my actions. But it happened a long time ago when I was a shallow youth. You said yourself that I should be forgiven for crimes committed as a stripling. I distinctly remember that you were unhappy with my brother for the very conduct you now seem intent on emulating.'

'That was before I knew what you had done.'

'You knew what I had done. I told you the day we met on the Level.'

His jaw jutted pugnaciously; he was damned if he would let her rewrite their conversation to suit her own quixotic ends.

She was beginning to unravel, but she pulled her defences together and fought back. 'You told me that you had failed friends. I did not know then the manner of that failure, or that it was my own very dear friends that you had treated so wickedly.'

'So your moral code is relative, is it? My actions are forgivable, but only if the wounded parties are people for whom you have no care.'

She realised he was right and that her stance

was illogical. But it did not change the way she felt. She had known too well the damage done to Richard, known how helpless she had felt to comfort him.

Her long silence seemed to encourage him and he softened his voice in persuasion. 'Christabel and Richard are happy now, are they not? Isn't that what is important? It was a bad deed, but good eventually came of it.'

She had no intention of disclosing that Christabel was staying just a few yards away and that a great deal of good had eventually come of it. But only eventually; so much unhappiness and suffering had gone before.

'If they are happy, can we not be happy, too?' he was asking.

That was simple to answer. 'I can never be happy with a man who would deliberately cause such heartache.'

'You refine too much on what is long past.'

'How can you dismiss your wrongdoing so casually?'

'I don't. I am well aware of my sin. But I was a stupid boy—and now I have grown up. My life is different.'

'Precisely how different?'

She was regaining courage. If he had shown true remorse, pleaded with her, asked for forgiveness, she might have found it impossible to resist. But he had done none of those things. Instead he continued to be at his most mocking and combative.

'Have we returned to my improper life and my fearsome reputation? Now let me see… You haven't exactly baulked at consorting with a rake these past weeks. And, if I were being ungallant, I might say more than consorting.'

'How dare you!'

'And nor did Christabel mind,' he continued inexorably. 'Don't forget it takes two. What happened was not my fault alone.'

'You should have known better and acted better.'

'I agree, but then so should she. It was she, after all, who was betrothed.'

Domino made to turn, hitching the skirts of her gown clear of the uneven strand. 'I have no wish to continue arguing.' And in the quietest voice yet, she added, 'It is too painful.'

He seized on that one small phrase. 'That would suggest that you still care for me.'

She said nothing and he pressed her, 'If that is indeed so, why are you doing this?'

'I have told you.'

Exasperated, he burst out, 'Are you sure it's not because you still love Richard Veryan and wish to punish me for the fact that he married elsewhere?'

It was an unkind stab. She turned back to him and, in a voice that wobbled only slightly, made her final adieu. 'I have nothing more to say, Mr Marchmain. This is goodbye. Please do not attempt to contact me again.'

And with that she was gone.

Left alone, Joshua stared sightlessly out to sea. He had wanted to make amends to Domino for disrupting her life so badly and had offered her his hand in the best of faith. It had not been easy to breach the detachment that had protected him for so long, but he had done it. Only for her to walk away on a whim; it could only be a whim. It was absurd, he thought. He was no angel. He had behaved badly, once very badly, but that had been years ago, years when he'd been barely more than a fledgling and had understood nothing, neither who he was nor what he wanted. Surely youth offered some mitigation. They had been years of heady excitement, of feeling that every day as he ventured forth he could renew his world. He had certainly done so when he met Christabel. Renewed her world and Richard Veryan's, too.

Fresh faced and inexperienced, he and Richard had launched themselves on the town in the very same month and become firm friends. Then one summer Richard had left for his home in Cornwall and returned with Christabel on his arm. A single look and he'd fallen immediately under her spell. She had been so alluring and so eager to seize life, so tempting and so easily tempted. He had cast caution to the winds, ignoring every demand of friendship. There had been nothing deliberate about the passion that had flamed between them; it had simply been too wild to control. That was no excuse, but why couldn't Domino forgive such an old tragedy?

He guessed at the answer and his rancour began slowly to subside, dissolving into the sea air and on the cry of the gulls. He had destroyed her belief in him. Only very slowly had she grown to trust. At the outset she had been mightily suspicious, writing him down as a dangerous individual and one to avoid. But she'd been unable to avoid him. He had rescued her from her follies, one after another, and gradually she had begun to see him for the man he was, to see beyond the label society bestowed. And it turned out that the man she saw fitted her so perfectly that she had tumbled into love with him. Now the image she held had been shattered by a moment of careless talk.

But how careless? he wondered savagely. It had all the marks of spite, the marks of the vendetta waged by Charlotte Severn since first she became aware of the girl as a rival. The woman was stupid as well as vindictive. How could she not realise that the affair between them had ended months ago, that the plots she had been busily engineering against Domino were pointless? He would never return to her.

But she had wreaked all the damage she could possibly desire. It mattered not to Domino that Christabel and Richard were content. He had caused them pain, and there could be no defence for that. But if they had suffered, so, by God, had he. For years he had wandered Europe, seeking the most sublime art it could offer. He had taken solace in the beauty he'd found and tried to blot out the ugliness he'd known. Women had come and gone, his physical needs satisfied, but always there was beauty to strive for, a beauty just beyond his reach. He had begun to paint in the hope that here at least he would find what he so desperately desired. The seascapes he painted, one after another, the endless seascapes with their limitless horizons, spoke of escape from the unlovely life he led and the person he had become. But there could be no escape. For a brief moment, rescuing Domino from her plight had offered the prospect of a new wholeness, but that too had turned to ashes. He was not made for beauty. His decision to marry had been foolish, a transgression duly punished. The doubts that had bombarded him ever since he'd proposed were justified. He took a deep breath and began the climb to the promenade. He would live as he'd always done, he thought grimly, and go to hell in his own way. For years he had been doing just that and with some success.

'Mr Marchmain and I have bid each other farewell, Papa.'

Domino stood just inside Señor de Silva's office, ready to flee the room as soon as she was able. She was humiliated by this confession, for she was telling her father that she no longer wished to marry the man she had been mad to have only a matter of hours ago. This was an interview she wanted to be over before it had begun.

'Farewell? What do you mean, *querida*?'

'We have decided that, after all, we do not suit,' she said as composedly as she could, silently praying that there would be no questions.

'And are you quite sure of this, my dear?'

'Yes, quite sure.' But her heart was breaking. Surely any moment her father must hear the pieces falling to the ground.

'You do not wish to marry him?' Alfredo repeated, almost to himself.

He felt suddenly a good deal lighter. Domino's determination to wed a man he considered grossly unsuitable had shocked him. It had been a struggle to appear complaisant, not wanting to be alienated from his only child. But now it looked as though her plans had come to nought. He would not have to suffer Joshua Marchmain as a son-in-law.

'No, Papa, I no longer wish to marry him.' *Please*, she begged inwardly, *please don't ask me why*. Then thinking she should offer a little more to her long-suffering parent, she added, 'I am sorry to have caused confusion.'

'No confusion, my dear. You are right to draw back if you have doubts. And it seems that you do.'

She nodded miserably. Her father put his arms around her and gave her a comforting hug.

'You have made a sensible decision,' he said consolingly. 'And now you must put it out of your mind and think what is to be done. Have you had a chance to consider?'

She had no idea what her life was to be. How very different to just a day ago! But she must not upset her father and, freeing herself from his arms, she fixed him with what she hoped was an unwavering look.

'Lady Veryan will soon be travelling to London to consult a practitioner in Harley Street.

She is wishful that I accompany her before I return to Spain.' She congratulated herself that she spoke with hardly a tremor.

'As her friend, that would naturally be a kind thought.'

'Then I will do so, but she is to know nothing of this, Papa', and she gestured vaguely in the air. 'I mean nothing about Mr Marchmain. It cannot interest her and may cause her distress if she feels that I am upset.'

'I will say nothing, you have my word. And Carmela knows nothing, so your friend will stay in ignorance of these doings. But *are* you upset, *querida*? You seem very calm.'

'I know that I am doing the right thing, Papa,' she answered obliquely. He must never know that her heart was crushed.

Her stay with Christabel in London would be brief. Beyond that, she hardly dared to think. Once her father was back in the capital, he would no longer need her services, for Lady Blythe would once more act his hostess while he remained in London. And Domino had no desire to linger in a place where at any moment she might come upon the man she most wished to avoid. She supposed that she would return to Spain—where else could she go?—but it would not be to marry as her aunts wished. Of that she was sure. After Richard she had been indifferent, ready to marry whatever husband they chose. But that was no longer possible. The sorrows of youthful infatuation had given way to an all-consuming passion, but for a man she could not wed. And if she could not wed him, she would wed no other. Always in the deepest recesses of her heart there would be this pain: sharp, nagging, insistent. A pain with Joshua's name written on it.

Her father was speaking again. 'I shall not be far behind you in leaving Brighton, my dear. But there is an important event to consider before we are finished here—the Regent's birthday celebrations. I am sure you won't have forgotten that the palace is throwing a grand dinner and ball in the Prince's honour.'

The gentle reminder left her dazed. Her mind shrank from the idea of ever setting foot in the Pavilion again.

'Friday's celebrations are to be the most sumptuous occasion, I believe, and we have been greatly honoured by an invitation. It is fortunate that you will not have left for London by then.'

Surely she might be spared this further anguish. But, no, her father clearly expected her to accompany him. And she owed him that at least, for she had caused him nothing but trouble this summer. If he had an inkling of her true feelings, he would not wish her to go within a mile of the palace. But he saw a composed face and heard a calm voice and suspected nothing.

'I shall be pleased to attend, Papa.' Her voice seemed to her to travel from a great distance.

'Then it is settled. After the ball you and Carmela will accompany Lady Veryan to London. From there, you can journey with your cousin on to Spain. I shall make sure that I am back in town in time to see you both safely on your way.'

Her father began idly to leaf through the sheaf of messages on his desk and she judged it time to go. The interview was thankfully at an end, but she still had to face the forthcoming encounter with Christabel. That would be far more difficult to negotiate, for women had much sharper antennae. She must prevent her friend from tuning into any hint of the distress that was tearing at her soul.

She was to be allowed a few more hours of grace. Christabel had endured a disturbed night and did not appear in the drawing room until almost noon, and, when she did, Carmela was in attendance. From the moment Lady Veryan had arrived at Marine Parade, Carmela had taken the expectant mother under her wing. Delighted to have a charge to coddle, she was busy now fussing over the likely need for shawls or slippers or footstools. She seemed intent on wrapping their guest in thick coils of cotton wool.

'You will never go to the parade, Lady Veryan,' she said in a shocked tone when Christabel mentioned that she was looking forward to visiting the Level that afternoon to view the Regent's birthday parade.

'I don't see why not.' Christabel's musical voice held a note of amusement. 'I cannot sit indoors forever and I'm quite sure that my young friend will be looking forward to the spectacle as much as I.'

Her young friend, coming into the drawing room at that moment, felt herself grow heavy with despair. She had counted on hiding herself away until Friday when she must endure the Regent's party before a final escape to obscurity. It was not to be.

'You would like to go, Domino, wouldn't you?' Christabel asked coaxingly.

'Naturally we must not miss such a display,' she returned bravely. 'We can stroll to the Level after luncheon. I believe the ceremonial marching is to begin around two o' clock.'

They arrived well before that hour, hoping to secure a good vantage point. Alarmed at Lady

Veryan's imprudence, Carmela had insisted on accompanying them. The dowdiness of her dress contrasted almost jestingly with the flamboyant colour that was everywhere around. Her severe distaste for ostentation was well known and Domino watched in surprise at her cousin's interest in the preparations that signalled a beginning to the military display.

The square on which the soldiers were to parade was the Regent's old cricket ground, now transformed by a hard covering underfoot and decorated with fluttering flags and bunting of every shape and hue. Crowds were gathered along the intersecting pathways leading to the marching square and a tiered stand had been built at one end for the more genteel visitors. The little party made their way to seats on the front row from where they would enjoy an uninterrupted view. The chattering throng and a military band already playing with gusto added to the sense of anticipation. The sun was bright for a late August afternoon, but a cooling breeze blew inland from the sea and the striped canvas awnings, which had been erected over the stand, stood ready to protect delicate complexions.

Christabel looked around her in appreciation. She had been living retired from *ton* society so long that she had forgotten the exciting

hum of people intent on pleasure. Glancing
right and left at the fashionable silks and satins,
the poke bonnets, the little pieces of gauze and
tinsel masquerading as hats, she began to feel
a complete dowd. Life in the countryside was
wonderful but it had its drawbacks, particularly for one who had long been considered a
diamond of the first water. She must make sure
that she returned from London with new gowns
as well as medical advice. She need not have
worried. Whatever she wore, she was instantly
the centre of attention. Her flame-haired beauty
ensured that. A number of people recognised
her and she nodded in response. A woman
three rows back craned her neck to see who
accompanied Domino de Silva.

The music made it impossible for anyone to
be heard and nobody sitting nearby attempted
to strike up a conversation. Domino was thankful since she had lost all desire to socialise. Her
anxious scan of the stand revealed no sign of
Joshua and she could only hope that his role in
planning the event would remain backstage.
He must have deliberately absented himself,
guessing that she would attend. He would not
know of Christabel's presence, of course. And
it must stay that way. The thought of a meeting
between the two was unbearable.

'Isn't that the Dragoons?'

Christabel leant forwards in eagerness as the band struck up an altogether more martial note. The Light Dragoons had arrived, decked in their resplendent ceremonial uniform. They marched proudly towards the square, a thousand limbs moving as one. A drum major strode at their head, beating time with his golden mace. Their show of military prowess began with a display of intricate marching patterns, dizzying in their complexity and breath taking in their co-ordination. There followed individual feats of daring and skill until finally the stupendous conclusion of a mock battle complete with enemy infantry and a troop of cavalry.

An hour had slipped easily by before the last hurrahs of the crowd were sounding and they made ready to leave.

'Domino, my dear. How agreeable!' A perfumed figure crossed their path. 'I forgot to ask when we last met if you intended to come to the parade, but somehow I knew the uniforms would bring you!'

Carmela glared at the newcomer and Domino bowed stiffly. 'As you see, Your Grace, we have been enjoying the display.'

Slightly in the rear of the group, Christabel caught up with them at that moment. She smiled shyly at the duchess and Domino had no alternative but to introduce her.

'Your Grace, this is Lady Veryan.'

'Veryan?' the duchess queried faintly.

'That's right,' Christabel said warmly, 'Christabel Veryan. How do you do? Was that not a most magnificent spectacle?'

Bewilderment, mortification, naked fury flitted across the duchess's face in rapid succession. But her rigid training stood her in good stead and a mask of indifference slipped into place as she responded levelly, 'The Dragoons can always be relied on for a superb exhibition. The dear Prince dotes on them, you know.'

Christabel marked the condescension but as the woman appeared to be a friend of Domino's, she felt it incumbent to be courteous. Her two companions seemed to have been struck temporarily dumb. She waded gallantly into a smooth stream of small talk. The duchess ably played her part in the charade, automatic responses issuing with ease from her practised lips, while all the time questions laid siege to her mind. Why was Lady Veryan here? Surely after what she had divulged to Domino de Silva, this woman should not be her friend! Something had gone badly wrong. She broke off what she was saying and looked wildly around. She needed to see Leo Moncaster urgently.

Christabel was nonplussed by the older woman's evident disquiet but hoping the duchess would soon recover her composure, she persevered. 'I spend my life in the depths of the Cornish countryside, so you see today has been a most wonderful treat.'

Charlotte Severn pulled herself together with enormous effort. 'And what brings you to Brighton at this time, Lady Veryan?'

A last hope had flashed into her mind and she was clinging to it. Christabel had come to Brighton to commiserate with Domino, to reiterate that she too had suffered from Joshua Marchmain's iniquity. She had come to tell her that the man was bad through and through and that Domino was right to separate from him forever.

'I'm on my way to London,' Christabel said happily. 'My husband insists that I see someone in Harley Street, though goodness knows why. Everything...' and she patted her expanding stomach lovingly '...seems to be progressing just as it should.'

The duchess's hope flickered and died. 'And will you also be travelling to town, Domino?'

Desperate to appear unperturbed, Domino found her voice at last. 'I will, Your Grace.

Lady Veryan's arrival is timely. We can enjoy at least a sennight together in London before she returns to Cornwall.'

The duchess digested this. 'Then you are staying in England?

'I imagine so,' she lied.

'And not returning to Spain?'

'Not for the moment. My father has need of me still. And I am enjoying my stay greatly and would be loth to cut it short.'

She had the satisfaction of seeing the duchess blanch. Let her think that she and Joshua were still together, that the return to London signalled a deepening of their relationship. This spiteful woman had recounted her poisonous news for one reason only. She had wanted to ensure their separation. She had succeeded but Domino would never give her the pleasure of knowing it. Let her feel chagrin that her plan had not worked, let her feel anguish that Joshua would never return to her. In time of course he would. That was inevitable but every moment of pain inflicted on this malevolent creature was worthwhile. The strength of her own venom shocked her. If she could have heard the duchess's embittered conversation just a few hours later, she would have prized the small triumph.

* * *

'It hasn't worked!'

Leo Moncaster looked ruminatively at the furious woman opposite him.

'Why is that, my sweet one?' he asked drily.

'Do not call me that.'

'I cannot think why I did.' He glanced at the sour expression distorting her face. 'Anything less sweet would be hard to imagine.'

'It hasn't worked,' she spelt out angrily. 'Christabel Veryan is here in Brighton and quite clearly friends with that chit. The girl has no shame. Wasn't she supposed to be desperately in love with Richard Veryan? Yet she is happy to consort with the woman who broke his heart and unconcerned that Joshua was the willing accomplice. She is shallow beyond belief.'

Moncaster raised his eyebrows and seemed about to comment, but evidently decided otherwise.

'I know what you are about to say. Don't! I may be shallow, but at least I am consistent. The girl is happy to entertain Lady Veryan in her own home; more than that, she's happy to accompany her to London in a few days' time. What would you wager on her being equally happy to see Marchmain there, whatever ill she knows of him?'

'Let it go, Charlotte,' he advised her roughly. 'I would like to punish the girl as much as you, but we have failed at every attempt and done nothing but make ourselves look foolish. It might be as well simply to let her disappear to Spain.'

'That's because you haven't heard the best of it. The chit is staying in England!'

Moncaster's brows knit together in annoyance, but he spoke calmly. 'So what do you want to do?' His equanimity infuriated the duchess.

'Do! Do! I want to get rid of the girl forever. You know what I want to do.'

'Then we must hazard a final throw of the dice, my dear. No hesitation this time. No misgivings.'

'You are right. I have been too kind to her.'

Lord Moncaster grimaced, but the duchess went on. 'Far too kind. I have allowed her to flourish instead of nipping the life out of her from the very outset. We will do what we've had in mind for weeks. Are you ready?'

'I can be ready at any time, dear lady.'

'Good. Then the Regent's ball, the day after tomorrow?'

He took her hand and slowly brought it to his lips. 'A perfect occasion, I feel. It will prove a splendid finale to an overlong drama.'

Chapter Nine

By the time they wended their way back to Marine Parade, Christabel was feeling very tired. It had been an entertaining afternoon, but a long walk and prolonged sitting had taken their toll. Once in Domino's own small parlour, she cast off her bonnet and sank gratefully into a comfortable chair.

'You should rest in bed, Lady Veryan,' Carmela scolded. 'It cannot be good for the baby to be forever on your feet.'

'Thank you for your concern,' she replied sweetly, 'but I can rest here.' She reached for a cup from the tray the housekeeper had just brought in. 'The tea is sure to restore my energy.'

'But, Lady Veryan…'

'I will stay.' Her voice was firm. 'Such a delightful room—it must catch every glimmer of sunlight and its view of the sea is unmatched. I can understand why you chose this for your own, Domino. And it's perfect for a comfortable coze.'

The last thing Domino wanted was a comfortable coze. She hoped that Carmela would remain and put paid to any chance of intimate talk, but her cousin rose almost immediately and announced that in that case she had many things to do, and all of them urgent.

'This afternoon has been wonderful,' Christabel began gently as the door shut, 'and thank you for taking me. It felt strange to be among a fashionable crowd again, but thoroughly enjoyable. Not that I would ever forsake Cornwall!'

'I don't imagine you would. Tell me about life at the Abbey.'

If Domino had hoped to deflect her friend from the personal, she hoped in vain.

'The best thing about this afternoon was sharing it with you. I've been waiting a long time for you to come to Madron and discover the house for yourself.'

'The moment never seemed right,' her young companion hedged. 'My aunts would not have taken kindly to my travelling abroad again. They only permitted my return to England

294   *Society's Most Scandalous Rake*

because Papa needed help.' A small white lie would not hurt, she thought.

'Perhaps once the baby is born you will feel able to make the journey to Cornwall.'

Domino smiled non-commitally. By then she would be back in Madrid and there would be little opportunity to venture far.

'We never had time to know each other really well,' Christabel was musing. 'But I'm sure if we had, we would have become the best of friends. One thing of which I *am* very sure—I have you to thank for my happiness.'

Her friend flushed and made haste to disclaim any such thing.

'My dear, yes. If it had not been for you, I might never have felt able to trust Richard. And with what result! We could not be happier together and this child will only bring us closer.'

Domino felt genuine pleasure. A few months ago, a few weeks ago even, her enjoyment would have been compromised by regret but that had melted like summer snow. She had a new and far heavier burden to bear.

'It's wonderful to see you so happy,' and she pressed Christabel's hand, 'but my role was very small—a silly letter only. You were always destined to be with Richard.'

'You made me see that and I cannot thank you enough. I did some foolish things but you made me realise that I could have a different future.'

The young girl swallowed hard, but said nothing.

'It seems that no matter how badly one has behaved,' Christabel continued thoughtfully, '—and I did behave badly—past events don't have to ruin the rest of one's life.'

There was again no response from her companion and Christabel paused and looked intently at the girl seated beside her. 'I hope you'll forgive me for saying this, my dear, but you have not been looking quite as carefree as I remember. I wonder—is there anything wrong?'

Danger leaped out in mile high letters. Domino knew that she must drive the conversation away from this treacherous ground.

'There's nothing wrong, I assure you. I'm just a little tired. Brighton is a town made for leisure and that can be hard work! This summer has been very busy.'

'I can imagine,' her friend said sympathetically. 'Wherever the Regent is in residence, there's unlikely to be a deal of tranquillity.'

She paused again, as if wondering whether or not she should say more. 'But *should* anything be causing you unease, Domino, my best advice would be to meet it bravely and then not look back.'

'There is nothing.'

'I'm glad to hear it. No doubt you are far too young to fall into anxiety.' She leaned back in her chair and gazed through the bow windows at the ruffled sea beyond. 'But, truth to tell, I was only your age when I managed to fall into a maelstrom of trouble that took years to resolve.'

Domino could hardly speak. If Christabel intended to confess her youthful folly, she did not want to hear. Or did she? There was a part of her that needed to know why this woman had abandoned an honourable man like Richard—the same part, perhaps, that needed to excuse her own all too easy fall into the arms of the same philanderer.

'How many years?' she heard herself ask in a constricted voice, though she knew the answer well.

'Six wasted years. I thought I could never forgive myself for what I'd done, nor forgive the man involved. But I was wrong.'

'How did you forgive?' Domino's throat was dry.

'I was foolishly naïve, on the town for the first time in my life. And so was he. We were both too young and heedless to bear the responsibility of our actions.'

Her words were almost an echo of those Domino had heard from Joshua himself.

'And you didn't blame the man?' she ventured. 'Should he not have taken responsibility?'

'But why? We were both to blame. In fact, I can thank him now. Until I met him I had taken Richard for granted. I was sleepwalking into marriage. A short-lived affair, for that was all it was, may have destroyed my betrothal but it made me realise that I had forsaken a deep, abiding love for a momentary passion, one that had no substance to it, no depth. If I were ever to meet that man again, I would shake him by the hand and thank him truly.'

Domino was shocked. How could Christabel speak so lightly of an event that had almost ruined her life and, even worse, almost ruined Richard's? Six wasted years, she'd said. But here she was exculpating Joshua and willing to share blame for the catastrophe, even grateful to him for showing her the true nature of her feelings!

Christabel put her teacup gently down on the table and rose to leave. 'Carmela may have been right,' she said softly, sensing that her words had in some way hit home. 'A rest in my room before dinner will refresh me. I will see you later, my dear', and she bent her graceful form towards her young friend and lightly kissed the top of her head.

Left alone, Domino wrestled with the conversation that had passed between them. A blissfully happy Christabel could afford to forgive the past, she thought churlishly. But it is *her* past to forgive, a small voice murmured, not yours. What have you to forgive? This sorry story took place when you were not much more than a child. Christabel is happy, Richard is happy. Why can't you be? But she knew she was confusing the symptom for the cause. And the real cause of her unhappiness was the fear that Joshua Marchmain was the rake everyone said he was, and that she could never trust him to be otherwise. For a moment she had believed him capable of changing. But how short that moment had been! Knowledge of the wicked path he had trodden six years ago had brought home to her the magnitude of his offences—his flagrant immorality, his uncaring selfishness—and had damned him in her eyes forever. Joshua had not changed, would never change, and if she gave herself to him, she would live a lifetime of heartache.

Fortune favoured her the next day when Carmela decided to forsake her household duties.

It was her cousin who escorted Christabel on a shopping expedition to Bartholomews market and her cousin who sat with their visitor sewing and reading in the small parlour. Domino was able to disappear for long stretches of the day, citing the necessity of helping Flora to pack her wardrobe. It was a job that appeared to take an inordinate time but while she sorted muslins and silks she tried to keep her mind a determined blank. The grand dinner and ball at the Pavilion was one more trial to face, the final trial, and she needed to keep at bay the thoughts that constantly harried her.

When she met her friend later in the day, she greeted Christabel with guilty warmth, infusing her voice with as much geniality as she could muster.

'It's a great shame that you cannot come to the ball. Papa would have been happy to obtain a ticket for the dance, if not to the dinner.'

Her visitor gave a rueful grin. 'My dear, look at me, I am in no case for dancing. Carmela and I will go on very well at home, don't fret. But if I can be of any help in getting you ready for the grand event, send your maid to me. I shall not be sleeping—merely waiting in readiness for the call!'

Domino was not to need her friend's expertise. Since coming to Brighton Flora had improved as a lady's maid by leaps and bounds and tonight's grand occasion was to be the fitting climax of her apprenticeship.

When her mistress presented herself in the drawing room a few hours later, conversation stopped and her audience gazed wonderingly at her.

'Dear Domino, you look gorgeous!' Christabel was lavish in her praise.

Her father nodded, his chest seeming visibly to expand with pride. Even Carmela gave her a brisk smile of approval.

'You are sure that you're happy to stay home?'

Domino wanted only one answer to her question. If Christabel remained at Marine Parade there would be no chance of her meeting her former lover.

'I am very happy to. Carmela and I have planned a light supper together and then we intend to do a little sorting of baby clothes before an early bedtime. In my present condition, it makes for a perfect evening.'

'Far better than junketing with the most undesirable people,' Carmela could not resist saying.

'Unfortunately, cousin, we are forced to partake of a little junketing, but I promise I shall have Domino home well before midnight.' Alfredo's voice was cold and crisp as though he, too, wished to get the evening over as swiftly as possible.

Domino had not wanted to dress finely, but Flora had been adamant. This was to be the last grand event of the Brighton summer. In her maid's opinion it was the time to shine, the time to leave a splendid final impression. When she looked at her mistress that evening, Flora knew Domino would do just that. The gown of orange blossom crepe worn beneath a tunic of bespangled gossamer clung lovingly to the curves of her lissom young figure. A shawl of spider gauze covered her bare arms and on her feet she wore cream satin slippers ornamented with cream roses. A circlet of orange blossom was threaded through the glossy curls that cascaded gently around her face. She looked every inch a young princess on her way to a magnificent evening of pleasure. Only the pale face gave a glimpse of her true feelings.

As before, they approached the Pavilion through newly planted gardens and alighted from their carriage in the shelter of the portico. As before, a footman escorted them to the Long Gallery, low-ceilinged, but as opulent as the rest of the palace. Here the guests who had been invited to dinner waited to be summoned to the table. In a swift glance Domino established that Joshua was not among them. Dinner was always served promptly at six in the evening and there were already upwards of thirty people in the gallery. She knew that many more would arrive for the ball, but first a copious meal, an essential part of the Regent's evening entertainment, had to be endured.

'This is extraordinary, Papa,' she whispered as they were ushered into the Banqueting Hall.

It easily rivalled the Music Room for drama. From the central dome hung the biggest chandelier she had ever seen, held in the claws of an enormous dragon. A host of smaller chandeliers shimmered light around the room, reflecting back and forth the sweeping decorations of silver gilt until the great space resembled nothing more than a huge treasure casket.

'Extraordinary!' her father whispered back, beginning a search for their place names.

Everything in the room was designed to overwhelm, from the painted canopies with their intricate patterns of moons and stars to the spectacular ormolu candelabra positioned in the centre of a dining table which stretched as far as she could see.

Almost immediately the first serving of food was brought to the table by a dozen uniformed footmen. Elaborate soups were followed by a choice of fish, then patés and meats, followed in turn by a dozen different entrées of meat and game. Should any of the guests feel the need for additional nourishment, seven rosewood sideboards positioned at intervals around the room groaned with platters of cold beef, venison, game and pies.

She cast a worried glance at her father. 'How on earth am I to eat even a fraction of this?' she asked in a low voice.

'Do your best,' was all he could offer in reply.

She picked her way delicately through the dishes offered, taking a very small helping of a very few of them. After nearly an hour she had done her best and was beginning to relax, when worryingly a second serving of food began to arrive. Four different roasts with their accompaniments and a multitude of sweet and savoury side dishes were scattered across the massive table. Her spirits sank as she encountered myriad jellies, tarts, ices, meringues and cream puddings. But by dint of engaging her neighbours in animated conversation, she managed to talk more than she ate.

Although many of her fellow guests seemed similarly disconcerted by the sheer volume of food, the Regent himself ate happily and solidly for the two hours apportioned to dinner. She was grateful to have been seated alongside her father at the lower end of the table and therefore unlikely to catch George's eye. After her last encounter with him, she was determined to remain unnoticed. There would be no Joshua Marchmain to rescue her from the Prince's clutches this time. He was still nowhere to be seen but she remarked the duchess and her husband occupying a prominent place to the left of the Prince. And when she heard a sniggering laugh ring out in a sudden interval of silence, it was clear that Moncaster, too, was in attendance. Only a few more hours to survive this monstrous evening, she shuddered, taking her father's arm on the walk to the ballroom.

'Thank heaven someone has had the presence of mind to open the windows,' Alfredo commented as the late August breeze, tangy with salt, wafted through the long glass doors of the ballroom. An ornamental front garden lay beyond, cool and green, a welcome foil to the overpowering heat within.

The orchestra, auditioned personally by the Prince, was already striking up for a country dance and dance pairs were being formed. Domino looked around the room and felt grateful that she hardly knew a person there. She could sit decorously with her father and watch from the fringes the revelling that Carmela so despised. But out of nowhere, it seemed, a string of young men materialised at her side. The enchanting young girl, barely known to them, had piqued their interest and become a prize to win. With one accord they rushed to claim her as a partner. In a moment almost every dance on her card had a name beside it. Almost—not even an indulgent father would oppose her aunts' dictate that on no account must she ever allow herself to waltz. Over the next hour she danced with one young man after another, all of them personable, all of them eager to please: they found a safe place for her gauze wrapper, fetched her lemonade, sat out a country dance with her as she cooled by the open window. Obliging young men, delightful young men.

But she could not dance away the heart-ache. She must go through the motions, smile prettily, dance daintily, and hope for the hour to come very soon when Alfredo would consider that sufficient respect had been paid to the Prince Regent and they could retire. It was during a lively quadrille that she saw with a jolt that Joshua had joined the throng in the ball-room. His elegant figure marked him out from the crowd, his light-coloured satin breeches and dark coat fitting him where they touched. An embroidered waistcoat and lace cravat with one single winking diamond completed the modish ensemble. He was soon dancing. With the duchess, naturally. Who else? She could see he was eager to talk with her whenever the dance brought them together. He would have a good deal to say, she thought bitterly, after wasting so much time on a new and unsuccessful dalliance. Charlotte Severn would forgive him. She was hardly a stranger to dalliance herself. In no time they would be together again, the lovers they had always been. As the dancers traced the figures of the quadrille, the duchess's flushed face seemed to leer out at her. This was her victory.

Domino looked quickly away and bent an attentive ear to her partner. The social mask must never be allowed to slip, though her life was in ruins and the ashes of its destruction all around. She stumbled slightly and her partner steadied her.

'I am so sorry,' she apologised, 'I wasn't paying sufficient attention to my feet.'

'You are a most accomplished dancer, Miss de Silva.' The willowy young man guiding her round the floor was nothing if not gallant.

She began to watch her steps fiercely. She must try to concentrate even though her mind was determined to stray. Knowing him to be so very close, Joshua consumed every thought. So close and yet as distant from her as the jungles of Africa. Her body moved mechanically in time to the orchestra's tune, but another refrain played through her mind: the past need not determine the future. Christabel had followed that advice and freed herself of the past. *Unlike me,* Domino thought. For three long years she had allowed herself to be governed by a pointless infatuation with Richard. And the moment she had freed herself from that shadow, another had arrived to manipulate her life, only this time more painfully than she could ever have imagined. It was history repeating itself a hundredfold. The anguish she had felt in saying goodbye to Richard was in retrospect a mere pinprick. It was Joshua who had taught her real suffering.

The quadrille had come to an end and her partner departed on a mission to find refreshments. She sat down on one of the ebony chairs dotting the edges of the room. How could she ever follow Christabel's advice? She had learned to trust Joshua, to discount the label of rake that hung so easily on him. He had taught her to love. Then came the devastating details of his history. How could she put such knowledge behind her, forget it existed? It was impossible. In her heart she had made the image of a man she could venerate and he was no longer that man.

Refreshments arrived and she sipped at her second glass of lemonade. All too soon she must return to the dance floor and time passing ever more slowly. She danced on, partner after partner, her feet nimbly performing the correct steps, her face smiling just enough.

The evening was half gone when the orchestra struck up a waltz. This was the moment she'd hoped her father might deem it fitting to leave. But out of the corner of her eye she saw he was engaged in a deep discussion with some of the Court's political men. He must think she was enjoying the ball and had decided to delay their departure. She allowed herself to slip wearily towards a seat once more and hoped his conversation would soon flag.

At first she didn't notice the figure. He must have walked towards her in a wide arc and only when he was bowing courteously over her hand did she realise that Joshua stood before her.

'I hope you will do me the honour, Miss de Silva,' he began formally.

His beautiful gold-flecked eyes were as warm as ever but his gaze was challenging. She was utterly disconcerted. That he should dare to approach her this evening and then behave as though they had never endured a harrowing goodbye!

'Thank you, sir, you are most kind, but I do not waltz,' she managed at last, in a voice which hardly seemed to belong to her.

'I thought that possible,' he conceded, 'but I was hoping you might make an exception.'

Whatever possessed him to think that she would dance any dance with him, let alone a waltz? The answer to her question arrived swiftly.

'We have never danced the waltz together, much to my regret, and I imagine that this will be our only chance to do so.'

His voice was as smooth as crushed velvet and his bright hair glinted in the light of a thousand candles. His glance sought hers and she could not drag her eyes away. *Concentrate*, she scolded herself. *Keep your mind focused. Get him to leave.*

'I do not waltz, sir,' she repeated dully.

'But for old times' sake?'

He was refusing to take her refusal. He was incorrigible. He was also magnificent. Unwillingly she registered the power of his body, the satin breeches clinging in all the right places.

'There are no old times,' she snapped. 'And if you had an ounce of propriety you would not address me in this manner.'

'That's better, Domino!' he cheered. 'For a moment I was a little worried that you might have gone into a decline. But I see you are as spirited as ever. Come, my dear, a few minutes only.'

He was holding out his hand and several people near them had begun to look in their direction, sensing an unfolding drama. She must get away, leave immediately. But where was her father? She could have stamped with vexation when she saw that he and his companions were now nowhere to be seen.

'Domino?' Joshua's voice caressed her. The strains of the music had begun to thread their magic through her veins and she no longer seemed to own her limbs. His warm eyes glinted gold at her and her body softened dangerously. Why did her father not come?

Joshua was still holding out his hand, beckoning her to him. The people on either side were looking even more interested. She felt herself take a step forwards and then she was in his arms.

'I will dance,' she said angrily, 'but only because I do not wish to be the centre of a scene.'

'Naturally, why else would you dance with me?' he mocked. 'It was such a long time ago, was it not, that you were happy to do a great deal more than dance.'

'You are insufferable. Why can you not leave me alone?'

'One final dance and I promise all the solitude you could wish.'

She kept a resolute silence and in response his arms tightened and he swept her into the middle of the floor, manoeuvring her dexterously between couples and clasping her firmly against his chest. She tried very hard to hold herself at a distance, but her body was soft beneath his touch and growing softer with every minute. He smiled down at her, his honey-glow eyes bewitching in the subdued candlelight.

'You waltz well. That's a surprise. I had supposed you would not have been allowed to learn the dance.'

'You supposed correctly,' she found herself saying, the corners of her mouth crooking themselves into a small smile despite her best efforts.

'You never disappoint me!'

She was beginning to slide under his spell and she must resist at all costs. She saw Charlotte Severn standing at the side of the room in a small knot of people. The woman shot her a look of hatred.

'Do you not think, Mr Marchmain, that you would be wise to forgo this dance and ask another to partner you?' she asked in a voice that was deceptively steady.

He followed her gaze. 'I think not, Miss de

Silva. I had my fill of that particular pleasure many months ago.'

'I find that difficult to believe, so enthused were you in each other's company earlier this evening.'

'Enthused, no, irritated, yes.' And his arms tightened even more firmly around her.

'Why irritated?' she found herself asking.

'It is taking Her Grace longer than I had hoped to understand my changed feelings,' he said diplomatically. 'She did not take kindly to my reminding her.'

Domino said nothing. So they were not together again. Why did a sharp arrow of delight fly straight to her heart? It should not matter to her, must not matter. And yet it did, crushed as she was to his chest, moving with him to the enticing rhythms of the waltz. Their limbs shadowed each other, touching, separating and touching again. She felt his warmth through the light clothes he wore and savoured the indefinable musky smell of him. His lips brushed the top of her hair, coming to rest just behind her left ear. Slowly, delicately, she felt the tip of his tongue taste her skin. She was melting, melting, diffusing into liquid pleasure. His arm slowly slid down her back and pulled her body even closer until she felt his answering hardness. His mouth trailed kisses down her neck.

He was seducing her, here on the dance floor and in full view of a hundred pairs of eyes. And she was letting him! She could not bear it. She broke from him abruptly and fled, leaving him alone in the middle of the ballroom floor.

Incensed by her abandonment and caring little for the tittle-tattle that would ensue, Joshua made to follow but, as he drew near, a servant in the Prince's livery approached her with a message and he stopped in his tracks. He turned away, ignoring the interested stares from around the room. She had deliberately exposed him to ridicule!

But it was his own fault. He should have accepted her refusal to dance and walked away. He should never even have asked her. But an angry frustration was driving him: he had foolishly broken the unspoken law by which he lived. For longer than he could remember, he had avoided intimacy. The scourging he'd received from the Tallis affair had left him wanting no more such hazards. He might flirt with young women and acquire the reputation of a dangerous man, he might enjoy the challenge of confounding their duennas, but he was always careful never to step across the line. Discreet, and sometimes not so discreet, liaisons with well-born ladies bored with their husbands served his physical needs. Such relationships were often tedious, occasionally joyless and always sterile, but they caused him not one jot of discomfort.

His life had flowed smooth and unruffled—and then he'd met Domino. He had been resolute in his refusal to fall in love, but that hadn't prevented him being constantly by her side. Her youthful spirit had enchanted him, holding as it did the promise of beauty he had so long sought. He had been beguiled even into offering his hand. But the summer had proved a mere dream and after their last tempestuous encounter, he had vowed to put her from his mind. The fantasy was over and his old life awaited him.

But tonight, seeing her once more in all her loveliness, a slender flower of a girl, the craziest desire had overpowered him and all he'd known was that he had to be close to her again. One more time, one final time. And look where that had led. He would be the object of derision in the Court for days, but it didn't matter. Nothing mattered.

Domino rushed from the dance floor, her cheeks aflame and her heart hammering. She must find her father immediately, she had to leave this place and never return. But a footman in knee breeches and starched shirt was barring her way.

'Yes, what is it?' she asked impatiently, her breath still uneven.

'A message, Miss de Silva, from your father.'

'My father? Where is he?'

'He awaits you at the eastern exit of the palace. A coach will be ready to take you home.'

It seemed strange that her father should disappear without a word and send a servant to fetch her.

'Why has he not come himself?'

'I am to tell you that he has gone ahead to summon the carriage so that you will not catch cold awaiting its arrival.'

How very like Papa, she thought with sudden warmth, forgiving him his earlier desertion.

'But my shawl and reticule? I must find those first.' She smiled at the retainer. 'They cannot be too far away.'

'Señor de Silva has them already, I believe. They await you in the carriage.'

Her father had been unusually busy. She was surprised for she had thought him far too engaged with his political friends.

'Then I have nothing to do but find him,' she replied almost gaily in her relief that she was at last on her way home.

She made her way out of the ballroom and along the passage indicated by the footman. There was nobody to be seen, yet she had a nagging feeling that she was being watched. How very stupid. The alarms she had suffered that evening were making her overly sensitive to the atmosphere. The corridor itself was narrow and bare and meagrely lit by a few branches of candles at irregular intervals along its walls. It was an odd whim of her father's to have his daughter traverse the length of the Pavilion to the little used eastern exit. But he was there waiting to take her home. All would be well.

The colonnade which gave on to the gardens was smaller here and far more enclosed than the portico at which they had arrived. Tall trees shaded the building at this point and the covering of gravel was a mere path rather than a carriageway. Her father was nowhere to be seen, but in the dusk ahead she could make out the silhouette of a coach, and she made her way gladly towards it.

She walked swiftly through the small porch and out of the palace. Her footsteps sounded unnaturally loud in the silence which seemed to fill the air like a palpable presence. A few steps forwards and then two figures came looming from the darkness on either side of her. She started back but before she could regain the shelter of the Pavilion, they had grabbed her arms and pinioned her between them. Their clothes were unwashed and they smelt strongly of liquor. Terrified, she imagined she had been attacked by thieves but she had little on her person worth stealing. Their rough hands dug into her flesh as they jostled her forwards. Then she realised—they were dragging her towards the waiting coach. This was not a robbery, but an abduction! In a moment they had wrenched open the carriage door and made ready to bundle her inside. She struggled furiously, but she was no match for two hulking men and found herself being thrust into the coach. Then a loud shout sounded nearby. The hands loosened their grip and she was dumped, spread-eagled across the rear seat of the carriage.

She scrambled to her feet and down the coach steps. The dusk was dense, almost impenetrable, the moon shining only fitfully from between lowering clouds, and she could hardly see a foot in front of her. She could hear, though. There was a crack as two skulls were smashed expertly together.

'Run—back to the Pavilion and find your father.'

It was Joshua. As she turned to flee, she saw

that her assailants had recovered their footing only to be floored again, one after another with several punishing left hooks.

'Run!' he repeated.

She needed no second urging and rushed towards the Pavilion entrance, desperate to find help. Both attackers lay on the floor, prone and unmoving. Joshua, his cravat askew, stood back ready for a further onslaught. But their loud groans were heartfelt and they seemed unlikely to give more trouble. She was back in the Pavilion now and about to retrace her steps along the passageway when a sudden noise from outside made her turn again. Surely those villains could not have recovered so quickly.

But it was Leo Moncaster who stood to one side of the carriage, brandishing a sword.

'Get up, blockheads,' he swore at the men, 'and find the girl. Else what use are you to me?'

One of the men made a feeble attempt to stagger to his feet but then crumpled to the ground again. The other managed to crawl to the colonnade and haul himself upright on its wooden pillars. Domino felt him grab her skirt as she tried to whisk herself from sight. She had not run, could not run with Joshua in such danger.

Moncaster gave a growl of annoyance and turned to the cause. 'When will you learn,

Marchmain, not to interfere? I draw comfort from the fact that this is the very last time.' He slashed at the air with his sword, its evilly sharp point threatening the unarmed man.

'You are a cur, Moncaster. I don't fight with dogs.'

'Who said anything about a fight, dear friend? You will not have the chance. Regretfully I cannot allow you to regain the palace and tell your story. It would be too degrading.'

'What then do you intend, or need I ask?'

'I imagine not. Sadly, you will be found a victim of robbery. Such dubious creatures hang around the Pavilion these days, it will occasion few questions.'

'And Miss de Silva?'

'My plans for her must change. Your intervention has done her little favour. Instead of a few days' incarceration, she must now be lost for months. She may be allowed to surface in Spain eventually if she proves a sensible girl. By then no one will believe a word of any story she chooses to tell.'

The moon suddenly swam free of its cloudy cover and a shaft of silver illuminated the scene. It flooded everything in its path, glinting along the horses' glossy coats, embellishing the scratched panels of the coach and flashing its light on to a lone strip of glittering steel. In a second Joshua had seized the dagger from its resting place in the lining of the carriage door and made ready to defend himself.

'You will hardly inflict damage with that poor object,' his adversary mocked.

'We shall see. Any blade is gold if it destroys a mongrel such as you.'

The fight was ugly. No graceful swordplay, but a tense game of cat and mouse. They circled each other warily, each waiting for the other's move. Then Moncaster's sword was swinging through the air and Joshua nimbly retreating out of reach. Moncaster tried again, but with the same result. Again and again he struck and each blow Domino expected to be final. Both men were tiring in this inelegant ballet, but only when Joshua was sure that his opponent was sufficiently winded did he begin to advance. Then it was a swift run beneath Moncaster's sword blade and a desperate attempt to wound at close quarters. His enemy was too quick and retreated out of harm's way. The man who held Domino was gradually loosening his grip on her as he watched the fight, enthralled by its savagery. She thought she might manage to pull herself free but knew she could not leave. She was watching Joshua as though her life depended on it as much as his. She had to be there, stay with him, whatever their mutual fate.

Moncaster was growing ever more furious and began to slash wildly, circling the sword over his head, hurling its blade from right to left. But still Joshua evaded him. Years of practice with the most exigent of fencing masters had taught him skills of defence as much as offence. And he needed them. He could fight only at close quarters and the sword had a very long reach. Moncaster, tiring faster than his younger and fitter opponent, determined to make an end to his adversary. He saw his chance when Joshua for an instant came to a standstill. He lunged forwards to catch the younger man off guard. In the blink of an eye Joshua saw his danger and dipped beneath the oncoming sword so low that he almost knelt on the gravel. Then in a swooping movement from the ground he raised the dagger upwards and into the man's right arm. He pinked it neatly and Moncaster's sword clattered to the ground.

'Still so disdainful of a humble dagger?' Joshua's face was pale, but in the moonlight his eyes glittered with an unholy joy.

Leo Moncaster roared in pain and struggled blindly to free himself from Joshua's iron hold. But footsteps were running towards them from the passageway behind. The ruffian holding

Domino suddenly let her go and loped off into the darkness, the summer growth of bushes shielding him from view.

She was free and her father was by her side. Two of the Prince's guards had pinned Moncaster between them and were forcing him back into the palace. Joshua, his beautiful coat rent with sword slashes and his golden hair sadly dishevelled, faced her father.

'Take her home,' he said hoarsely. 'I believe she has had sufficient excitement for one evening.'

Alfredo nodded grimly and placed the spangled shawl around his daughter's shoulders. Together they stumbled through the back corridors of the palace to find again the familiar entrance. Domino sat back in the carriage, pale and exhausted. Only then did the tears begin to roll slowly down her cheeks.

Chapter Ten

She slept late the next morning. When she opened her eyes, Flora was bending over her, a look of concern on her face. Domino smiled and Flora smiled back.

'It's so good to see you awake, Miss Domino. You gave us such a fright last night.'

'I did?' She struggled to sit up, blinking at the brilliant light that was streaming into the room from chinks in the drawn curtains.

'It was as though you were sleepwalking, dazed like. You didn't seem to recognise any of us, nor your own room. I put you to bed and you slept straight away, real deep, too, and you've been sleeping like that ever since and it's past noon.'

'You sat with me all night, Flora?' Domino

propped herself up on one elbow and pressed her maid's hand affectionately.

'What else would I do, miss? We were so worried.'

'And my father?'

Flora piled the soft white pillows as high as she could and her mistress collapsed back on them with a sigh.

'My father?' she prompted.

'He's at the palace. He's gone to enquire of Mr Marchmain. Seemingly he did you a great service last night.'

'He did.' Her voice was barely above a whisper and the tears again began to flow. Her maid's face puckered in fright.

'Whatever is it, miss? You're safe and Mr Marchmain has come off with barely a scratch, or so I believe. That villain, they say, has packed up and gone back to London. He should be in prison, but Quality never goes to prison.' She sounded bitter.

Domino rallied herself and said in a far stronger voice, 'Are you saying that Lord Moncaster has left Brighton?'

'So Cook says. Her sister works in the Pavilion kitchens and such a to-do. The Regent himself was involved. After your father brought you home, *Lord* Moncaster—' and she emphasised the title with considerable scorn '—was taken to the Prince by the guards and had to confess what he'd been up to. Cook's sister says that Moncaster has been told he ain't welcome any more at the Pavilion, nor at Carlton House neither.'

Flora's acquired gentility was rapidly vanishing in the face of her honest indignation.

'Where has he gone, do you think?' Domino ventured, the thought tormenting her that her enemy might even now be waiting, ready to make another attempt on her.

'Apparently…' and Flora drew in her cheeks at the thought of the news she had to impart '…the Regent has advised his friend to go abroad for a space. Lying low, I call it. He should be in prison.'

'And all this has happened while I've been asleep.'

'Yes, indeed, miss. It's like you were under some kind of spell, but it's so good that you're back with us again.'

There was a gentle tap at the door and Alfredo looked into the room, his face drawn, but when he saw Domino sitting up in bed and sipping her morning chocolate, a wide smile lit his face. Flora quietly slipped away.

'How good to see you looking yourself again, *querida*.'

'I'm sorry I gave you such a fright, Papa. But as you see, all is well.'

He came to the bedside and enfolded her in a stifling bear hug. Her tears began to fall again and he pulled back, his face once more anxious.

She put her hand in his and squeezed it reassuringly. 'I am well, so you must not worry, but I cannot seem to stop crying.'

'You have had a terrible shock, my dear. I am not surprised you are deeply upset. When I think what could have happened!'

She would rather not think but she was desperate to know from him what had passed at the Pavilion. Had her father learned anything of the shameful history that existed between herself and Moncaster? She prayed not.

'Do you know why Lord Moncaster tried to abduct me,' she asked at last, 'for I presume that is what it was?'

'An abduction indeed. It makes my heart heavy to say this about any man, but he is evil through and through. And the Duchess of Severn is no better. She was in on the plan, too, it appears. I always thought her an indelicate woman, but I had no idea that she could sink to such wickedness.'

He fell silent as he considered the two miscreants.

'But what was their plan, and why should they plot against me?' she probed.

'Why they should do so, I have no notion. As for the plan, I do not think you need to know it.'

'I want to know, Papa,' she said stubbornly.

'My dear, how will it benefit you to know the depths of their villainy?' His voice was filled with misgiving.

'I have to know, Papa. I have to know the truth.'

He gave a heavy sigh. 'Leo Moncaster planned to hold you overnight in a house that the duchess owns in Worthing, just a few miles down the coast. He would have kept you there some days and allowed the gossip on your whereabouts to flourish. Or so I have learned from the Regent.'

'But how would that have served his purpose?'

Her father's face grew grimmer and his mouth tightened into a thin slit. He could hardly bring himself to speak the words.

'When Moncaster released you, he intended to publish to the world that you had voluntarily stayed with him as his mistress. It would be his word against yours and as a notable member of the *ton*, he expected to be believed. Even if he were not, the mere suggestion that his words might be true would ensure that your reputation in England would be shattered forever. No doubt he would spread news of your supposed affair as far afield as he could.'

Her mind swiftly processed this information, but she said nothing.

'Do you know why he would do such a thing, Domino?' her father ventured at last.

'I believe the duchess is for some reason jealous of me,' she extemporised. 'Perhaps Lord Moncaster has feelings for her and he planned this dreadful attack on her behalf.'

That, at least, was partially true. Charlotte Severn must suppose her intervention at the theatre had failed and she would be eager for the abduction to destroy Domino's reputation and make her a social outcast. The way would then be clear to seduce Joshua all over again.

'The crime seems out of all proportion to the cause,' Alfredo was saying thoughtfully.

Moncaster had his own reasons to hurt her, Domino knew, but she was not about to explain them.

Her father was still following his thoughts. 'But then these people cannot be understood by any normal standards of conduct, so perhaps we should not look too far for a motive.'

She closed her eyes, suddenly very tired again, but Alfredo had not yet finished. 'Lady

Veryan would very much like to see you when you feel able to receive her, my dear. She has been much disturbed by this terrible business and is wishful to be a comfort to you if she can.'

She nodded wearily. 'I should like to sleep a little longer but later perhaps we can take tea together.'

'I will tell her,' he said softly and took a seat by the bedside. It was evident that her father intended to keep watch as Flora had done through the night.

She sank back on the pillows and closed her eyes. But it was not to sleep for almost immediately a procession of shadowy figures began to dance across her vision. Blurred images of Christabel, her father, the Regent, Moncaster, and in their wake memories of Joshua: Joshua fighting for his life, Joshua fighting for her. Why had he been there? Why had he intervened? On that dreadful morning by the sea, she had rejected him, told him starkly that she never wished to see him again. But last night he'd ignored her dismissal, intent it seemed on proving that he could still cause her passion to flame: they had only to dance together. The shaming truth had been plain for all to see and in her anguish she had ruthlessly snubbed him and left him to face public humiliation.

Yet that had not weighed with him. He had continued to watch her, to watch out for her. He must have seen those brutal men waiting as she walked heedlessly into their trap. And he had gone into the fray with no more weapons than his own two fists. He could so easily have been killed. Moncaster would have denied all knowledge of the crime, glibly blaming it on the shiftless men who occasionally inveigled their way past the guards and into the Pavilion gardens. Such unsavoury people gather around the palace these days, she could almost hear him say. She would have lost her reputation but Joshua would have lost his life.

As if sensing that she did not rest easily, her father spoke again, his tone hesitant. 'This is a delicate matter, *querida*, but you owe much to Mr Marchmain. I understand that your—hmm, friendship—is at an end, but it is still right that you should see him. A few minutes only, sufficient to thank him for his bravery in your service.'

Her heart was beating too fast. She acknowledged how very much she owed Joshua but how could she meet him again, knowing that he had risked his life for her, but that she must still spurn him. The dreadful events of last night changed nothing. He was still the man who had deliberately betrayed his best friend, deliberately seduced Christabel Tallis. He was not the man she had hoped for, the man she had invested with her dreams.

'You will see him?'

She opened her eyes and saw her father looking anxiously down at her. 'It will be for a few minutes only,' he repeated, stroking her hand reassuringly. 'I can be with you. Or Lady Veryan if you prefer.'

'No!' She almost shouted the word. Her father looked astonished.

'I mean, Papa,' she said in a quieter tone, 'that it is I who owes Mr Marchmain such a debt of gratitude and it is I who should thank him. I will see him alone.'

'Very well, my dear. I will send a message asking him to wait on you tomorrow if that is convenient.'

Domino closed her eyes again. She was safe but not at peace. Tomorrow she must see Joshua and offer him her heartfelt thanks but still stay true to herself. It would be difficult. No, it would be utterly painful: to see his dear face, to look into his loving eyes, to desire his beautiful form and be unable to touch. She groaned inwardly. The pain was almost physical. But she was tired, so tired. Her eyes shut fast and sleep overcame her.

* * *

It was evening before she woke again and Christabel was standing in the doorway with a small tray in her hands.

'You've missed tea, my dear, but I've bought a little supper. Sleep is an excellent restorative but you need to eat.'

Her friend placed the tray on a nearby table and drew up a chair at the side of the bed. She bent down to kiss Domino's cheek and a subtle scent of roses filled the air.

'How are you, Domino? Such a fright you have given us!'

'So I understand. I'm sorry I have caused such consternation but as you see, I am fully recovered. Almost fully recovered,' she amended as Christabel's face registered doubt.

'I could hardly believe my ears when I learned what had happened. It is almost impossible to comprehend. Lord Moncaster is the most wicked of men. I understand that the Regent has banished him from Court for some time. That is mild punishment. He should be in prison.'

Christabel's normally gentle manner had given way to one of hot indignation, causing Domino to smile. Lady and lady's maid were evidently in agreement.

'It's so good to see you smile,' her friend

cheered. 'You will be back to your old self in no time.'

Domino thought otherwise but she had no intention of admitting Lady Veryan into the deepest and darkest of her secrets. Lady Veryan, though, it seemed had other ideas.

'And it was Joshua Marchmain who came to your rescue! I have not seen or heard of him for an age and then he appears out of nowhere, your very own guardian angel.'

Domino held her breath.

'I must tell you,' Christabel said a trifle self-consciously, 'that I was acquainted with Mr Marchmain in my youth.'

Her companion's face assumed an ignorance of the fact.

'It appears that he forms part of the Regent's entourage and that you have been in the habit of meeting him regularly. You never mentioned it.' There was a gentle scolding to Christabel's tone.

'I've met many people from the palace this summer.'

Her friend ignored the dissembling and continued blithely, 'I understand that he is to come here tomorrow. It will be good to meet him again.'

Alarm at these words was clearly written on Domino's face and Christabel offered a hasty amendment. 'Naturally you will wish to see him alone. You must have much to say to each other. But I would like to exchange a few words with him before he leaves the house. An opportunity to lay the past to rest comes seldom, you know.'

Domino felt her tongue stilled and her face freeze. She eased herself into a sitting position and looked directly at the visitor by her bedside. What exactly did this lovely young woman intend for the morrow? Whatever it was, she feared it could only make her meeting with Joshua even more tormenting. The air between them prickled.

In an attempt to diffuse the uncomfortable mood, Christabel spoke again.

'I should explain, Domino. As a young woman, I fell into trouble. I mentioned something of it when we talked yesterday. Mr Marchmain was involved and I fear that in the end he suffered unjustly for his part in our small tragedy.'

'And you wish to see him again?' Domino's chagrin fought with jealousy. Were these two old lovers to be reunited and under her roof?

'I turned out to be a very bad mistake for him. I would like to make my peace,' Christabel said simply.

* * *

Joshua threw down his brush in annoyance. He had been standing before a blank canvas all morning and getting nowhere. Normally his studio was a blessed retreat and painting a path to serenity. But today the magic was not working. He looked gloomily through the long glass windows into the garden. Since midnight the rain had been incessant and its dripping from the ornamental roof beat a repetitive tattoo on the gravel beneath. The world looked drear. The Regent had risen betimes, sending a collective shudder through the household, and Joshua had been summoned to his presence before the great ormolu clock in the Long Gallery had struck even ten. A lengthy interview had culminated with the Prince's command that Moncaster leave the Court immediately. His lordship was swift to make preparations for France and at Steine House the duchess was organising a hasty departure to London.

That was all very satisfactory, but this was not: he was unable to paint. If he were honest, he had been unable to paint for days. Ever since Domino had made plain that he was not her future. He wondered how she was faring after the frightening events of the previous evening. She was tough, he concluded, she would survive happily enough once the immediate shock had receded. As for him, he had a few bruises from the tussle with those ruffians, a few aches and pains, but in days he would be as new. His rawest ache was something that would not heal so easily.

His offer of marriage had stemmed from guilt at ensnaring Domino so badly, but once she made clear that he was the last man on earth she would consider marrying, any guilt should have vanished. After their disastrous meeting on the beach, he'd told himself that he could resume his old life with equanimity. He could feel free once more. But last night at the ball he'd known himself to be anything but free. He had wanted to master her, wanted to prove that she was not indifferent to him, no matter how much she might wish it. And he had succeeded so well that she'd fled without warning and left him looking a fool, alone in the midst of the dance floor. He had watched her storm from the room, watched her met by a liveried servant he did not recognise. That was strange in itself. In a furious mood, he had begun to follow her. He wasn't sure why, perhaps it was simply an inability to let go. But thank God he had. When she had taken the little used passageway, his instinct for danger had been alerted. How right he had been!

Two burly thugs had set upon her as soon as

she'd emerged from the palace and following close on her heels, he saw what they intended almost immediately: a coach and pair stood waiting in the shadows beyond. He hadn't seen Moncaster, the third villain of this blackguardly trio, but it would not have mattered if he had. Two men, three men, he would have intervened in any case. He would have intervened on behalf of any woman so threatened, but his blood had run cold when he saw it was happening to the girl he loved. And he did love her, he knew that now. His wish to marry had stemmed from love, not guilt. He had pretended otherwise, but after all the excuses, the justifications, the weasel words he'd told himself, he loved her. The minute he had seen her threatened he knew that she had all of his heart. But his case was hopeless: she would not change her mind. She was adamant that she could not forgive him.

He had been surprised, therefore, to get Alfredo's message asking him to call at Marine Parade. Unsure, too, whether or not he should obey the summons. The thought of seeing her again made his heart jump, yet it could mean nothing but distress for them both. Pride had strengthened his resolve that this unlucky love affair would not destroy him and a meeting would call on every ounce he possessed. Anger had proved useless. He had tried stoking it against her, telling himself again and again that she had dismissed him for no good reason— a past misdemeanour that had no currency in the present. When last night she had fled so precipitately, his wrath had reached its highest pitch; he had felt furious beyond belief. Furious that a chit of a girl should do this to him! But his rage had died the minute he had seen her in danger and he knew that for once in his life, his feelings were not playing him false. Whatever she did now and in the future, this was a woman he loved, truly loved.

His meeting with her tomorrow would be an elegy, a melancholy closing of the one good chapter in his life. The Court was busy packing for London and the leaves in the Pavilion gardens were already turning gold. It was a time for endings, and his own ending that would have no new beginning—for him at least. He would see her on the morrow, feel the turn of the knife once more, and walk away. He would return to his bare canvases and his bare life. He should not repine. This was the path he had chosen when he had betrayed his friend and seduced the girl he was to marry. From there he had gone from bad to bad. For a brief moment this summer he had glimpsed a different life, but that was at an end. He must not repine.

* * *

'Flora, lay out my cream figured muslin, please.'

The maid stared in surprise. 'The cream muslin?' she questioned, thinking she must have misheard.

Domino nodded. 'And the deep red satin ribbon we bought the other day in Barthlomews. I shall wear it threaded in my hair.'

'Are we going somewhere important, Miss Domino?' the maid ventured.

'We are going nowhere, but I am to have a visitor today and I wish to look my best.'

Why? she asked herself. It mattered not how she looked when Joshua came to call. She planned to be with him a few minutes only before he disappeared forever. It was mere whistling in the wind. A façade to cover her misery, a boldness when she felt fatally weakened.

Flora scurried around laying out underwear, stockings and the figured muslin along with matching satin slippers. She could see that her mistress was hardly herself but that was not to be wondered at. Such a dreadful experience she'd gone through. And now this Joshua Marchmain coming. She supposed it was right that Miss Domino should thank him prettily for his rescue but the man meant trouble in Flora's view. Ever since Miss Domino had met him, she'd been on a wild carousel, first happy and exultant, then cast down with dejection. It would be better for all of them once they were free of Brighton and free of him.

Domino dismissed her maid as soon as she could. She wanted time to collect her wits before Joshua arrived. She had formulated the words she needed to say. He had only to respond in similar vein and their ordeal would be finished.

But when an hour later she faced him across the drawing room, the words died on her lips. He looked a picture of quiet elegance, his clothes as always moulding themselves to perfection around his athletic form. The dark blue of his coat set off his shining gold locks and a waistcoat embroidered with small grey and blue flowers worn over dove grey pantaloons completed a more than alluring picture. But his eyes, that familiar colour of melting honey, held a reserved expression.

'I am delighted to see you so well.' His tone was neutral.

'Thank you, I am well,' she managed and then as a scattered afterthought, 'and you?'

'I've suffered no lasting damage—at least from the fight,' he offered drily.

She tried to keep her mind on the words she

had rehearsed. 'I am so glad you were able to call, Mr Marchmain. I wanted very much to thank you.' Her voice began to break as she met his shrewd gaze.

She tried again. 'I must thank you for your bravery', and then finishing in a rush, 'and of course your skill.'

'It's comforting to know that my experience in Italy has proved useful at last.' He fingered his scar and his voice sounded a caustic note.

'If it had not been for your intervention,' Domino doggedly followed her script, 'I would be in a sorry case.'

'We must not think of that.' He brushed aside her thanks. 'You are well and safe and that is all that matters.'

She felt stupidly annoyed that he seemed determined to make light of his rescue. How nonsensical of her. She should be glad that he was willing to pass over the event so quickly for it could only mean that his visit this morning would be mercifully brief.

'But still,' she persisted, 'I am conscious— my father and I are conscious—that we owe you a great deal.'

'You owe me nothing, Domino, unless it's a fair hearing,' he said harshly.

The interview was not going the way she had imagined. Why had she ever thought it would? A painful silence filled the room for what seemed an age but when he spoke again, his voice was deliberately indifferent.

'May I ask what your plans are?'

'I am to go first to London and from there I will travel on to Spain. Carmela will accompany me.'

'Ah, yes, to Spain and the unknown suitor. I imagine he has been resurrected.' They were back on dangerous ground and his gaze was derisory.

'There will be no suitor,' she said shortly.

'How can that be?' His eyebrows rose in mocking question.

She decided to fight back, to call his bluff. 'Surely, Mr Marchmain, you of all people should know the answer to that question.'

'But I don't.' His eyes had lost their sardonic amusement. 'If you no longer intend to marry, it isn't because you love elsewhere. A week ago I would have said differently. I would have said you had sought and found an abiding love. But now? I think you want only the illusion of such a love.'

She was desperate to end this dreadful conversation but was stung into exclaiming, 'You are unfair, sir!'

'I think not. You don't like reality, Domino. You prefer illusion and when the real world comes too close, you retreat. Your love for Richard Veryan was empty emotion. And now your love for me has gone the same way. You don't want a flesh and blood man with all the good and bad that that implies, you want a man that doesn't exist, a fantasy lover. Veryan filled that role until he inconveniently married. My tenure was even shorter. I fell from my pedestal almost immediately.'

For a moment the breath went out of her and she looked as though she was about to collapse.

'If it's not to be the unknown bridegroom, then what?' he asked as if he had not just uttered the most wounding words possible.

Wasn't that the question she returned to endlessly? What *was* she to do once back in Spain? Once they knew she was not intending to marry, her aunts would be eager to suggest a convent.

'A convent, perhaps?'

She stared at him. 'Well, isn't that one of the few acceptable choices for a virtuous Spanish girl? The altar or the cloister, or so I understand.'

Rage fought with tears. How dare he predict her future? What she did was no longer his concern. But suddenly his voice was soft.

'Don't choose a convent, Domino. You were not made for such.'

He began to walk towards her and she seemed paralysed to move. But before he reached her, the door opened and Christabel walked into the room. Domino had thought this encounter could not get worse but she had been wrong.

Joshua stared blindly at the vision that had entered. Though well into pregnancy, Christabel was able still to stun any man who crossed her path. But Joshua's mesmerised gaze was not for the woman he saw before him, but for the one he had long ago bid farewell.

'Christabel?' he queried in amazement. 'Christabel Tallis!'

'Christabel Veryan,' she corrected him gently.

'Of course. Lady Veryan, my apologies, and my very good wishes on your marriage.' He bowed politely. 'And on your forthcoming happiness,' he added, smiling at the noticeable bump Christabel carried.

'Thank you, Mr Marchmain. You are most kind. And I am delighted to see you again.'

Domino remained silent and unmoving, hardly able to believe the turn of events. It was as though she was watching a play enacted, with herself the sole audience.

Christabel continued unperturbed, 'Domino

told me you were to call today and I was hoping that I might speak with you.'

He looked enquiringly and she said with hardly a pause, 'I am sure she has thanked you profusely for the service you rendered her. But I would like to add my own thanks. Your courageous action saved her from the most dreadful fate.'

He nodded an acknowledgement but she had not yet finished and her quiet voice seemed to fill the room. 'There is something else. I wished to thank you for the service you rendered *me* many years ago. I know that as a result you must have suffered harm.'

Joshua was looking dazed—as well he might, thought Domino, burning with righteous anger.

'If you had not intervened in my life so dramatically,' Christabel went on, 'I would have wed Richard, but for all the wrong reasons. I would not have the happy marriage I have today. I needed to find out where I truly belonged, and you did that for me.'

His expression was wry. 'You are most kind, Lady Veryan.'

'I speak only the truth. But what of you, Joshua? I hope you, too, have found where you belong.'

'I thought I had but apparently I was mistaken,' he said curtly.

He picked up his gloves from the small table beneath the window and bowed to each of the women in turn.

'I believe it is time I left. Christabel, Lady Veryan, it has been most pleasant to meet you again. Domino, my very best wishes for your future happiness.'

And with a brief nod, he was gone. The front door shut with loud finality and Domino could no longer maintain her veneer of detachment. Careless of what Christabel would think, she rushed from the room and up the stairs to her bedroom, locking the door behind her.

She sank down on her bed. She was out of reach of friends and family alike, but not out of reach of torturing thoughts. The carefully scripted encounter had gone very wrong. All she had to do was express grateful thanks for her rescue. A few words on either side would have sufficed. Instead, what had happened? Joshua had not wanted to be thanked for his endeavours. He had wanted her to know that her priorities were wrong. The rescue was unimportant; what she did with the rest of her life was what mattered. He had brought home to her in bald terms just what her choices were and she had not liked them. And he had chopped her into the smallest of pieces by claiming that she had no idea what love was; that all she was capable of feeling was a pretence of love.

And then there was Christabel greeting him as a long-lost friend, behaving as though they were meeting at some dowager's tea party. She had clearly astonished Joshua with her words. She had absolved him, Domino thought savagely, so that he no longer need feel a shred of guilt for his past sins. She had even come close to praising him!

The churn of thoughts flooding her mind brought her to her feet. She could not rest and began aimlessly to pace the polished floorboards. Joshua had done a dreadful thing; he had almost destroyed the man she once loved. According to him that love had been nothing but illusion—and he was right. She had recognised that weeks ago. But he was so very wrong about this love. The love she felt for *him* was no illusion. He had taunted her that she didn't want a flesh and blood man. If that meant that she didn't want a man who carelessly inflicted hurt, then he was right. Yet both Richard and Christabel were happy now. Their baby would soon be with them, an added joy in the life of love they already shared.

And what of her, Domino de Silva, heiress and sad, sad girl? What was to become of her? Just a few days ago her world had been full to overflowing, then Charlotte Severn had dripped poison into her ears, and suddenly her life, her future, was changed forever. The duchess had won their battle of wills.

But why should she? She was allowing her to win—no, willing her to win. She was behaving exactly as Charlotte Severn had anticipated. The woman had judged her correctly to the last inch. How mortifying to be the duchess's creature. But if she were to defy Charlotte's malign calculations...

She paused her restless wandering and gazed out of the window. For several long minutes she stood there, watching the waves endlessly tumble to shore. Joshua Marchmain was a fallible man, a man who had lived a far from perfect life. But it was a life that had given him strangely little happiness. She remembered how puzzled she'd been that someone who seemed to have everything could be so bored and discontented. Yet from the moment they'd met, he had appeared quite other. Was it really possible that his days of philandering were over, that with her he'd finally stumbled on fulfilment?

She rested her forehead on the cold glass of the window pane, thinking, thinking. Minutes ago she'd heard him say that he thought he'd found where he belonged but that he'd been mistaken. But he hadn't been. He did belong with her and she belonged with him. Not with an unknown husband, nor behind a veil. She belonged with him, a strong, tender man who had once been an unloved child. He'd lost sight of where he belonged and before he'd properly matured, had committed the fatal error determining his life's path. Why couldn't she accept that?

There was no reason, no reason. She snatched up her bonnet and pelisse. The wind was blowing strongly and dark clouds threatened the return of an early autumn storm, but she took no heed. In a minute she was tripping down the stairs as quickly as she had run up them. Flora was crossing the hall and made to speak to her. She held up her finger for silence and slipped out of the front door.

The wind sent her skirts skirling but she bent her head against its force and pushed on towards the Pavilion. The guard on the gate recognised her from previous visits and though surprised at her solitary state, allowed her through into the gardens. She quickly found her way around the side of the palace, making for where she knew Joshua would be. Where else but in his studio?

He looked up as she appeared in the open

doorway. The wind had whipped colour into her pale cheeks and her dark, dishevelled curls framed a luminous face. Her graceful young figure was silhouetted against the stormy sky outside and she looked heartbreakingly lovely. He drew in a sharp breath but resisted the impulse to reach for her. He had no idea why she was here. It was yet another confusion in a vastly confusing day.

Meeting Christabel after so long had been astonishing and his mind still grappled with her sudden arrival. He could make little sense of it except that her presence had forced him to be circumspect. When she'd entered the room, he had been in a fair way to forgetting his resolve to remain coolly polite. He'd wanted to grab Domino, shake her, make her see the foolishness of her decision. He would have done it, too, if Christabel had not opened the door at that very moment. In the end he had been forced into a cold, mechanical farewell: a fitting end for a doomed love affair.

But now here she was, teetering on the threshold of his studio, her face wistful, her eyes shining.

'I had to come,' she said simply.

'And...' A small flicker of expectancy started deep within him.

'I'm sorry. I was wrong.'

'About?' he prompted, the flicker growing stronger.

'About everything. I've been obsessed with what happened all those years ago. You behaved very badly but so did Christabel. She has forgotten the bad memories, Richard too, and you—all of you have forgotten. I don't know why it became so important to me.'

'Perhaps because I was not the man you imagined.' His voice was guarded and he remained standing aloof from her.

'I have been very stupid.'

She walked further into the studio, moving closer to him, her gaze clear and unwavering. 'I don't know why I got it so badly wrong. I started out thinking you were the worst kind of man, a thorough rake, irredeemable. But then I fell in love and thought the world had wronged you and treated you callously. You became the best kind of man there could ever be. I placed you on an impossible dais.'

'And now you know that I am neither?' For a moment he looked tired and brushed away a lock of hair which had fallen over his forehead. Her heart stirred in tenderness.

'I know that you're the only man I ever want to be with,' she said with a catch in her voice.

He was beside her in a step, his tiredness

forgotten. He held out his arms wide and she walked into them.

'Is that true?' he breathed into her ear.

'I've never stopped loving you, Joshua. But for a while I lost my trust.'

'And now?'

'Now I've come to realise that your past is truly dead and I was wrong to doubt you.'

'Does that mean you still wish to marry?'

'I do with all my heart—though what Papa will make of it, I cannot begin to imagine.'

He smiled down at her, the familiar glint back in his eyes. 'And not only Papa,' he mocked gently. 'How will Carmela survive the news?'

Domino pulled back from him a little and said in a considered tone, 'I think perhaps we should wait until she is back in Spain before we formally announce our betrothal.'

'Then let us make her travel arrangements as soon as possible.'

She gurgled with laughter. He had thought he would never hear that sound again and pulled her close, holding her fast against his body, his suppressed longing overtaking prudence and destroying the carefully forged restraint. The palace was full of interested observers and the studio doors stood wide open to the garden. It mattered not.

He tipped her face to his. Her dark eyes

were radiant and filled with love for him. This is where they both belonged. Gently and insistently he began to kiss her. Over and over again, at first soft and exploratory and then demanding, ever more demanding. Blind to everything around them, they crashed a path through the studio until they came to rest on the well-worn couch pushed against its rear wall. Laughingly they disentangled themselves and surveyed the carnage. Canvases were scattered here and there, an easel had been overturned and paint streaked the floor and soaked though their footwear.

'We seem to have managed a pretty good demolition.'

'Since we've made such a satisfactory start, perhaps we should finish,' she suggested, her full mouth curving into a provocative smile.

In response he folded her tightly into his body. 'Do you not think we should wait until you have a wedding ring on your finger?'

He was nibbling delicately at her ear but she detached herself sufficiently to take him to task for such heresy. She ran a finger lovingly down his face.

'I would never agree to such a foolish notion.'

'How foolish?' He kissed her eyebrows one at a time.

'Unbelievably foolish! Every girl knows that once she's caught her rake, she must make it impossible for him to escape!'

'Is that so?' His hands were making light work of the muslin's fastenings. 'I've obviously left it far too late to save myself.'

'I fear so.' Her voice faded into a sigh as she felt his limbs pressing fiercely against her, imprinting her with his form.

'Sadly your beautiful gown is like to be ruined,' he lamented as the crushed dress was swiftly undone and cast to one side. Shirt and breeches soon went the way of the muslin.

His lips were moving across the bare skin of her neck in sweet, fiery kisses. She heard her breath coming fast as his mouth reached her breasts, tasting them, teasing them, moulding them into sharp pinnacles of desire.

'I cannot think of dresses just now,' she panted, small groans of pleasure emanating from somewhere she had never before known.

'And why would you?' he murmured, his body hard and hot. 'While I am so very close, what need have you of a gown?'

Epilogue

'*Las Meninas* has to be the most flawless picture ever painted.'

Joshua was squinting at the large canvas, trying without success to detect an imperfection. The young Infanta Margerita, surrounded by her entourage of maids of honour, bodyguard, two dwarfs and a dog, looked out at him from a room in Philip IV's palace.

Domino smiled knowingly. 'It depresses you.'

'Only a very little. Nothing so perfect can depress me for long. Do you see Velázquez himself in the painting, just behind this group here, working at his canvas but looking out at the viewer. He's mocking me for my very poor efforts.'

'He's greeting you from across the centuries,' she said consolingly. 'You must have seen the picture many times before. I remember your saying how much you loved coming to the Prado to see Velázquez. Does he always have this effect?'

'Far worse. I'm finding the painting much less dispiriting today. That's because you're by my side.'

'*Las Meninas* looks different with me?'

'Everything looks different with you.'

'You are a shameless flatterer', and she held his arm more tightly. 'At least I assume that was a compliment.'

'It could be nothing else. I feel as though I've been walking on clouds for the last six months. I want to paint the most exquisite picture which will say everything I feel for you. But Velázquez reminds me how far I am from achieving that.'

She smiled up at him, her face aglow with happiness. 'Whatever you paint for me will be better than anything hanging in the Prado, for it will be done with love.'

'An understatement, my darling.' And he dipped his face beneath the brim of her bonnet and kissed her soundly.

'You shouldn't do that! No London manners here! And I am fearful that any time soon you will come down to earth with a bump.'

'I am almost sure that you're wrong. I find that married life is exactly what suits me.'

Their fellow visitors shuffling their way around the white-walled room stopped for a moment to glance with curiosity at the couple. A tangible lustre surrounded them and everyone in their vicinity felt its warmth.

'Only almost!'

'I cannot allow you to get too puffed up,' he teased, adjusting the rose-satin ribbons of her villager hat and surreptitiously slipping his arm around her waist. He squeezed her tightly and an elderly lady wrapped in black glared at him through her pince-nez. In response he smiled sunnily back.

They began to move away from the picture that had taken their attention for so long, strolling slowly through each succeeding salon, their bodies brushing as they walked together, side by side, over the thick red carpet. In this fashion they made their way to the huge polished wood door guarding the front entrance. Domino could see ahead the fresh blue of a spring sky. Beside her Joshua's flaxen locks glinted in the sun's rays as they penetrated the gallery's long windows.

'Madrid in spring is heavenly.'

'The city has made a perfect end to our

journey,' he agreed. 'But now it's time to head home—to my home, rather.'

'My home, too,' she reminded him.

'You will miss your father.'

She looked a little troubled. 'We will miss each other. We have had such a short time together but he is very happy to have been posted to Spain. I think he found London life a deal too complicated. And he will visit us in England for sure.'

'And your aunts?'

'It's strange,' she conceded, 'but I will miss them too. I never thought I would say that but they have been so welcoming. It must be your charm, you've won them over completely.'

'But not Carmela, I fear.'

He reached over to take their outdoor coats from the attendant and helped his wife into her rose velvet capote, shrugging himself into a greatcoat with upwards of a dozen capes.

'You never will,' Domino said sagely. 'For her you will always be the dangerous rake. But she is happy enough in Santa Caterina. The convent is where she has always wanted to be, you know. Brighton was a horrible deviation and I am sure she wishes to forget that she ever visited the town.'

He took her hand and guided her down the

long flight of steps. 'That's something *we're* not likely to do, I fancy.'

'Forget Brighton? No indeed, though I don't think I would ever wish to return.'

'But why not? In the end everything came right, and since we found happiness there, the town should have a place in our hearts.'

A shiver prickled the surface of Domino's skin as they began to walk slowly along the wide pavement, the trees on either side sprouting their first greenery of the season.

'The place has as many bad memories for me as good,' she said as easily as she could. 'Lord Moncaster, for instance.'

'He need never concern us again.'

For a moment they were forced to abandon their conversation in order to negotiate a path round a group of chattering acquaintances, intent on enjoying the mild sunshine and blissfully unaware of the obstacle they presented.

'I received an intriguing message yesterday,' he continued once they had rounded the group. 'I forgot to tell you—it came from an old friend at Carlton House. The duchess has married Moncaster!'

Domino looked shocked but said with some spirit, 'They deserve each other. But it is very soon after the duke's death. Only a few months. Surely that cannot be right.'

'Charlotte has never been one to spend too much time observing the proprieties,' he said wryly. 'I imagine she was desperate to find another husband—marriage gives at least the semblance of respectability—and Moncaster was free. She grabbed him while she could.'

Domino remained silent, watching the stream of stylish carriages making their way along the wide boulevard at a smart trot, but with her mind far away.

'And they are in London,' she said finally, the strain in her voice betraying her anxiety.

'Don't fret, my darling. They may be in London but that's where they'll stay. Being close to power is all that interests them and now that Moncaster has been allowed back into Court, they will be eager to resume their places in the Regent's entourage. They're sure to hang on to George's coat tails forever and we're just as sure never to see them again.'

'Norfolk is not that far from London,' she reminded him, still anxious but willing herself to be convinced.

'It's far enough, particularly in the depths of winter. The climate can be inclement and the roads sometimes impassable. I only hope you won't find it too quiet.'

That galvanised her and she turned impulsively towards him. 'I am so looking forward to seeing Castle March and setting up house with you there.'

'It will be a house for someone else too,' he reminded her, gesturing lovingly to the gentle swell of her stomach.

'Indeed. It will be the perfect place for children and the perfect place for us.'

'No chance there of falling back into my wicked ways, you mean.'

She nudged him playfully. 'You know I mean nothing of the sort. I am very sure that your wicked ways, as you call them, are long dead.'

'You should be sure. It's you that has tamed me.'

'I doubt that', and she blushed at the thought of the night they had just spent together. 'Not that I would want to!'

He bent to kiss her full on the lips, ignoring the scandalised glances of their fellow strollers along the broad walkway. 'Together we'll make Castle March a real home, Domino. At last I can hang my da Vinci. It's the very first thing I shall do. Actually, the second,' he corrected himself. 'There's a small matter of carrying you over the threshold.'

'You must make sure that you don't drop the pair of us!'

'I will be taking the greatest care of you both.'

He looked at her blooming cheeks and shining dark eyes. 'You are more beautiful than ever,' he murmured and then stopped short and pulled her to himself, almost roughly. 'I think we should be thinking of quite a large nursery.'

'Do I get any say in that?' She smiled roguishly up at him.

'Not a word. It's already decided. But I do need your advice with something that has me in quite a puzzle.'

Domino, still smiling, raised her eyebrows.

'It's a matter of the greatest importance, so take care before you answer. Where exactly *am* I to hang the Leonardo?'

* * * * *

A sneaky peek at next month...

HISTORICAL

IGNITE YOUR IMAGINATION, STEP INTO THE PAST...

My wish list for next month's titles...

In stores from 1st June 2012:

- ❏ The Duchess Hunt – Elizabeth Beacon
- ❏ Marriage of Mercy – Carla Kelly
- ❏ Unbuttoning Miss Hardwick – Deb Marlowe
- ❏ Chained to the Barbarian – Carol Townend
- ❏ My Fair Concubine – Jeannie Lin
- ❏ Weddings Under a Western Sky –
  Kate Welsh & Lisa Plumley

Available at WHSmith, Tesco, Asda, Eason, Amazon and Apple

Just can't wait?

Visit us Online

You can buy our books online a month before they hit the shops! **www.millsandboon.co.uk**

0512/04

MILLS & BOON® Book Club

2 Free Books!

Join the Mills & Boon Book Club

Want to read more **Historical** stories?
We're offering you **2 more**
absolutely **FREE!**

We'll also treat you to these fabulous extras:

- 🌹 **Books up to 2 months ahead of shops**

- 🌹 **FREE home delivery**

- 🌹 **Bonus books with our special rewards scheme**

- 🌹 **Exclusive offers... and much more!**

Treat yourself now!

Visit us Online
Get your FREE books now at
www.millsandboon.co.uk/freebookoffer

0112/H2XEA/REV

MILLS & BOON Book Club

2 Free Books!

Get your free books now at
www.millsandboon.co.uk/freebookoffer

Or fill in the form below and post it back to us

THE MILLS & BOON® BOOK CLUB™—HERE'S HOW IT WORKS: Accepting your free books places you under no obligation to buy anything. You may keep the books and return the despatch note marked 'Cancel'. If we do not hear from you, about a month later we'll send you 4 brand-new stories from the Historical series priced at £4.50* each. There is no extra charge for post and packaging. You may cancel at any time, otherwise we will send you 4 stories a month which you may purchase or return to us—the choice is yours. *Terms and prices subject to change without notice. Offer valid in UK only. Applicants must be 18 or over. Offer expires 31st July 2012. **For full terms and conditions, please go to www.millsandboon.co.uk/freebookoffer**

Mrs/Miss/Ms/Mr (please circle)
_____

First Name
_____

Surname
_____

Address
_____

_____
                                    Postcode
_____

E-mail
_____

Send this completed page to: Mills & Boon Book Club, Free Book Offer, FREEPOST NAT 10298, Richmond, Surrey, TW9 1BR

Find out more at
www.millsandboon.co.uk/freebookoffer

Visit us Online

0112/H2XEA/REV

Book of the Month

MILLS & BOON

We love this book because...

Dark, determined cowboy Jake fights against the odds to keep his newfound family safe in this pulse-racing romantic suspense from Intrigue star Carla Cassidy.

On sale 18th May

Visit us Online

Find out more at
www.millsandboon.co.uk/BOTM

0512/BOTM

 ## Special Offers

Every month we put together collections and longer reads written by your favourite authors.

Here are some of next month's highlights— and don't miss our fabulous discount online!

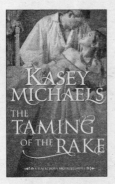

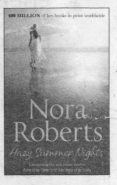

On sale 18th May   On sale 1st June   On sale 1st June

Find out more at
www.millsandboon.co.uk/specialreleases

Visit us Online

0512/ST/MB375

Mills & Boon® Online

Discover more romance at
www.millsandboon.co.uk

- **FREE** online reads
- **Books** up to one month before shops
- **Browse our books** before you buy

...and much more!

For exclusive competitions and instant updates:

 Like us on **facebook.com/romancehq**

 Follow us on **twitter.com/millsandboonuk**

 Join us on **community.millsandboon.co.uk**

Visit us Online | Sign up for our FREE eNewsletter at **www.millsandboon.co.uk**

WEB/M&B/RTL4